Trained as an actress, Barbara Nadel used to work in mental health services. Born in the East End of London, she now writes full time. She received the Crime Writers' Association Silver Dagger for her novel *Deadly Web*. She is also the author of the highly acclaimed Inspector İkmen series set in Turkey.

Praise for the Francis Hancock series:

'An atmospheric and entertaining brew' *Mail on Sunday*

'She confidently and convincingly paints a grim picture of a bombed-out east London . . . curious and memorable' *Time Out*

'Nadel has created an atmospheric setting and a fascinating insight into the lives of Londoners struggling against the Luftwaffe's nightly onslaught. The book's intelligent original theme and empathetic characterization make for a compelling read' *Good Book Guide*

'Excellent' *Birmingham Post*

'Undeniably gripping. Her description of life under the Blitz is extraordinarily vivid and intense' *Morning Star*

'Ingenious premise and goosebump-inducing finale. Great pace and atmosphere . . . thoroughly recommended' *Shotsmag*

'A rattling good thriller set in the uncertain early years of the Second World War' *Bolton Evening News*

By Barbara Nadel and published by Headline

BARBARA
NADEL

Sure and Certain Death

headline

First published in 2009
by HEADLINE PUBLISHING GROUP

First published in paperback in 2010
by HEADLINE PUBLISHING GROUP

1

Cataloguing in Publication Data is available from the British Library

ISBN 978 0 7553 5760 4 (B Format)
ISBN 978 0 7553 3625 8 (A Format)

Typeset in ACaslon Regular by Palimpsest Book Production Limited,
Grangemouth, Stirlingshire

Printed and bound in Great Britain by
Clays Ltd, St Ives plc

HEADLINE PUBLISHING GROUP
An Hachette UK Company
338 Euston Road
London NW1 3BH

www.headline.co.uk
www.hachette.co.uk

To all of those whose minds have been taken by war

Prologue

February 1941,
Plaistow, East London

Nellie knew she shouldn't have taken that drink. She shouldn't have taken any sort of alcohol at all. Dr Stansfield would have been appalled! What was she thinking?

She was thinking that actually it was very nice. It was cold, she was cold and she was lonely. Her daughter was evacuated out to Essex, leaving Nellie with her mother and her sister and the endless droning of Dr Stansfield in the pulpit of their church every Sunday. Dr Stansfield didn't believe in drink or fags or fun of any sort really. If the minister had had some time for the after-life – as in finding out what it was really like – Nellie could have understood it. But there was no questioning the letter of scripture in any way at all. You died, and if you were good and loved Jesus you went to heaven; if you were bad or you didn't love Jesus you went to hell. Quite where that left people like all the Jews she'd grown up around, Nellie didn't know. According to Dr Stansfield,

1

they were going to burn in hell! Not that that could be right. They were nice people. Nellie liked Jews, they were a laugh.

When it was offered, Nellie took another swig of liquor, which made her glow inside. Feeling a bit wobbly too by this time, she just naturally followed on into the bombed-out house on New City Road. When the terrible pain first hit her, initially in her stomach, and then everywhere, and then the blood came, she was shocked. Shocked and then afraid and then terrified, and then, mercifully, Nellie fell to the floor and died.

I came across what was left of Nellie Martin completely by accident. Not as I knew that great hunk of meat I saw in that house was Nellie Martin at the time. Neither me nor my young apprentice, Arthur, could tell whether what we saw was even human. But it stank, and as I tried to get closer to it to find out what it was, the shattered floorboards underneath the thing made it quiver like a piece of liver on a butcher's chopping board. I felt sick. Poor Arthur *was* sick. In spite of my profession being what it is, I hadn't expected anything like this. What even I do rarely brings with it such horror.

I'm an undertaker. My name is Francis Thomas Hancock and I'm forty-eight years old. A veteran of the Great War of 1914–18, I still find it difficult to take in the fact that we're at war with the Germans once again now. I thought I'd seen everything out in the trenches of Flanders. But ever since the Luftwaffe have been trying to bomb our poor old London into surrender, my mind has been tortured all over again. Not that it ever really healed after the First Lot.

I'm a man who isn't 'right', a man whose brain is so broken it can't always be trusted. I am a lunatic who sees and hears things that are not there. But not this time. This time when I went into what was left of that house in New City Road, Plaistow, I knew that the horror was real because Arthur was seeing it too.

'What the . . .' the boy started once he'd finished being sick. 'Mr H, what the . . .'

'I don't know what it is, Arthur,' I said as I carried on looking at the thing, unable to take my eyes off it.

We'd come to do a job, me and the boy. An old character called Herbert Wills had passed away in the house next door to the one we were in now, and we'd come to take his body back to my shop up on the Barking Road. But Herbert had been a big man, twenty stone at the very least, and so we'd decided to take his body out via the passage that runs along the back of the houses on New City Road. The reason we were in the house next door at all was because we were taking a short cut. After all, if a place is empty and in ruins and your motives are pure, as ours were, then why not?

'Do you think it's human?'

'Yes, it's my belief it is a person, Arthur,' I said. The thing was on a chair, and dangling in a place where a leg would probably be in the normal course of events was a human foot. I looked at it hard just to make really sure, but it was definitely a foot.

'This house was bombed out weeks ago and so this . . . person can't have died in a raid,' I said.

There hadn't been a big raid on London for two weeks.

The last really big one, on the 11th of January, had been the direct hit on Bank station. Before that we'd had the terrible 29th of December 1940 set-to. The night of the firestorm when St Paul's Cathedral, and yours truly with it as it happened, was almost burnt to a crisp. People were saying that maybe because he failed to get the cathedral, Hitler was losing the will to keep on pounding at us. I didn't trust that idea myself. I still don't.

'Died?' Arthur, now just about able to look at the terrible thing on the chair, said, 'What kind of thing can have made someone die like that?'

'Maybe,' I said, 'it wasn't some*thing* but some*one*.'

Arthur was about to turn eighteen at the time. Only a kid. He looked at me, struck. But then Arthur hadn't seen active service, and unlike me, he hadn't seen murder be it on or off the field of battle.

'Get back up to the Barking Road and go to the police station,' I told him. 'Tell them we've found a body in a bombed-out house.'

He made to go without another word and with a lot of haste. I couldn't blame him for that, but before he went I said, 'And pop your head around the Willses' door before you go. Tell them we've got a bit of a problem but we'll be back round to pick up Herbert just as soon as we can.'

As he moved bits of shattered door and other unidentifiable pieces of wood out of his way, Arthur said, 'All right. But Mr H, what will you . . .'

'I'll wait here,' I said.

'With . . .'

'With some poor creature who met its end in what would seem to be a bad way,' I replied. 'We can't leave it alone here in case it frightens others. And anyway, Arthur, getting the dead where they need to be is what we do, and this poor soul does not need to be here.'

Arthur pushed his way out of that crumbling house without another word. He knows my philosophy. Undertaking is about care. The dead, helpless as they are, need assistance to reach their final destination. It's our job to make sure that they get there without undue molestation or just plain useless interference from the living. Between the living and the dead, the undertaker, in my opinion, is not wholly in one state or the other. That suits me fine.

I stood over that bleeding mound of what had once been human, the wrecked floor beneath my feet shifting and splintering in the wind and under the weight of the dying house that was threatening to crush it into the earth below. As time passed, I became accustomed to the sight of the body, just like I became accustomed to the possibility of the building falling and taking my own life from me.

Chapter One

It didn't take long for the Plaistow gossip mill to grind into action. I'd said nothing to anyone, apart from the coppers and young Arthur of course, about what we had found in the house on New City Road. But although they may not look too countrified, a lot of London boroughs still have the souls of villages – with all the attention to gossip and rumour that goes with that. This is especially so in the East End, and very particularly in my borough of West Ham. Plaistow, which is in the middle of the borough, is a place where people know a lot about their neighbours. By people I mean, of course, women mainly, and by women I mean particularly women of an anxious turn of mind. Like my sister Nancy.

Two days after my and Arthur's grim discovery, she came to me with an even more drawn and frightened-looking expression on her face than usual. Nancy is older than me; she's a spinster, and in common with a lot of older single ladies, she worries. She listens to gossip with what could be viewed almost as relish, but she rarely hears news that doesn't either outrage or frighten her. I was out in the shop yard grooming the horses when she came down from our flat and leaned against the water butt.

'Why didn't you tell me you found Nellie Martin dead up New City Road?' she said. As usual, she got right to the point. Nancy is a very good-living and sincerely religious woman, but she doesn't know very much about how to talk to people – not even her own brother.

'It wasn't my place to talk about such things,' I replied. 'I didn't know what the coppers wanted said, if anything. And anyway, what's it all to you?'

'I was at school with Nellie is what it is!' Nan responded aggressively. Her face, which like mine and like our mother's is brown, was, I could see, flushed with the anger she felt inside.

'Oh, Nan, I'm s—'

'Never liked her,' Nan continued as she folded her arms underneath her thin, almost nonexistent breasts. 'She was one of them who called me names. But that ain't the point. You should've told me!'

As kids we'd gone to different schools, Nan to New City Road School and me to the grammar. We'd both of course suffered our share of bullying. Only my younger sister, Aggie, had not come in for any of that. But then Aggie hasn't taken on the darkness that Nan and I get from our Indian mother. Fair like our English father, Aggie is also a completely different character. She doesn't take any nonsense from anyone. I'm not a pushover myself, but Nancy just goes into herself and broods when people are unkind to her. Ill equipped for the knocks

8

and blows of life, she keeps herself to herself and spends most of her time looking after our widowed mother. Not that she isn't bitter about being a woman alone. She feels her 'misfortune' acutely, and if Mum, or the Duchess as we all call her, on account of her very proper manners, were not so sick with her arthritis, I think that Nan could be a very bored and nasty busybody. As it is, she rarely has time to pass on what she hears from other bitter and twisted spinsters after Mass on Sunday or on the local grapevine. This time, however, she'd known the person the latest gossip was about.

I finished brushing Sita, the larger of our two geldings, before I turned to Nancy and said, 'Look, even if I'd known you'd known her, I couldn't have said anything. I didn't know who she was myself until the coppers managed to identify her the following day. She didn't live in that house, you know.'

'No. Iniskilling Road. Her family all live there.'

There was a pause. Nan looked down at her feet and for a moment I thought that she might be crying.

I began to move towards her. 'But if you didn't like this woman . . .'

'Don't mean I can't mourn her!' Nan said as she very quickly pulled away from me. My older sister doesn't take affection easily. 'Frank, they say she was murdered, skinned alive!'

'Well I don't know about . . .'

'My Uncle Woofie told my mum that a lot of the old people down our manor are saying that it's Jack the Ripper come back again.'

The voice that had interrupted me was female, smoke-dried and came, unmistakably, from our office girl, Doris

Rosen. Doris lives in Spitalfields, where the famous murderer Jack the Ripper had done his evil deeds back in Victorian times. No doubt some of the old people over there did remember those days. And given the state of Nellie Martin's body when Arthur and myself found her, I could clearly see where the idea that the Ripper was on the loose again had come from. I hadn't seen much beyond just a big piece of meat with a foot hanging from it at the time. That the body had been skinned hadn't actually occurred to me. But that detail wasn't just gossip; the coppers themselves had told me it had happened. Jack the Ripper, albeit only once, had skinned one of his prostitute victims, Mary Jane Kelly in 1888. I wondered what, if anything, Nellie Martin had done for a living. I also began to think about a lady close to me in that profession too.

'Horrible!' Doris dragged heavily on her fag and shook her head slowly.

'I knew Nellie Martin from school,' Nancy told her.

'Oh!' Doris was clearly shocked. 'Oh, Miss Nancy, how horrible for you!'

'Yes.'

I was on the point of mentioning the fact that Nan and this Nellie hadn't actually been friends when my sister said, 'She was a spiteful girl as I remember her, but it brings me no pleasure that she's dead. She must've suffered. I wonder what she can have been doing in a bombed-out house on New City Road?'

'Well it's only about a minute away,' I said. Iniskilling Road, Plaistow, crosses the top of Jedburgh Road, which is

10

then cut in half by New City Road. It's no distance at all. 'Maybe she was looking for someone or something in there.'

'And gets horribly murdered for her pains!' Doris said. 'Blimey! She have any family, did she, Miss Nancy?'

My sister frowned, visibly thinking it through. 'She married,' she said. 'But I think her old man died. There's a daughter somewhere or other.'

'Oh. Shame.'

'Her father had a greengrocer's down Prince Regent Lane. The whole family always worked in there. Unless Nellie was on war work, of course . . .'

There *was* a greengrocer's called Martin's down Prince Regent Lane. Several tired-looking women worked there as I recalled. Had a woman brutalised and skinned until she died really once worked in such an ordinary place? But then if she had, why not? Extraordinarily bad things happen to very ordinary people. In fact more often than not the victims of strange and terrible crimes are very poor and very workaday folk. Nellie Martin had not, however, as far as I knew, and unlike the Ripper's Mary Jane Kelly, been a prostitute. I was relieved about that.

Just because the Jerries had seemingly given up on destroying our city didn't mean that Hancock and Co., Undertakers, were not busy. This is a poor manor. Even without the bombing, death comes sooner rather than later here. The Royal Docks, probably West Ham's biggest place of work, takes a big toll. Loading goods on and off ships is hard work for men who also play hard in the pubs that line the streets down to the docksides of Canning Town, Silvertown and Custom House. Those not worked to death die in fights or just drink themselves into an early grave. An example of the latter was a bloke called Sidney Shiner. He'd just turned fifty when he keeled over in a pub called the Chandelier in Canning Town. No one noticed for quite a while because apparently he quite often fell unconscious in his local of an evening. It was, so local legend had it, the funny colour Sidney seemed to take on after a while that finally gave the game away. That had been the day before I'd been called. Now, just over twenty-four hours later, Sidney was about to be buried in East Ham Jewish Cemetery. Unlike Christians, like my family, the Jews put their dead away with utmost haste.

So then I had a lot to do to take my mind off what I'd found in that house in New City Road. Once I'd prepared the horses and the hearse, I made sure that my bearers, young Arthur and an old geezer called Walter Bridges, were as smart as these strange times allow. Time was, when my old dad was still alive, funerals even in West Ham were ornate affairs. We had a team of very elegant-looking young men bearing for us in those days, not to mention the mutes some of the wealthier families used to insist upon. But with all the men gone to the forces, we're left with kids like Arthur, well-meaning if a bit dozy at times, and old men like Walter, whose love of a good pint can be a bone of contention between him and me. That said, we picked up Sidney Shiner from the boarding house he'd lived in in Canning Town and got over to East Ham just before the Reverend Ritblatt, the officiating rabbi.

Sidney Shiner had never married, and so the only family in attendance were a brother, a sister and their various children. Some of the blokes he'd worked with down the docks had taken the time to come and pay their respects. Apart from those, there was just one rather elegantly dressed middle-aged lady. When I saw her, slightly set apart from the family and the workmates, I went over to her. I did I confess have a frown on my face by this time.

'What are you doing here, Hannah?' I said as I sidled up to her and put one of my hands on her slim, black-clad shoulder.

She looked at me and smiled. 'I knew him,' she answered simply.

'Sidney Shiner?'

'Canning Town ain't a big Jewish area,' she said. 'Me and Sidney, we . . .'

'You didn't . . .'

'Give him one?' Her face darkened as I looked around to make sure that no one was listening. But the Reverend Ritblatt had started his spiel and so everyone else was attending to that. 'Sidney lived inside a booze bottle. He weren't interested in anything I had on offer,' Hannah continued angrily. 'Jews know each other just like Italians, the Maltese, you lot . . . I've told you this, H, we've talked about it before.'

We had, and her rebuke made me hang my head. But it didn't cure me. Nothing I don't think ever will. I've been in love with Hannah Jacobs for years. In fact she is the only woman I've ever loved romantically, and although she was when I met her and continues to be a prostitute, I know that she loves me too. To Hannah, I am 'H', a wounded, mad and besotted old soldier. I am also the only constant person in her life. Nothing, however, comes for free, and so much as our time together is spent now as man and lady friend in the normal way of things, I know that there are other men she 'sees' for business purposes. I'd pay her rent for her, I'd marry her if she would only let me. But Hannah is an independent woman, and so I remain a very jealous man.

Once Sidney Shiner was in the ground and I'd offered my condolences to his family, I sent Arthur and Walter back to the shop with the hearse. Hannah hadn't even tried to approach any of the Shiner family on account of her being very well known amongst the folk of Canning Town. She didn't want to embarrass them, and so she just waited for me to come and see her, as she knew I would, outside the cemetery on Masterman Road. She'd worked out that despite the fact I'd sent the hearse on ahead, I probably couldn't stay for very long. By that time it was already almost midday, and I had another funeral to do over at the East London Cemetery at half past two. But in spite of the bone-aching cold of that day, it was nice just to be out and about with her, even if it was only for a few minutes or so.

'How have you been?' she asked as she took my arm and began walking slowly with me towards East Ham High Street. 'You been sleeping now the bombing's eased off?'

Hannah isn't the only one who asks after my health. Ever since I came back from the Great War with my mind in so many pieces, my body a shade of what it once had been, people have always asked me. But then even once my physical wounds had healed, my brain remained as it is to this day. Damaged, it makes me see and hear things that aren't always real, vile things from that horror in the trenches. To be honest, had I not had Arthur with me when I found it, I would have been inclined to think that Nellie Martin's body wasn't real. What the trenches have also left me with is a fear of being buried alive. So when the sirens go off to let us know the Luftwaffe are on their way, I don't go down to any shelter. I just run – anywhere, everywhere, as fast as I can. Sleep, therefore, over time, becomes a stranger to me, and my insanity grows accordingly.

'I get the odd hour or so,' I said as I pulled Hannah close in to my side. 'Slightest noise still wakes me, but . . .'

'Seeing what happened to that poor woman down New City Road probably didn't help,' Hannah said.

I stopped, turned towards her and looked into her strong, handsome face. 'Who told you about that?' I said. 'God blimey, my own family have only just found out about that!'

Hannah shrugged. 'Everyone knows about the skinned body.'

'Yes, but me finding it and . . .'

'Listen, with few bombs to talk about, people have to gossip about other things,' Hannah said. 'So we'd all heard the story but it was Bella who said she'd heard that it was an undertaker who'd found the body.'

'So how did you know that it was me?' I said.

Hannah gave me a slightly pitying look. 'Now, H . . .'

I sighed. It's stupid not to acknowledge it, but sometimes it is hard to accept I'm as instantly recognisable as I am. 'So was it the colour of my skin or the way I behave?'

Hannah gave me another look. What my sister Nancy would call an old-fashioned look.

'That mad wog undertaker, wasn't it?' I said.

Hannah didn't answer. She didn't have to. But then by the time the coppers had turned up to that bombed-out house in New City Road, I had been talking to myself. Or rather I'd been talking to what we now knew had been Nellie Martin. A man with hair the colour of coal and coffee-brown skin talking to a mutilated corpse. Even I can't blame people for the fact they pass things like that on. By means of either the coppers, their families or young Arthur, word had reached Hannah's mate Bella and probably all the rest of Canning Town too. We started walking again then, and Hannah, sort of, changed the subject.

'The dead woman was in her fifties,' she said.

'Went to school with my sister,' I replied. 'Bullied her.'

'Nancy?'

'Yes.'

Hannah shook her head. 'Still, terrible way to go. They say, so Bella told me, that she was a bit of a religious type.'

'Was she?' Nan hadn't mentioned it and so it hadn't occurred to me that Nellie Martin might be a churchy person.

'Always in and out of some church on the Barking Road.'

'There are lots of churches on the Barking Road, Hannah,' I said.

'I suppose there are,' she replied. Then just before we got

16

to East Ham High Street she said, 'But you're all right now? You're over the shock of it, aren't you?'

I smiled and said that yes, I was. But Hannah still looked worried and she was right to do so. I've a bit of a history of getting involved with the ins and outs of strange deaths that come my way. But I did feel all right at the time and I was quite sincere when I said that I was to Hannah.

Chapter Two

*S*he shouldn't have said so much! Running off at the mouth like that! No one wanted to know about her concerns, especially not about such intimate things. And what if Nancy were to find out? She'd be hurt, and that would never do. Nancy was her friend!

Fiddling in the handbag down by the side of her chair, she fumbled for her rosary. Maybe if she were quick she could get a couple of Hail Marys in, make some sort of penance before her guest came back from the privy. But instead she sipped some more tea and she waited. She'd had such a nice time, and really unexpected too. It had been a pity to spoil it with that sudden rush of bitterness about poor Nancy. Wringing her hands didn't help either, but she did it anyway. Dear Queen of Heaven protect me, she thought. If I lose Nancy because of my silly mouth, I will die! Rita will kill me if I lose Nancy and I go into myself and she has to look after me! Sisters, as Rita had told her on the few occasions they did spend time together these days, were not supposed to look after each other once they were grown up.

She looked up at the clock on the mantel and noticed that it was getting late. She noticed also that the face of the clock was somewhat blurry. Bad housekeeping, that! She got up from her chair with the full intention of going over to the mantel and wiping the face of the clock with a rag. But as she stood, she came over all funny in her head, and the next thing she knew she was lying on the floor. Embarrassed and really feeling quite peculiar by this time, she did try to get to her feet before her visitor returned from the privy. But she didn't make it.

'I'm sorry,' she began as she tried to push herself up on to one of her elbows, 'but—'

The sharp slash of a knife across the bottom of her throat stopped any further words she might have had to say for ever.

I didn't find the body of Violet Dickens, but then it could be said that it didn't need to be found. It sort of made itself apparent.

Three weeks before, her old man had reported her missing to the police. Not that they will or even can do much about people going missing these days. Nothing, according to the story that went about afterwards, happened until nearly a week after I found Nellie Martin's mutilated corpse. There'd been a big raid on the night of the 29th, and it was after that that Violet's husband noticed the smell. He thought at first it came from the lodger's room upstairs. But it didn't. It came from the attic. She was, so my sister Nancy informed me, in a 'shocking state' when she was found.

'Rotten,' Nancy told me just before the Duchess came in to the kitchen to have her breakfast with us. 'She was completely rotten. But then not enough, or so they say, that the coppers couldn't see that all her insides was pulled out all over the attic floor.'

My younger sister Aggie took her fag out of her mouth and said, 'If her insides had been all over the attic floor, her husband or the lodger or someone would've seen blood coming through the ceiling.'

'Maybe,' Nan said. Then after a short pause she added, 'Maybe they did and never told no one. Maybe it was her old man as done away with her! You know what some of them are like down there.'

'Down where?' I asked. We still didn't know anything much beyond the fact that some woman called Violet Dickens had been killed in the East End somewhere.

'Freemasons Road,' Nan said. 'You can't miss it, it's one of the only houses still standing.'

She was right there. Ever since the bombing started back in September 1940, the area around the docks had taken the worst of the attacks. Manors like Custom House, where Freemasons Road was, had been almost razed to the ground.

'Rough old handfuls down that way!' Nan continued.

'But human beings who have suffered very greatly,' said my mother, who had now very slowly entered the kitchen.

'Duchess.' I put my fag out and then got up to help her. Her arthritis was bad before the war but now it's even worse. Especially, as now, in the winter, it's so bad it makes her joints swell up, which causes her terrible pain. But even in difficulty she waved me away. My mother doesn't like to be dependent even though she knows, as I do, that it is just the way her life is now. She sat down slowly next to Aggie while Nan poured her out a cup of tea.

'Well of course they have, they've had a shocking time down that way,' Nan said as she put the Duchess's cup and saucer down in front of her. 'But Mum, you know as well as I do that down Freemasons they're a rough lot.'

Aggie, who works by the docks at Tate and Lyle's sugar factory in probably even rougher Silvertown, said, 'Oh you think everybody's rough!'

'No I don't!'

'Yes you do!' She gently patted the pile of bleached blonde hair that sat in loads of curls on top of her head. 'All you lot always on your knees saying your rosary, you're always so quick to call other people . . .'

'Agnes!'

My mother doesn't often lose her temper, but when she does it is usually because my sisters are arguing. Nan is over fifty, even young Aggie is nearly forty, and yet the two of them fight like cats. It's always over, basically, the same thing, which boils down to the fact that Nan thinks that Aggie is common and 'fast' and Aggie finds all religion and religious people hypocritical.

'Well, I get sick of it!' Aggie said to the Duchess. 'Her passing judgement on everybody!' Then, in the absence of our mother saying anything more, she attacked Nancy once again. 'Who do you think you are? The Pope?'

Nan, outraged by such blasphemy, was left speechless. The Duchess however said, 'Now, Agnes, that isn't a nice thing to say . . .'

'Mum, I'm a married woman with two kids!' Aggie said. 'I can have my own opinions!'

'Yes, but . . .'

'You do what you like, it's your soul!' Nan, who had found her voice, now said bitterly. 'But to take the name of the Holy Father in vain . . .'

It went on. I smoked and drank my tea and tried not to get involved. Like Aggie, I'm not religious, but I know that the church is all that Nancy really has. She believes, and that belief helps her. After what I saw in the Great War, as well as what's been going on since the bombing started up here, I can't see that any sort of loving God can exist. Aggie, whose husband left her for another woman, alone and unprovided for with their two kids to bring up, can't take to that idea either. Her little 'uns are evacuated out in Essex and she makes the little money she does have working at Tate and Lyle's sugar works down in Silvertown. On a Friday night she likes a drink or two in one of the local pubs. She even gets, and likes to get, some little attention from men from time to time. She's an attractive girl who takes care of herself, and so I think, why not? But Nancy thinks it's wrong, that Aggie is loose and sinful and that her immortal soul is in great danger. Poor Nan is jealous – there's never been anyone special in her life – but she does genuinely care about her sister too. Not that Aggie appreciates it.

As usual the argument ended with Aggie storming off to go and put her face on up in her bedroom. After that came a tense silence. Knowing that I was probably the only person who could put a stop to it, I said, 'Nan, you were telling us about the woman found dead on Freemasons Road . . .'

Nancy, as is very often her custom, acted as if she hadn't heard until she was absolutely ready to speak again. I'd almost given up hope of a reply when she said, 'People are saying that she was murdered.'

If, as Nan had told us, people said that Violet Dickens's insides had been torn out, then murder was probably the most likely cause.

'They're saying it's the Ripper again, like they did with Nellie Martin,' Nan continued.

The Duchess, who hadn't come to live in England since long after Jack the Ripper's career had ended, but knew the story nevertheless, said, 'But those murders took place in Whitechapel, Nancy. And many years ago now, before you were born. Jack the Ripper must be dead now, I think.'

'Some people think that the Ripper weren't human,' Nan said with a gleam of superstitious fear in her eyes. That Jack the Ripper had been some sort of ghost or demon wasn't a new story. When a crime remains unsolved, the mystery takes on a life of its own, and Nan, for one, was the sort who took on that kind of thing. But I didn't want to put her down myself. She'd just had enough of that from Aggie.

'Well, Ripper or not,' I said, 'there's nothing to say the two women were killed by the same person.'

'That's very true, Francis,' the Duchess agreed. Whether she actually believed what she was saying or not, I didn't know. Like me, she was mainly interested in calming Nancy down.

'And besides,' I said, 'much as you disliked her, Nan, Nellie Martin wasn't a, well, a . . .' I hesitated to use the word 'prostitute', 'a loose woman, was she?'

'No.'

'And Violet Dickens?'

'Don't know about her,' Nan said. 'She was married but there was a lodger, and coming from down near the docks . . .'

'But it's unlikely,' I said. 'Nan, the Ripper's victims were all ladies of easy virtue. There's no connection.'

'Mmm.' Nan looked down at the floor while the Duchess stared anxiously across at me. My older sister is tortured by agitation about things like this.

'These two poor ladies died horribly,' I said as I got up from my chair and began to make my way towards the kitchen door. 'But there's nothing supernatural going on, Nancy. There's no Ripper or . . . There's some horrible people about, love. That's all.'

And then I went off down to the shop to look at the diary for the coming week with Doris.

Nothing else happened in what had become the very quiet and almost calm streets of West Ham for another two days. Then, a Thursday night it was, I was just about to go to bed when there was a hammering on the front door of the shop. Looking down out of the parlour window, I saw a group of coppers standing outside the shop. When he heard the window open, one of them turned his head up to face me. I knew him.

Sergeant Hill from Plaistow police station isn't exactly a friend, but I know him and he and I have quite a bit of time for each other. We've helped each other out in the past and there is a respect there in spite of both our various shortcomings. Basically he knows I'm not all I should be sometimes in my head and I know a few things about him he'd rather not talk about too. But this wasn't a social call.

'Mr H, I won't beat about the bush,' Sergeant Hill said after I let him and his lads into my shop. 'We've got a body we want you to look after for us.'

I frowned. At the height of the bombing, I had taken bodies in from the police and from families bombed out of their houses who couldn't have the deceased at home. There had been a lot of pressure on mortuary services, and so because I do have a small room where bodies can be stored, it was in constant use during that time. But since the bombing had stopped, the backlog was being dealt with. One of the consequences of this was that my little room was currently empty. I was however puzzled as to why the coppers should suddenly fetch up with a corpse when there was space in the mortuaries. Turning up at night didn't seem normal either, and I said so.

'I know it's unusual, Mr H,' Sergeant Hill replied, 'and in the normal course of events I wouldn't be doing it. But this body is . . . well, it's . . . We think the lady has been murdered. She is to be honest in a bit of a state . . .'

'Sarge, why don't you just come out and tell him it's the Ripper!' Percy Adams was an old copper, a perpetual constable and a bloke incapable of keeping even the most innocent confidence. In peacetime he'd have had his cards years ago, but in these strange days people who do all sorts of jobs are simply the only people who happen to be available. Sergeant Hill shot the old geezer a furious look.

'Constable, we don't . . .'

'All her insides ripped out of her body!' Percy Adams looked at me and said, 'That's why you have to have her, Mr Hancock. Can't be at home in the family parlour with half her body in a hessian sack, can she?'

'She's a shocking state!' one other, slightly younger constable said while several of the others nodded in agreement.

'Will you button it, Adams!' Sergeant Hill roared. Then, waving an arm at his little group of coppers, he said, 'Get out of it, the lot of you! Go on! Get out!'

They moved quickly for men whose average age was probably fifty. Once they had gone, I pulled the blackout curtain over the shop door once again and looked at Sergeant Hill.

'So there's been another of these Ripper murders, has there?' I said as I took a packet of Park Drive fags out of my pocket and offered it to the sergeant.

He sighed before taking one of my smokes and lighting up. 'Bloody Adams!' he said, and then he sighed again. 'But yes, the body is in a state, which is why the family can't have her at home. I was going to tell you, Mr H, but in my own time and in my own way.'

We stood looking at each other in silence then, both of us smoking.

'You can refuse, of course,' Sergeant Hill continued. 'I mean, it's a sealed coffin but, well, it's, er . . .'

'Was she, whoever she is, murdered?' I asked. 'Was it, do you think, this, er, this Ripper as they call him?'

'Well yes, the lady was murdered,' Sergeant Hill said gravely. 'And as bloody Percy Adams said, it was done in a very violent and blood-soaked fashion. Not that I go along with all this Jack-the-Ripper-come-back-to-life business.'

'But someone is killing women.'

'Middle-aged ladies, yes,' Sergeant Hill said. 'And he is most definitely carving them up a treat, as I know you know, Mr H.'

Nellie Martin, the skinned victim of New City Road, had not been a pretty, or for me, unfortunately, a forgettable sight. I'd seen quite enough unrecognisable lumps of flesh on the Somme. The nightly bombing had brought its horrors too. Although this war, though vile in every way, lacks the personal enmity that I saw in the First Lot, that all came back to me when I saw Nellie Martin. That, like the hand-to-hand combat on the Somme, was something deliberate, personal and venomous.

'Part of the problem here,' Sergeant Hill continued as he sucked heavily on his fag, 'is that the lady this time was a spinster. Lived alone up on Green Street. No family to actually have the body at home except a married sister who lives up Ilford way. Nice house apparently she's got. Husband works in the print. She don't want her sister's body messing up the place.' He shot me a look of obvious disapproval. Even in wartime there are still those for whom unscratched lino is more important than life or death. 'Post-mortem's been done,' he carried on. 'Had her throat cut before all the mutilation went on, so the doctor reckoned. Thank God!'

'Sergeant, I've heard nothing about this murder. When . . .'

'Oh, it was a neighbour who found her,' Sergeant Hill said. 'A warden. Saw the back door of her place open yesterday morning, went in and . . .' He shrugged. 'Luckily because it was a warden we managed to keep it a bit hush-hush. Something like this . . . well . . .'

People panic. Whether this apparent halt in the bombing of London will hold or not, no one knows. But if Hitler has even temporarily given up, then Londoners should be able to enjoy a bit of a breather. No one wants that spoiled by a run of murders by one of our own – least of all the coppers. There's not even much, by their own admission, they can do.

'People know about the other two,' I said. 'Nellie Martin and Violet Dickens.'

'And they'll know about this one in time, too,' Sergeant Hill said on yet another sigh. 'But if we can keep it as low-key as possible . . .'

'Did they know each other, the women?' I asked.

'I don't know,' Sergeant Hill replied. 'Of course, living in the same area they probably saw one another and . . . But Nellie Martin was a widow, Violet Dickens a married lady, and now this spinster. All very different.'

'Except in age.'

'Oh, they're all of an age,' he said. 'Early fifties.'

Like my sister. I told Sergeant Hill she'd been to school with Nellie Martin. I was, albeit without getting hysterical, a little worried.

'But not with Violet Dickens?'

'No.'

'Oh well.' He put his fag out then and looked up at me.

'So, Mr H, can my boys bring the body round the back? We've got it in a van, and if you can unlock your yard . . . Of course, if you . . .'

'Yes, bring her in,' I said as I put my fag out and went to get the keys to the yard. 'What's her name, by the way?'

'Dolly O'Dowd,' Sergeant Hill replied. And then, seeing the probably very pale colour I had taken on, he frowned and said, 'You feeling all right, are you, Mr H?'

Chapter Three

I didn't get a wink of sleep that night. Not that I often do have what most would call proper shut-eye. But even my poor brain doesn't usually boil over all the time like it did that night. Dolly O'Dowd was one of Nancy's best friends! Two old spinsters together, they went to Mass every Sunday and took part in every sort of church social and good-works thing that was going. My Hannah had said that Nellie Martin had been churchy too. Nan and Dolly O'Dowd went, I knew, to St Margaret's in Canning Town, which was on the Barking Road like, it was said, Nellie Martin's church. Had Nellie attended that church too, and if so, was that what was connecting these women?

Of course I couldn't find out anything in the middle of the night. The Duchess and my sisters had seemingly slept through the coppers delivering Dolly O'Dowd's body through the back of the shop. The coffin lid was nailed right down and there was nothing to indicate who might be inside. But that didn't mean I was off the hook about telling the family. They would want to know who was in there, why the coffin was closed and why it had turned up in the middle of the night. Also, as far as Nan was concerned, I had a duty. Dolly, funny old character that she'd been, had been her friend and now she was gone. Nan was going to be upset even though I knew that she was unlikely to show it. My older sister keeps most things in, it's her way.

Because I couldn't sleep, I sat up in bed and lit a fag. There's a gas-lamp bracket over my bed which works when there's gas to power it, but mostly we use candles in our bedrooms. Thin, dusty candles that give off a light the colour of old lemons. Most of the time it's not worth having, especially if you're trying to read, and so I just lay in the darkness, puffing, trying not to peer too hard into the total blackness around me. Like most people's bedrooms, mine is cold, damp and filled with heavy Victorian furniture. At night, made pitch dark by the blackout curtains, it's a place where all sorts of horrors can rise up in the mind. I made to push them out of the way by thinking in what I hoped was a logical manner.

Dolly O'Dowd had been very obviously religious. Wherever she'd gone, she'd taken a handbag full of religious stuff along with her. Rosaries, religious pictures, crucifixes and holy medals – it wouldn't have surprised me if she'd had a bottle of holy water in there too. As I remembered her, she'd been religious as a kid, one of those girls always wanting to become a nun. But then her mum had died when she was still at school and she'd stayed home to look after her dad from then on. Quite when he'd died I didn't know, but it had been some years back. Her sister, Rita I think she was called, had obviously hopped off to Ilford and her printer at some point in the proceedings. Dolly, alone in the house on Green Street, had said her rosary, knitted for the annual church fete and tried to ignore the fact that her only great beauty, her once flaming red hair, had faded to the colour of dust. Apart from her friendship with my dark and very foreign-looking sister, there was nothing that hadn't been totally conventional about Dolly O'Dowd. So why would anyone want to kill such a quiet and inoffensive woman in such a wild and violent fashion? Was it that the murderer didn't like little spinster women, or that he didn't maybe like Catholics? Neither of the other two victims had been spinsters, and I didn't know, as yet, what if any religion they had followed. But I determined then to find out. Assuming that the killer of Dolly O'Dowd was one and the same as the killer of the other two women, there had to be some sort of connection between the three of them. If that wasn't the case, then it was possible that more than one murderer was working the streets and houses of West Ham. I shuddered at that thought. My bedroom may always be cold but I'm a tough old soldier and so I don't generally notice the chill too badly. But that thought, of more than one killer being amongst us, did what no London winter could and made my whole body shake and freeze right down to its bones.

Nan was mixing up powdered egg for everybody's breakfast when I walked into the kitchen the next morning. The Duchess was still dressing in her bedroom and Aggie was sitting at the table reading a copy of *Picturegoer* and smoking a fag. I was going to try and discreetly get her to leave so that I could speak to Nan on my own, but Aggie had questions she wanted answered and which she came straight out with.

'There was a lot of noise downstairs last night, Frank,' she said. 'What was it all about?'

'Oh . . . uh . . .' I'm not very quick off the mark with either Nan or Aggie. I developed a stutter back in the Great War which gets very bad during bombing raids, and sometimes during conversations with my sisters.

Nan turned away from the saucepan on the range and said, 'I heard some sort of kerfuffle too.'

'And there's a coffin down in the back room sitting on one of the stands,' Aggie said. 'That wasn't there yesterday.'

'Haven't had quite so many of the dear departed with us since the bombing stopped,' Nancy said.

'Yes, but people are still bombed out,' Aggie said as she flicked the ash from her fag into an old tobacco tin.

'That's true,' Nan said. 'Not everyone's still got a parlour to rest the one who has passed over in. I mean, we're very lucky in a lot of ways . . .'

'It's, it's D-Dolly O'Dowd!' I blurted. I didn't mean to. I hadn't intended to be so blunt about it. But that said, I knew that my sisters weren't going to shut up and let me speak unless I made them do so. Nancy and Aggie may not get on for much of the time, but what they both have in common is a huge ability to bloody rabbit.

There was probably half a minute of silence. As both my sisters looked at me with disbelief on their faces it felt like a bleeding lifetime.

Nan took the saucepan of powdered egg off the range and put it on the table. 'But . . .'

'You do mean Dolly O'Dowd from Green Street, don't you, Frank?' Aggie asked. And then tipping her head towards Nan she said, 'Her churchy mate?'

'Y-yes.'

Nancy sat down, staring at the saucepan as the sticky yellow goo in it began to congeal. Aggie flashed me a concerned look and so I sat down next to Nan and put one of my hands over hers. Any more contact than that would have upset her. My older sister doesn't like to be touched.

'Nan, love,' I said, 'I know that Dolly was your friend . . .'

'She was my best friend.' Nan looked across at me, her face long and taut with the strain of holding in a lot of tears. She said, 'I never heard Dolly had passed away. Why ain't she at her Rita's? Why's she here?'

I didn't know where to start. Of course, in spite of the best efforts of the coppers, some people already knew about Dolly O'Dowd and very soon the whole manor would be buzzing with the news. I had to tell her.

'I want to see her,' Nan said as she jumped up from the table and began to walk towards the kitchen door.

'Nan!' I stood and made to follow her just as the Duchess came in for her breakfast. She caught the wild look in Nan's eyes immediately and looked at Aggie and me.

'Francis?' she said. 'What's going on?'

'Duchess, it's . . .'

'Dolly's dead,' Nan said matter-of-factly. 'Downstairs. Frank's just going to show me her now.'

35

'Dolly O'Dowd?' my mother asked. 'My goodness! How . . .'

'Frank's just going to show me her now,' Nan repeated as she began to shove against the Duchess in order to get past.

Aggie, alarmed at Nan's fierce, insistent behaviour, looked over at me and bit her lip.

'Frank . . .' Nan began.

'Nancy, sit down and let me tell you about it,' I said.

'Frank, I want to see Dolly, I . . .'

'Nan . . .'

'Frank . . .' As she pushed against the Duchess, Nan began to cry. My mother put one of her arms around her. She's the only person who can do anything so intimate with my older sister. 'Frank, I want to see . . .'

'Nan, you need to sit down,' I said. Then, looking over her head at my mother, I added, 'We all need to sit down for a moment.'

'I'd better turn the gas off,' Aggie said as she walked over to the range and put out the flame that had been heating our eggs.

Nan looked at me with such fear in her eyes I began to feel sick just at the thought of telling her what had happened to Dolly O'Dowd. But once she, Aggie and my mother were settled at the table, I did it anyway. I didn't have any choice. When I'd finished I said, 'So you can't see Dolly, I'm afraid, Nan. She's just in . . . in too much of a . . . mess, if you know what . . .'

'Do they know who . . .' Nan began. 'The coppers, do they know who, who done . . .'

'No.' I shook my head. 'No more than they know who killed Nellie Martin or Violet Dickens.'

'Coppers think it's the same person, do they?' Aggie asked.

'They think it's possible,' I said. 'Although of course only Dolly and Nellie died in Plaistow. Violet is down to Canning Town.'

'Jack the Ripper!' Nan said, and then she began to cry once again.

I looked at the Duchess, who shrugged and then said to Nancy, 'But dear, Jack the Ripper is long dead.'

''Course,' Aggie agreed. 'But Mum, someone's cutting women up like the old Ripper used to do. Someone's copying him.'

'Maybe.'

'Anyway, even if somehow it is the old Ripper, as long as he's caught that's all that matters,' Aggie said. 'Frank, you say the coppers brought the body in last night?'

'They're looking into it,' I replied.

'Yes, well, they've been looking into the other two women's deaths as well,' Aggie said darkly. 'Don't mean nothing's been done. You know what they're like, Frank.'

I did, but I didn't say anything to either confirm or deny Aggie's low opinion of the police. In truth of course they are overworked and there aren't enough of them. All the A1 young blokes have gone off to fight or work in the mines, leaving our few sad old coppers here to deal with a hell of a lot of misbehaviour. To be fair, most people have pulled together with their friends and neighbours for the war effort, but a lot haven't. Even with this lull or whatever it is in the bombing the looting still goes on. There's murder too, old and not so old scores settled in the blackout, away from the beats of our very few coppers. Ordinary folk do their best and their bit. I've done my share in the past. In fact I have been quite successful, something that my sister Aggie alluded to now.

'You should look into it, Frank,' she said. 'You've a better head on your shoulders than any copper I've ever come across.'

'Ag—'

'Agnes, your brother has a job!' the Duchess said firmly, her eyes blazing in anger at Aggie. 'It is a job he does well. He doesn't need to do any more. Let the police do their job and allow your brother to do his!'

'Yes, but Mum,' Aggie said, 'he's helped the police out before! Blimey, it was our Frank who found out who killed that gypsy girl up in Epping Forest last year!'

It was true. I had indeed helped to bring the murderer of the gypsy girl Lily Lee to justice the previous autumn. And that wasn't all I'd done.

'Then there was that bother with them sisters from over the West End,' Aggie said. 'Our Frank found out who was killing them . . .'

'That is enough!' My mother held up a small, brown silencing hand and stared very hard into Aggie's eyes. 'In case you have forgotten, Agnes, your brother is not a well man.' She looked over at me and smiled. 'Wounded in the trenches. Francis needs calm and harmony, not this madness!' She rose from her seat, and as she did so, she smiled down at Nan. 'I am so sorry that Miss O'Dowd has died, Nancy. I am sure that the police will catch the person responsible.

I think that now I must go back to bed. I . . . I don't feel too well and . . .'

'Mum, do you want me to take . . .'

'No, no, please stay where you are, Nancy,' the Duchess said as she patted Nan's hand and then slowly began to walk towards the door.

'What about your breakfast?' Aggie called out just before the Duchess reached the door.

My mother turned slowly and regarded my sister with a very cold eye. 'I don't feel hungry now,' she said, and then she left.

I was wounded in the trenches, but not badly, not in a physical way at least. What really went on out there went on in my mind. The look, the smell, the sound of violent death in all its forms was what did for me, and the Duchess knew it. But how does anyone talk about such damage to the mind? My mother doesn't use the word 'lunatic' about her son. What mother would? That said, how else can you talk about a man who sees and hears things that aren't there, who runs in the street when the bombs begin falling because anything, *anything* is better then risking being buried alive under bricks and wood and mud? I am not right and I shouldn't do anything that might make my condition worse. I should not put myself in danger or under strain.

Once the Duchess was out of earshot, Aggie looked at me and said, 'Frank, I'm sorry, if you don't want to . . . It's just that you're good at finding things out, and . . .'

'Look, Ag,' I said, lowering my voice, just in case the Duchess could hear, 'it's down to Nan, all right?'

'Nan?' She looked at our older sister, who was still staring fixedly down at the kitchen table.

'If Nan wants me to try and find something out about Dolly O'Dowd and maybe the others, then . . .'

'Dolly never done no one no harm ever,' Nan said as she lifted her head up and then looked over at me. 'She was a good woman!'

'Yes, love, I . . .'

'She loved God and the Blessed Virgin and . . .'

'Nan!' Aggie put a hand on top of Nancy's and looked deep into her eyes. 'Do you want Frank to try and find out what happened to Dolly, or do you want to trust the bloody stupid coppers?'

I gave Aggie a look that wasn't exactly approving while we waited for the answer. I knew what it was going to be, mind. Aggie hadn't exactly left Nan too much room to say anything else.

Nan looked at me and said, 'Frank, will you find Dolly's killer?'

Rita Bentham, Dolly O'Dowd's sister from Ilford, turned up at the shop just before midday. A smart, matter-of-fact woman in her mid-fifties, Rita knew all about the circumstances of her sister's death and so she had no expectations about seeing Dolly in her coffin.

'You'd think that in wartime we'd stop turning on each other, wouldn't you?' she said as she sat down with Doris to check on possible dates for her sister's burial. 'But the police say they'll find who did it and so you have to trust in that, don't you?'

'Yes,' Doris said. She's very good at reassurance, Doris; she said it very warmly.

I was at the back of the shop while this was going on, behind the black curtain that divides where the public go from where they do not. Once Doris had made the arrangements I'd go and give Mrs Bentham my condolences. In the meantime I dusted down my hats and tried to shake some of the muck from my gloves. We had a funeral at the East London Cemetery at two, and the boys and myself needed to get ready. During the bombing it was almost impossible to look clean and presentable. Now it wasn't quite so bad, but there was still dust and dirt everywhere from all the bomb sites and from the damage done to the existing buildings and the streets. Sometimes I find it difficult to remember how this manor looked before Hitler and the Luftwaffe started trying to flatten it. There are whole streets I can't even bring to mind now.

'Father Burton says he can do next Thursday,' I heard Rita Bentham say.

There was a pause during which pages of the diary were turned. Then Doris said, 'We can do next Thursday morning, Mrs Bentham.'

'Good.'

'At the East London?'

'Yes.'

I went through the curtains and offered my hand to the lady.

'Mrs Bentham,' I said, 'I am so sorry for your loss.'

'Yes, well . . .' she sighed. Dry-eyed, more inconvenienced

than distraught, or so it appeared. Like her sister, Rita Bentham had once had very red hair which, unlike Dolly, she now dyed a sort of blondish ginger colour. Heavily made up, she was stylish rather than attractive and wore a large sombrero hat with a very brightly coloured feather curled around the brim. She took my hand but she didn't get up.

'As you know, Mrs Bentham,' I said, 'we have your sister here.'

'The police have explained.'

'Yes, well, of course,' I continued. 'But if you'd like the funeral to start at Green Street . . .'

'Oh, that won't be necessary,' she said.

'Oh. I just thought that because your sister had always lived there and your parents before . . .' I shrugged. She didn't respond. 'For neighbours to pay their respects . . .'

Mrs Bentham rose to her feet. 'My sister was a sad, lonely spinster, Mr Hancock,' she said. 'She didn't see people.'

'She was friends with *my* sister,' I said.

She looked down at the floor and said, 'Yes.' It's not often I've heard someone damn another with one such simple word. I wanted to ask her what she felt or imagined was wrong with my sister. But I didn't. Doris looked over at me and widened her eyes.

'I'd like the cortège to go from here,' Rita Bentham said. 'There won't be many mourners.' She waved a dismissive hand in the air. 'Your sister can come if she wishes . . .'

'I'm sure that Nancy would want to do that,' I replied, careful not to actually thank her for her grudging invitation. She was older than even our Nancy, and so I hadn't known

42

Rita O'Dowd, as was, when we were children. But as an adult I knew I didn't like her. I wasn't alone.

Once she'd finished making arrangements for her sister's funeral, Rita Bentham left and Doris spoke. 'Blimey, she was a right cold fish!' she said to me as she watched the woman walk eastwards down the Barking Road back towards Ilford way. 'And what was all that being sniffy when you talked about Miss Nancy?'

'I don't know, Doris,' I said. But I thought that maybe I did. Nancy is the darkest of the lot of us and it is Nancy, if anyone, who has to take any stick that's going because of it. The Duchess, to be fair, doesn't come in for much colour trouble. But then she is an Indian, she couldn't be anything else. Anglo-Indians like my sisters and me are another matter. Some people, Rita Bentham maybe included, see us as tainted – Nancy much more than me and Aggie hardly at all. Blonde Anglos like her can get away with it.

Later, when Nan came back from the shops, I told her when Dolly's funeral was going to take place. She took in what I was saying but it was obvious that she didn't really want to talk about Dolly. Just before I left for the cemetery that afternoon, she did however speak to me one more time.

'Frank, you asked me if I knew whether Violet Dickens went to me and Dolly's church,' she said.

She'd already told me that the first victim, Nellie Martin, had attended the Baptist church.

'Yes?'

'Violet Dickens never went to any church,' Nan replied.

'More comfortable in the pub, so it's said. I asked around like you told me to.'

I looked at her and smiled. So thin and tired and unhappy. How could I not help her find out who had killed her best friend? 'Thanks, Nan,' I said as I put my top hat on and started walking towards the door out into the yard.

'Thank you, Frank,' my sister replied. 'I think you'll find who murdered Dolly. I really think you will.'

I did appreciate her confidence, even though I didn't share it. Having said that, I had already made some little progress, because the churches the ladies had attended were maybe not what, for the murderer, connected them. At that moment the only thing that did that was their age. As I climbed up on to the hearse behind the horses, I looked down at my middle-aged sister and I frowned.

Chapter Four

Blood, thick and scarlet red, ran down every wall inside the stable and then rushed, as if charging, towards the horses. I didn't cry out because I knew what this was and I didn't want to alarm the horses. But I shook, and when I saw that there was also a man's head bleeding in the straw by the horses' hooves, I had to push my fist into my mouth to stop myself from screaming. God alone knew what the horses, my geldings Rama and Sita, thought of me with my shaking, my sweating, my mad terrified eyes.

'Mr H, you've got a visitor.' Doris's voice behind me only partially broke the spell that old visions from the trenches had temporarily cast over me.

'Oh, er, Doris, er . . .' I didn't turn around even though I knew that Doris was quite accustomed to seeing me like this. I've been tormented in this way ever since I came home from France in 1918. But since the bombing began last year I have got worse. Doris and everyone else is well aware of this.

'It's Mr Cox,' Doris said.

'Oh . . . right.' I turned briefly towards her, wiping the sweat away from my face as I did so. 'Tell him I'll er . . . I'll be in in a mo.'

'All right.'

She left. Albert Cox runs an undertaking business down in Canning Town. A few years younger than me, he too inherited his business from his old man. Like Hancock's, Cox's provides a full funeral service but to rather different people from those that we usually serve. Plaistow is a poor place where disease and hunger, even now, probably take the lives of more young children than the bombing. But we also get our share of local tradespeople, doctors and priests, men and women who've left good money for a good slap-up send-off. Canning Town, though, is real docklands. In other words it's noisy, dirty and poor in a way I've been told my mother's home city of Calcutta is. Although she was pregnant with me before she and my dad came back to England with Nan, I've never seen my mother's country. But she talks about it often. She loves it, and when we were nippers, myself and the girls used to enjoy her stories about gentle elephants and brightly coloured temples. But there was another side too. There were beggars and lepers, people dying in the street from hunger or disease. Dad told me once in whispered tones about the number of young girls 'on the street' and how dead in the eyes they always looked to him. Hannah, my Canning Town girl, can look like that sometimes. In Canning Town there are women and girls on the street. The men who go to them come from all over the world, delivering goods that mean wealth for the Empire, which means, in reality, money for a very, very few. I'm no Commie, God knows, but when I look at the hungry faces of the women and kids round here, particularly in the docklands, it makes me want to hit someone. Half the men down there only have casual employment, and although since the war began rich and poor alike have pulled together to do their bit, it's still those at the bottom who seem to do, and suffer, the most.

After securing the horses and then wiping my hands, I walked through the back room and into the shop. Albert, a short, fair-haired bloke, quite lined in the face, stood up and took my hand.

'Hello, Frank,' he said.

'Albert.'

Doris, who was sitting at the back of the shop at our now battered-looking desk, said, 'You and Mr Cox like a cuppa, would you, Mr H?'

'That'd be lovely, Doris,' Albert said cheerily as he took his fags out of his pocket and offered me one.

I said I'd like a cup of tea too, and so Doris left the shop and went upstairs to the kitchen.

'So, Albert,' I said, 'to what do I owe the pleasure?'

The smile that Albert Cox had had on his face when I'd come in from the yard dropped.

'Thought I'd better warn you,' he said as he lit up his fag and mine and then threw the dead match into Doris's ashtray, 'there's a nutter about, mate.'

'A nutter?' The word covered a multitude of mad people as far as I was concerned, including, even I had to admit, myself at times.

'Just finished burying an old girl up the East London,' Albert said. He looked around to make sure that no one was coming in either from out in the street or from the yard at the back. 'While I was there I went over to see the grave of a woman I buried two days ago. There'd been quite a lot of flowers and I was checking they were still there. You know how people can be . . .'

I nodded in agreement. War or no war, the theft of flowers from cemeteries still, sadly, goes on.

Albert took a drag on his fag and said, 'Well, I'm having a butcher's, like, and the flowers are all still there, and then I see something new.'

'Something new?'

'A little posy it was. Pretty little thing. So I bends down to have a look and I sees that there's a card with it. I read it.' Albert let his breath out on a whistle and then he said, 'Bloody horrible, Frank! No rest in peace or none of that!' He lowered his voice. 'Things like "evil slut", "Nazi bitch" and "rot in hell"!'

'Blimey.' I've come across some less than complimentary last messages to the dead in the past, but never that sort of thing. 'Was there anyone about? What did you do?'

'No one, apart from my mourners and the priest, as far as I could see,' Albert said. 'Normally I would've asked around a bit, discreet like, but in this instance . . .'

I frowned.

'It was on the grave of that woman what got murdered,' Albert said. 'Violet Dickens.'

'Bloody hell!'

'I took the whole shebang down the cop shop,' Albert said. 'Let them have a look at it. But it give me the creeps, Frank, as you can imagine. Then I thought of you burying that other woman, that spinster from Green Street, up there on Thursday, and I thought I'd better let you know. Just between us, though, and the coppers, as you know.'

'What about Father Burton?' I asked. 'Does he know?'

'Oh yes, I had to tell him,' Albert said. 'But shtum to everyone else, all right?'

I puffed on my fag and said, 'Yes, Albert, I understand. Thank you, I appreciate that.'

Albert went on with other nutter stories while I came to grips with this information about one of the so-called Ripper victims. Someone had put something very personal on Violet Dickens's grave. Whether or not it was the same person who had killed her, I didn't know. But even beyond the grave, it seemed, Mrs Dickens had at least one enemy.

Doris came in then with our cups of tea, but almost immediately she went off to powder her nose. Once she'd gone I asked Albert a question.

'What was Violet Dickens's funeral like?' I said. 'Did it go all right or . . .'

'Well attended. Luckily not by, I don't think at least, too many of the ghoulish types who like to go to funerals of them who've been murdered. But like I said, a lot of flowers for these days,' Albert said. 'Not from the family, though.' He leaned in close to me and lowered his voice. 'Skint, the lot of them. Friend of the family paid me, the priest, the flowers, everything.'

I was shocked. Families, even of the poorest docker, usually pay for their own relatives' funerals. If necessary they put their possessions in the pawn shop to do so.

'A friend?' I said. 'It wasn't the lodger they had, was it?'

'Ronnie Arnold? No,' Albert said. 'He ain't got a ha'penny to bless himself with. Like poor old Violet's husband, Ronnie's a drinker. That's why he was living there.' He moved in closer once again and said, 'I know there's been some talk about Ronnie and Violet maybe . . .' He winked suggestively. 'But there was none of that. It was Ronnie and Fred Dickens, Vi's husband, what had interests in common, if you know what I mean.'

For a moment I wondered whether Violet Dickens's husband and this Ronnie bloke had been involved in some sort of male love, something homosexual . . .

Seeing the look of nervousness on my face, Albert smiled and said, 'No! They was never iron hoofs or nothing, Frank! No, Ron and Fred got drunk together! When they couldn't get work down the docks they went down the pub while poor old Vi did whatever she could to earn a crust – taking washing, cleaning, you know.'

I did. Some say that the dockers' women work harder than their men, and in lots of cases that is true.

'Violet liked a drop herself, don't get me wrong,' Albert said. 'But she worked *and* had her Friday nights in the pub, if you know what I mean.'

'So who paid, then?' I asked. 'For the funeral.'

'A lady called Mrs Darling,' Albert said, and then he pulled a strange, almost disgusted face. 'Priest weren't happy.'

'Father Burton?'

'Yes.'

'Why not?'

'Well, she's one of them spiritual mediums,' Albert said.

'Mrs Darling?'

'Yes. Violet liked all that table-turning and talking to the dead, apparently,' he said. 'Been going to this Darling woman for years, so Fred said. Schlepping all the way up to East Ham twice a week.'

'Oh, it's not that far,' I began.

But then Albert said, 'It is if you're a cripple, mate. Vi wore callipers all her life. Something wrong with her bones, they say. Staggering up East Ham twice a week must have taken it out of the poor cow. But anyway, all that's by the by,' he continued. 'Main thing is, Frank, be on the lookout when you bury the Green Street woman. Maybe whoever is killing these ladies is leaving little messages for them in their flowers.'

Doris returned from powdering her nose then, and so Albert and I talked of other things.

Although our firm was the nearest one to the late Nellie Martin's home on Iniskilling Road, I hadn't actually buried the body that myself and Arthur had found. Nellie's family, who I had discovered when I'd been asking around about the women's various religions were devout Baptists, had insisted on using a family firm known for their affiliation to that faith, namely Haigh's of Barking. There had been a service for Nellie up at the Memorial Baptist on the Barking Road followed by an interment at the City of London Cemetery in Manor Park. That *had* been a big affair, with lots of what Albert Cox calls 'ghouls' in attendance. But then whereas Violet Dickens's family had been made up of basically poor drinkers, Nellie's were business people. She herself had been a decent Baptist widow, and sympathy for her was high. There was, I felt, a little bit of a feeling that Violet Dickens, with her drunken husband and loud-mouthed lodger in tow, had somehow deserved what had happened to her. Not so Dolly O'Dowd, however, although her funeral, as Father Burton told me later on that day, was going to be small for other reasons.

'The sister wants to keep it very quiet,' he said. 'People have only been invited by word of mouth.'

'My Nancy's going,' I said as I followed him into his parlour and then sat down.

'I should think so, they were good friends,' Father Burton said. Thin and rather monk-like in appearance, I've always thought, Father Burton folded himself into the armchair in front of me and then steepled his fingers underneath his chin. 'She was a good woman, Dolly O'Dowd. What she did to deserve such a fate, well . . .'

'Do you think it might be the same person killing all these ladies?' I asked him.

Father Burton shrugged. 'I don't know, Francis,' he said. 'It's the police you'd have to ask about that. I'm just a priest.' He took a sip from his teacup and then put it down on the table beside him. 'But it seems odd to me that if the same person is killing these women he should choose such different victims.'

'They're all around about the same age.'

'Yes, but a spinster, a respected widow and someone like Violet Dickens . . .'

He left what Violet Dickens was or had been like hanging in the air. Father Burton is not one who talks easily about what he generally expresses as 'immorality'. Not that, from what Albert had said at least, Violet could have been considered exactly immoral. Although no churchgoer myself, I knew this priest well enough to know not to push him, and so I just waited for him to talk, which eventually he did.

'Of course poor Violet had a cross to bear in the form of her husband,' he said after a very long pause. 'In a place of drinkers like Canning Town, it's quite something to be known and almost made into a figure of myth for your drinking. But Frederick Dickens is such a man.' He shook his head slowly. 'When the police told me that the poor woman had been dead in the attic of that house for weeks and Frederick and that other creature completely unaware, I wasn't surprised.'

'You weren't?'

'Blind drunk the pair of them! God Almighty, Francis, I wouldn't have been surprised if Violet had been dead since before the bombing started! All those men have done for years is drink. Not even sober at her funeral!'

'I didn't know they'd been . . .'

'Oh, it was the woman who claims to speak to the dead who ran the funeral,' Father Burton said. 'God help us, Francis, that a Catholic woman like Violet should seek counsel from such people . . .' He stopped briefly in order, I imagined, to collect himself once again. His normally colourless face was pink with fury. 'Table-turning and ectoplasm and what have you! God help us!'

Albert had said Father Burton hadn't approved of Mrs Darling. Not that I had really come to see him about her.

'Father,' I said, 'I know that Albert Cox told you about the posy he found on Violet Dickens's grave . . .'

'During Mrs Salazar's funeral, yes,' Father Burton said. 'A vile note! He gave it to the police, I believe.'

'He told me about it because I'm doing Dolly's funeral with you, Father, and Albert, well, he says we should be on the lookout maybe . . .'

'For what? Deranged people carrying flowers with offensive cards attached? Why would anyone want to do such a thing to Dolly O'Dowd?'

'Why would anyone do such a thing to Violet Dickens?'

'Francis, she drank her drop too, you know. And it is well known that the first of her seven children was born only three months after her wedding . . .'

'Father, whoever wrote that note called Violet a Nazi!' I said. 'That's nothing to do with her love life or her drinking!'

'No, but . . .'

'Well, I'm sure she wasn't a Nazi! But what if this horrible flower-sender sends something unpleasant to Dolly's funeral?'

The priest looked down for a moment as if he was a little ashamed of what he had said about Violet Dickens. I didn't think he was in reality, but I hoped that he'd taken my point anyway.

'Albert told you, and me, so that we can keep an eye open,' I said. 'Mrs Bentham wants her sister's funeral to be quiet and discreet, as do all of us.'

'We don't know when that ghastly posy was put on Violet's grave,' Father Burton said. 'I don't think it was at her actual funeral.'

'I don't suppose it was,' I said. 'But Father, if we see something suspicious . . . if it means that maybe we can catch someone in the act . . .'

'Francis, that is a matter for the law, not us,' Father Burton said coldly. 'You commend the dead to the earth, I commend them to God. Neither of us can dispense justice.' He fixed me with one of his not infrequent 'you're a mad person, Francis' looks and said, 'Especially not you, my son.'

I looked down at the floor of Father Burton's parlour and noticed, calmly, that the rug was swimming in blood from Passchendaele.

The Duchess went to bed early that night, and with Aggie on the night shift down at Tate and Lyle's it meant that I was left on my own with Nan. By this time, of course, she was in mourning for Dolly O'Dowd, and so even by her dark standards she was a deeply black presence in our flat. As night began to fall that afternoon I sat by the window in order to get the last of the daylight before we put up the blackout curtains. But soon the fog came down and there was nothing left to be seen and so I entombed us for the night while my sister cooked up a potato pie in the kitchen. Later, as I tried to read the *Evening News* by the light of a single candle, she came and stood next to me. So shrouded in black was she that I hardly knew she was there until she spoke.

'Frank?'

'F . . .' I put a hand up to my chest and only just stopped myself from cursing. 'Gawd above, Nan, what . . .'

'Frank, have you found anything else out about poor Dolly yet?' she asked. 'Oh, and the other women who, er . . .'

I lit a fag up to calm my nerves and then I said, 'No. Not really, love, I . . . Nan, this really is something for the coppers, love . . .'

'Oh, what do they do?' She sat down beside me and then shuffled her thin backside on the chair in an agitated fashion. 'Terrible things go on all the time, but they don't do nothing about it.'

'Terrible things?'

'Looting and all that what goes on down the public shelters.' She gave me a significant look. 'You know.'

Some say there's been more kids conceived down the London public shelters in the last six months than in the whole of the country for the last year. Makes me smile, but to someone like Nan it's an outrage.

'Nan, love, murder's a long way off from a soldier and his girl having a bit of a cuddle in the blackout.'

Even by the thin light of the candle I could see Nan blush with anger. 'They ain't doing nothing about murder and you know it!' she said. 'Frank, think about all the dear departed you've had to follow up on in the last year. Think about that bloke who got stabbed and only you knew!'

My old dad used to talk about the undertaker's 'third eye'.

How to express that in words I don't really know, beyond the notion that it is a feeling you get when a dead body isn't right. When a person has met his or her end in a way that is premature or violent, a good undertaker, dedicated to the care of the dead, does know. At the height of the bombing back in 1940 I'd had such a feeling about a bloke who died apparently from the effects of bomb blast. I'd seen him by chance just minutes before he died and he told me he'd been stabbed. But there was no evidence that the police doctor could find of this, even though I knew the dying man hadn't been lying. And I'd been right. He had been stabbed, but with a lady's hatpin, which had left almost no mark on the outside of his body. The poor bloke had bled to death inside – a slow and apparently very painful death. That said, Dolly O'Dowd and the other women were known to have been murdered.

'Nan, the police . . .'

'Aggie was right. The coppers ain't doing nothing, Frank, and well you know it!'

'Do I?' I lit up a Woodbine and said, 'How do you know? Have you spoken to them? Sergeant Hill at Plaistow is a good bloke. I'm sure he's doing his best.'

'Yes, but you . . .'

'I'm finding out what I can,' I said. I wondered whether to tell Nan about the posy with the insulting card that had been placed on Violet Dickens's grave and then thought better of it. Her low opinion of the dockers' women in general would only make her dismiss that anyway. 'And Nan, you must tell the coppers anything you might know about Dolly, and the others, too.'

She turned away slightly then and said, 'I only really knew Dolly.'

'You knew Nellie Martin,' I said. Then, because all of the women were around about the same age and because I couldn't remember anyway, I asked her, 'Did you go to school with Dolly, Nan?'

'Yes.'

'So you went to school with Dolly O'Dowd and Nellie Martin?'

'Yes.' She was still turned away from me, into the darkness.

'Violet Dickens? What about her?'

'She lived down Canning Town,' Nan said.

It wasn't really an answer and so I said, 'Yes, but Dolly lived almost in Upton Park, but she still went to New City Road School. Did . . .'

'I dunno.' She turned still further away from me, and she shrugged.

I got up then and moved around so that I could see my sister's face. The old third eye was apparently working with the living at that moment and I knew that what Nan was telling me wasn't right in some way.

'Nan, I have looked for connections between these ladies and I haven't found any yet,' I said. 'They differ on religion, on whether they're married and have kids or not and on whether they've got any money. All they have in common is their age. Now, if they all went to the same school . . .'

'I don't know where Violet Dickens went to school!' Nan said. Her face I could see now was screwed up with tension. She wasn't telling the truth about something, either that or she was leaving something out of what she was saying. 'Frank . . .'

'Because if you do know something, then you've got to tell the coppers.' I bent down to look more closely at her and added, 'Because, Nan, if this killer is murdering middle-aged women who went to New City Road School forty years ago, then that could mean that you're in danger.'

She looked up into my eyes and I swear I saw a bead of sweat form on her top lip.

I stood up straight again and said, 'And I don't want any harm to come to you, Nan. None of us do.'

'I don't know anything,' she said as she got up from the chair and ran out of the parlour back to the kitchen. 'Nothing!'

Just over an hour later the sirens went and Nan headed for our Anderson shelter. I went out in the street.

Chapter Five

Her thick mane of strawberry-blonde hair had always been Marie's best feature. Now it was twisted cruelly around a hand that was strong and determined and which she knew meant her harm.

'Please!' she said softly. Her head was pulled back so that she was looking up at the ceiling. Upstairs, just above the parlour, was where her dear old dad was sleeping. Even now, even with this monster in control of her beautiful hair, she didn't want her dad to wake up. 'Don't pull out my hair! Not my hair!'

'Not your hair.'

'No! Please!'

There was a pause. No slackening of the grip upon her hair happened, but Marie began to feel her attacker's other hand take hold of her blouse at the back and pull it upwards, away from her skirt. Panting with fear, Marie tried to move one of her hands around to her back, but doing that just resulted in her hair being pulled almost out by its roots once again.

'No!' she hissed again, still trying to be quiet, still so aware of her father asleep upstairs. 'No!' She felt groggy. When the cold air *in the parlour hit her now naked back, the shock of it made her feel sick. 'Oh God.'*

Another tug on her hair. This time Marie just groaned. Stupid, stupid, stupid woman! Why had she allowed herself to get into a situation like this? She wasn't silly, she was a bright girl, a good girl, a girl who would have made something of herself if her poor old dad had been more of what he should have been. 'Not my hair! Not my hair! Please, please, please, not my hair!' she murmured.

Her hair was left alone after that. The knife that her attacker had taken from Marie's very own cutlery drawer first slid into the skin on her back and then scraped it off her flesh and her bones in one smooth, hard movement. Still not wanting to wake her sleeping father, Marie screamed silently as she felt pain like she'd never experienced in her life before.

The murder of Marie Abrahams from Plashet was believed to have taken place later on that night. Not that anyone knew about it for a good eight hours until after it had happened. I was out and about when I heard.

I'd done some thinking since I'd had that conversation with Nan the previous evening, which made me even more certain that she was concealing something, probably something quite unimportant, from me. Nan's a strange creature when it comes to things of a moral nature. Even when it doesn't directly concern her, lack of morality can upset her enormously. It's why I can't tell her about my Hannah and why, possibly I thought, she might not want to admit to having gone to school with a drinker like Violet Dickens. But I didn't see Nan that morning, as I had an early appointment to see the landlord of the Tidal Basin pub in Canning Town. His mother had just died, and although he was strictly on Albert Cox's territory, he'd known my old dad and so he wanted Hancock's to do his old girl's funeral. Even in those rough parts I was still surprised to see a couple of blokes outside the pub as I went round the back to get to the flat up above. I commented on it to the landlord after we'd made our arrangements and I was leaving.

'Oh, that's bloody Ronnie Arnold and Fred,' he said as he shook my hand on the back doorstep. 'I tell you truly, Mr H, if Fred's missus hadn't just died, I'd tell the pair of them to fuck off.'

There's no beating about the bush in pubs like the Tidal Basin. An oath is an oath and it is never apologised for. I can respect that. I tipped my hat to the landlord and went around to see the men, who I had, in a way, some interest in. Getting into conversation with Fred Dickens and Ronnie Arnold was not, however, a thing easily done. It was only nine o'clock in the morning and they were already three sheets to the wind.

Because the landlord's mother had died the previous day, he'd been loath to leave her body in the pub when the sirens had gone. There hadn't been much of a raid compared to what we're used to, but most people, if not myself, had sheltered, including apparently Ronnie and Fred.

'He let us go down his Anderson,' the darker and older of the two men said as he jabbed a blunt thumb back towards the pub and, presumably, the landlord inside.

'We took a couple of pints down with us,' the other, red-headed bloke put in. 'There was only us and Tilly, like.'

'An' Tilly too,' the older man said. 'Yes, Tilly . . . Tilly with a gin and lemon and . . .' His eyes began to close.

'Sir, is your name Fred Dickens?' I began. 'I . . .'

The eyes opened. They were bloodshot and now quite suspicious. 'Who wants to know?' he said.

'Well, I'm . . .'

'He's a fucking undertaker by the look of him,' the younger man said.

Well there was no denying that fact. I'd come out to visit a bereaved family and so of course I was dressed in a suit with a top hat on my head. There aren't many people outside my profession, in the East End, who wear clothes like that. Even drunks can identify us.

'He ain't Cox,' the other man said, alluding to my mate Albert.

'No, my name is Hancock,' I said. 'I work in Plaistow.'

'Oh, Barking Road,' the younger man said to the older. 'Fred, he's that darkie undertaker.'

'Oh!' Fred Dickens smiled, showing me very quickly his complete absence of teeth. 'Oh, you're that one who runs about when raids are on, ain't you?'

I do, and so I didn't bother to deny it. After all, even if people are roaring drunk they generally deserve the truth about matters. I run out into the street when bombs start to fall because I fear being buried alive. I make no secret of it.

'Mr Dickens,' I said.

'Mate, do you have any drink about you?' the other, presumably Ronnie Arnold, asked me.

'I don't, I'm afraid,' I said. 'Although I can offer you and Mr Dickens a fag.'

Fred Dickens's drink-sodden face assumed a serious expression. 'You got Passing Clouds or something else posh, have you?' he said.

I put my hand in my jacket pocket and took out a packet of Capstan Full Strength. 'No . . .'

'Oh, Capstans'll do lovely!' Ronnie Arnold said as he leaned across and took two fags from my packet.

'I'll have some of them!' Fred Dickens said. But as his mate began to shakily light up one of his smokes, I withdrew my hand and the fags to one side for a moment.

'Mr Dickens,' I said, 'I know that you've recently lost your wife . . .'

'Gi'us a fag!' Fred Dickens pushed against me, trying to grab the Capstans from my hand.

'Mr Dickens, you're still in mourning, I know . . .'

'You gonna give me a fag then, wog?'

Ronnie was smoking contentedly away in his own little booze-soaked world. But Fred was getting aggressive. One thing that he wasn't, however, was upset, at least not visibly so, about his late departed wife.

Still holding the fags out of his reach, I said, 'Mr Dickens, what school did your wife go to when she was a kid?'

'What school?' Still looking up at the Capstans, he licked his dried-out lips and then said, 'Why do you want to know where Violet went to school?'

'I just do,' I said. I didn't want to have to stay and talk to these two for any longer than was necessary. Fred obviously wasn't mourning his wife any more and I needed to carry on trying to find out if any connections existed between the Ripper murder victims – and maybe my sister Nancy too.

'Why'd you want to know?'

'If you tell me, truthfully,' I said as I held the packet of fags up in front of him, just a little out of his reach, 'you can have the whole packet.'

He stared at me for a bit then. Small black eyes surrounded by bloodshot whites tried, without success, to stare in what he probably imagined was a menacing way at me. But then he just caved in as drunks tend to do and said, 'New City Road School. Give!'

I gave him the Capstans, which he shoved into the pocket of his jacket so quickly I almost didn't see them go. I hadn't wanted that particular answer, but I was glad nevertheless to have some sort of reply, even if it made me suspicious of and anxious about my sister. I was just about to go when Ronnie Arnold piped up and said, 'Ripper done another one last night.'

'What?'

'Ripper,' the red-headed man said. 'Killed another woman last night.'

I leaned towards him and said, 'Where? How do you know?'

'Tilly talked about it,' Fred Dickens said. 'Talking nonsense!' Then he turned to Ronnie Arnold, slapped him on the arm and said, 'She's a drunk! What you listen to her for? You should keep away from Tilly, like I told you!'

'Fuck off!'

They started to fight.

I didn't know who Tilly was or how she knew what these

men claimed that she did. But I wasn't going to find anything more out from either of them and so I left. I didn't have long to wait to discover what the truth of the matter was, however. As soon as I got back into the shop, Doris pulled me to one side and said, 'Mr H, a woman's been killed up Plashet. They say she's had her liver cut out and the skin peeled completely off her back! Can you imagine?'

Having seen the body of poor Nellie Martin, unfortunately I could.

By early afternoon, gossip had it that the Plashet victim was a fifty-one-year-old woman called Marie Abrahams. Because Plashet is to the north of Plaistow, and comes under East Ham actually, it's not a place me and mine know too well. However, because the surname was, I at least imagined, Jewish, it wasn't long before Doris was making contact with her friends and family living out that way. And so by the early evening we knew that poor Marie had in fact been a Jewish lady, that she'd grown up in Stepney and that she and her father hadn't gone to live in Plashet until just before the start of the Great War.

'My cousin Betty went to school with her,' Doris said as she picked up her handbag and her gas mask and made ready to go home to Spitalfields.

'Jewish Free School?' I asked.

'Where else?' Doris smiled and then her face fell very quickly once again. It was only a few months since her husband Alfie had died in a raid, and so she still had sudden, quite disconcerting, patches of melancholy from time to time.

'Doris . . .'

'The coppers are all over the house up Plashet,' Doris said as she pulled the shop door open and began to step outside. 'Took this Marie's old father away, they say.'

'He was in the house when his daughter was murdered?' I asked.

'Poor old bloke's simple, apparently,' Doris said. 'Off his nut, you know.'

And then she left. I looked down at the copy of the *Evening News* Arthur had brought in for me earlier and saw, with no surprise, that there was no mention of any murder anywhere. Same as Nellie Martin, Violet Dickens and even poor old Dolly O'Dowd. Censorship is used to cover up stories that might depress the population at large, bring down the mood of the war effort. It means that the East End is often alone in its mourning – its children bombed to bits in their own schools, whole dockside manors emptied of all human life. I don't care if the King and Queen come and visit us down here every day, we're on our own in the East End, I don't mind what anyone says.

As I shut up the shop I thought about poor Marie Abrahams's father. 'Simple' was how Doris had described him, but that covered a multitude of sins. Was the old man retarded or senile or was he just really, really shocked? If he had been in the house when his daughter was hacked up and skinned, was it surprising the old man was not himself? I wondered whether the police had taken Mr Abrahams away for his own safety and sanity, which had to be part of the reason certainly. But were they questioning him too? And if they were, what, or who, more to the point, had he seen? One thing that was starting to worry at my brain was the seeming fact that all the women killed so far had gone quietly to their horrible deaths. Nobody round and about had heard anything even resembling a scream on New City Road around the time it was thought Nellie Martin had died. Violet Dickens, living in what was now the middle of nowhere with two alcoholics, didn't count, but no one had heard Dolly O'Dowd die or even seen anyone go into her house. Now, apparently, Marie Abrahams had been slaughtered while her father was in the house with her. The murderer was getting in and doing his business very easily and very anonymously. Even if all the victims knew the killer, why was he not being spotted by anyone else?

'Hello, Frank.'

The door I'd just shut opened and my cousin Stella walked inside. Stella, who is the daughter of my dad's brother Percy, was bombed out last October. Uncle Percy died in that raid and Stella, a funny old spinster at the best of times, went a bit shell-shocked for a while afterwards, which is why she now lives with us. For the past couple of weeks, however, she'd been staying with my dad's sister Hester down in Margate. Thin and plain, Stella, who is just a bit older than Nan, is generally a very pale creature. But as soon as she came across the threshold I noticed that unusually she had a bit of colour in her cheeks.

'Sea air must have done you good, Stella,' I said as she hunched her way over towards me.

'Yes,' she said flatly, like she does. 'Couldn't get down the beach though because of all the wire and the mines and that.'

'Well, it's the coast, isn't it?' I said. Then, as it occurred to me how odd her presence in the shop was, I said, 'Was the back gate closed?'

The girls and the Duchess and to a large extent Walter and Arthur use the gate in the back lane into the yard to get to the rooms behind the shop and up to the flat. It was unusual for Stella to come in from the street.

For a moment Stella looked away, and then she said, 'Well, I didn't like to . . .'

Walter sometimes has a few bottles of beer in the yard before he goes home of a night. Sometimes he has more than a few, and when he does that, he gets loud and not a bit intimidating – particularly to nervous middle-aged spinster ladies.

'Was Walter drunk, Stella?' I was prepared to go and read him the riot act. I can't do without him but at the same time I won't take any nonsense.

'No, no, Frank, it's not that,' Stella said. Then she sighed a little before putting one of her hands on my arm. 'Nancy and Aggie were in the yard when I came along,' she said. 'Frank, Nancy was crying. Crying so her heart would break. They never saw me and so I left. Aggie was trying to comfort her.'

It had to be about Dolly O'Dowd, in which case Aggie was probably the best person to comfort Nan. But there was a niggling doubt in my mind about this even then. I was very tense that evening until the girls came in from the yard, and with good reason.

* * *

I'd just made the Duchess a cuppa and taken it to her in the parlour when Aggie, pushing a still tearful Nan in front of her, came into the kitchen.

'Cuppa?' I said as I held the teapot up for my two sisters to see.

'No thank you, Frank,' Aggie said. She pushed Nan rather roughly, I thought, into one of the chairs at the kitchen table and said, 'We have to talk to you.'

I poured myself a cup and then lit up a fag. 'What about?' I said. 'Dolly's funeral's all in hand and . . .'

'It ain't about Dolly O'Dowd's funeral,' Aggie said as she too lit up a fag and then sat down next to Nan. Nan, I noticed, didn't look at Aggie as she did any of this. But then Nan can sometimes be awkward with our younger sister. Pretty, blonde and always up for a good time, Aggie likes to wear what Nan describes as 'racy' clothes – short skirts and dresses and tight little jackets that show off her figure. Nan finds this unacceptable in a woman who has children and is still officially married even though her old man is off with another woman.

Aggie it was, therefore, who turned to Nan. 'You gonna tell him or am I?' she said harshly.

'Tell who?' I said. 'Me? And what?'

Nancy began to softly sob. Aggie stared at her with tight lips, and then she looked up at me and said, 'She knows all the women what've been murdered.'

'What . . .'

'Even this Jewish girl they found today,' Aggie said. She looked across at Nan and said, 'Knew her too, didn't you?'

Nan just hung her head. I sat down opposite her and began

to tell her I'd suspected as much because of her reluctance to tell me about the fact that she'd been to school with Violet Dickens. Now of course I knew that Violet had been to New City Road . . .

'Oh, that ain't all of it,' Aggie said with a lot of aggression in her voice. She and Nan don't see eye to eye a lot of the time, but this was downright nasty as far as I could see.

'Aggie,' I said, 'let her speak . . .'

Nancy snapped her head up and looked me straight in the face with her tear-soaked eyes. 'Frank,' she said, 'you have to remember we was all just girls at the time. You was already at the front and . . .'

'Hang on a mo,' I said. I didn't understand what she was talking about and I said so. 'You talking about the Great War, are you, Nan?'

'Yes.' She put her head down again now. Nan had been twenty-four when the Great War began. She, like me at the time, had been an enthusiastic supporter of it. Dad, who'd lived a bit and seen what had happened with the Boers in Africa, hadn't been so keen. Nan and myself were proved the fools. Her maybe, as I was shortly to find out, more so even than me.

'So . . .'

I could see that she was really struggling. Words were there but they just wouldn't or couldn't come out of her mouth. Eventually, unable to take it any longer, Aggie said, 'She was a White Feather girl, Frank. Her and the others, they all did it together.'

I felt nothing at first. It can be the way of things when a

shock is so great it's almost unbearable. All but one of the mates I joined up with in 1914 died in the trenches and I don't think I really broke down over any of them. It was all too unimaginable for that. Like this.

'Frank, I . . . We was young and silly and . . .'

'You sent men to their deaths!' Aggie said to her. 'You and all them other silly bitches! What did you think you was doing?'

Nan began to cry again, but Aggie just went on.

'Giving every bloke out of uniform a white feather to tell him you think he's a coward?' She put one fag out and then immediately lit up another. 'Nancy, men not fit enough to walk across London Bridge went off and enlisted because of stupid women like you! They died!'

'Aggie . . .'

'Frank, I have only just found out,' Aggie said to me breathlessly. 'She never told no one, and with good reason! Dad would've been furious. *I'm* furious. What you must think of her . . .'

The White Feather movement, as it came to be known later on, began in September 1914. A retired admiral from Folkestone organised thirty women to present white feathers to any man of serving age they saw out of uniform. All fired up by stories of rape and murder as the Germans invaded Belgium, these women saw themselves as doing essential work shaming cowards in defence of innocent civilians – themselves, they imagined, included.

The white feather itself, as a symbol of cowardice, comes from cock-fighting. I've never been to such a thing myself, but it's said that some cockerels have white feathers in their tails which they show when they 'turn tail' as it were, when giving up a fight. 'Showing the white feather' therefore is showing your fear and cowardice in the face of the enemy.

Once I'd been approached by a White Feather girl, when I was home on leave. I was out of uniform at the time because I wanted and in fact needed to forget about the bloody trenches for the sake of my sanity. It was early 1916, I'd been fighting for just over a year, and most of my mates were already dead. When the woman gave me the feather I was first stunned, then I felt such violence in me that I had to just run away from her as fast as I could. I'd wanted to rip her head off. It hadn't occurred to me that maybe I might try to explain my situation to her or perhaps even shock her by telling her tales of men drowning in mud and giant rats feasting on corpses. I'd just wanted to end her.

I looked over at my older sister and saw immediately the fear in her eyes.

Aggie put a hand on my shoulder and said, 'Frank . . .'

'You have to tell the coppers about this,' I said to Nancy.

'What, about me being involved?'

'You've got to tell them who was in your . . . your group,' I said. 'If that is why these women are being killed . . .' I stopped to swallow. My sisters both looked at me, knowing that I wanted to say so much more about how that made me feel. 'Women are in danger.'

'Including her!' Aggie said as she looked across at Nan, and then she added, 'How could you be so stupid? All the men who could fight were doing so! Your own brother was out there, for Christ's sake!'

Nan has never been one to back down when Aggie has a go at her. She changed from weeping misery to outright fury. Her face, reddened already by crying, became almost purple with rage. 'What do you know, Agnes!' she screamed. 'You was just a kid at the time! Our men were fighting for their lives against the Hun and yet there were blokes all over this country who were too weak and too cowardly to do their duty!'

'Oh, and it was up to you and a load of other mad bitches from West Ham to go out and put that right, was it?' Aggie said. 'Christ, you make me sick, Nancy! Sick!'

'What is going on?'

We looked up and saw the Duchess standing in the kitchen doorway. She must have been disturbed by all the shouting.

'Nancy?'

As soon as she saw the Duchess, Nan began to cry once again. My mother looked over to me for answers, but I couldn't give her any. I didn't know what I felt at that moment – about almost anything. I ran out of the kitchen, down into the yard and headed west towards Canning Town.

Chapter Six

I was in Hannah's bed when the sirens went off. Dot Harris, her landlady, has an Anderson in the back yard of the house she shares with Hannah and the other 'old girls on the game', as Hannah calls them. Not that Dot ever bothers to use it, or in fact any of the other women either. Prostitutes, even when not actually working at the time, are a fatalistic bunch. But that said, I asked Hannah if she wanted to go down the shelter anyway.

She shook her head. 'No. But H, if you want to go out running . . .'

I'm generally pounding the streets during raids, but this time I was so exhausted, mainly by the emotions I was feeling, that I said I'd really rather stay put.

'I've one of them tins of vegetable soup we can share if you like,' Hannah said as she pulled a small saucepan out of the inside of her range and then put it up on the hob. She only has one damp little room in Dot's house, but it does have a range and so Hannah can always have heat and hot – or rather

77

more usually lukewarm – food and drink almost whenever she wants it.

'That'd be nice,' I said, as I reached one naked arm over to the table at the side of the bed and picked up my fags and matches.

'Capstan?'

'No, not for the moment,' Hannah said as she rifled in the small cupboard over her sink and took out a tin of Heinz soup. God alone knew where she'd got that from, but I knew better than to ask. Like it or not, my lady friend is a prostitute and so her life is made possible often by means I prefer not to think about. After a bit of a struggle with the opener, Hannah got the tin undone and then poured its contents into the pan on the range. She added a bit of water from the kettle to make the soup go a little further.

'I know you're feeling angry at the moment,' she said as she stood by the range and stirred the soup with a wooden spoon. 'But I know you and so I know how much you love your family.'

I'd told her about Nan just before she'd pulled me into her bed and made it all, temporarily, better. Now, in the calm that always follows our lovemaking, she was getting me to talk about it. She's a very wise lady, my Hannah. It's one of the many reasons why I love her.

'Your Nancy was a silly girl,' Hannah said. Outside, the drone of Luftwaffe bombers could now just be heard. 'But a lot of girls were silly then. There was what I suppose you could call love of soldiers among them.'

'Not all girls handed out white feathers,' I said as I lit up my fag and then lay back down in her bed once again.

'No, I know that,' Hannah said. 'And H, I can see why you're angry, believe me. But however you feel about it, you're going to have to talk to Nancy.'

'I don't want to!'

'No, I know you don't, but you're going to have to!' Hannah looked over at me with a very straight, no-nonsense expression on her face. 'If, as you think, this killer is going after the White Feather girls in Nancy's old group, then she could be in danger. And whatever you might feel about her now . . .'

'I could kill her myself!'

'Whatever you say now,' said Hannah, shouting above the roar of the Heinkels and Messerschmitts up above, 'you do love her and . . .'

A massive explosion from somewhere very, very near cut short Hannah's words as the blast threw both her and the saucepan in her hand across the room. Stark naked as I was, I jumped out of that bed and ran over to her. The gas was out by this time but I could just make her out as she groaned at the foot of the door leading on to the landing.

'Hannah!'

For a few seconds she made no further noise. I began to panic.

'Hannah!'

'Christ Almighty, H!' I heard her say. 'Bloody . . .'

Another explosion that was far too close rocked the house again and I heard the sound of something splintering somewhere up above. Either the plaster on the ceiling or the boards up above were under strain from the blast.

Dot Harris from downstairs called up, 'Hannah love, you and Mr Hancock all right, are you?'

I heard Hannah take a deep breath and then she yelled, 'Yes, Dot, all all right here!'

'Fucking Nazis!' Dot said, and then I heard what was obviously the sound of her shuffling back into her parlour once again.

'Hannah . . .'

'Well, all I can say, H, is that it's a good job that old range don't work properly,' Hannah said breathlessly. 'Being covered in cold soup, I can stand. Hot soup . . .'

'Hannah,' I said as I began to pull her up to her feet, 'are you hurt?'

'Nah!' The sleeve of her dressing gown was damp and a bit lumpy too, but that was probably the soup. 'Blimey, H, are you wearing anything or are you in the buff?'

'I'm, well, I'm, er, I . . .'

She laughed at my so very obvious embarrassment. Then, still in the pitch blackness, she found my lips and kissed me. So it was that I made love in a raid with a woman covered from head to toe in Heinz vegetable soup. Mad as it seems now, we laughed and joked a lot as we did it then too. Only in the morning, when the thin winter dawn broke over yet more death and destruction in the city, did Hannah and I speak of the White Feather girls again.

Just as I was leaving her, Hannah said to me, 'H, if you don't know who the other girls in the group were, then you have to find that out. Speak to Nancy. Take her to the coppers. Marie Abrahams must be the last to die like this. She must!'

I knew that.

There had been nine of them. All under twenty-five and all with a passionate love for 'our boys', as they had called them, brave men in uniform. As well as Nancy and the four murdered women, there had been twins, Esme and Rosemary Harper, from Forest Gate, a Margaret Cousins from East Ham and another girl from Canning Town who Nan could only remember as Fernanda.

'Her people was Portuguese,' she said. 'I don't remember what her surname was.'

It had taken a fair bit of courage for Nan to speak to me first when I'd come home that morning. I was still wild with her, which showed in how I responded now. 'Well, you'd better try and remember,' I said. 'Because all these old mates of yours could be in danger.'

'Frank, we don't know that it's because of the white feathers . . .'

'How did you all get together?' I asked. 'How did you come to do this, this . . .'

Nancy, Violet Dickens, Dolly O'Dowd and Nellie Martin had all been to New City Road School together. Although Nan and Nellie had never got on, Nellie had been a good friend of Dolly O'Dowd and of Violet Dickens. Marie Abrahams also came in via Dolly O'Dowd, who met her shopping on Green Street and became her friend. The Harper twins were cousins of Nellie Martin, and Margaret Cousins had worked with Violet Dickens when they'd been in service together in a house up in Woodford.

'Violet's maiden name was Watts,' Nancy told me. 'One of the Harper girls, Esme I think it was, got married after the Great War, but I don't know what her name became. Marie became very close with Margaret and later with Fernanda too.'

'What about this Fernanda woman?' I asked.

Nancy frowned. 'I think she was a friend of Margaret's first off,' she said. 'I expect Margaret got married in the end. She had a sweetheart in the forces.'

'Do you know what his name was?'

She smiled. 'Same as yours. Frank.'

'Frank what?'

Nancy shrugged. 'I don't know. Can't remember.'

I sighed. 'Nan,' I said, 'you're going to have to tell the coppers all of this.'

Her face turned white. 'What, that I was a . . .'

'Sergeant Hill knows you and so it'll be . . . well, it'll be all right,' I said. A lot of the old coppers had been in the Great War and most of them felt much the same as I did about the White Feather girls. Even with Sergeant Hill over at Plaistow, who was basically a friend, Nancy wasn't going to have an easy time of it.

'Will you come with me, Frank?' she asked.

I only made a pretence of thinking about it before I said, 'All right.'

As much as people in general don't like conchies, there isn't the complete lack of understanding of those who don't care to fight and kill as there was back in the First Lot. Now if a man is unfit to fight he'll be found something else to do to aid the war effort. And there's no shame in that, amongst normal sensible people. But the attitudes we have now are as a result of what happened between 1914 and 1918 and the aftermath of that war. I am lucky. I don't always know what is and isn't real but I can do a job of work and feed my family. How can you do that with no legs, or no face, or if indeed you're stone dead in some blood-sodden field in Flanders? Girls still worship soldiers now, but they do that at the back of public shelters and in shop doorways in the blackout. They don't hang around in gangs and make blokes out of uniform want to take their own lives. Maybe it's because not so many girls now are as pure and untouched as they were back in those days. Maybe they're not so frustrated any more. I watched Nan put her coat on as we both got ready to go to the police station and I found that my face was still set into a sneer of disapproval.

'Never had time for White Feather girls meself but I can't see why anyone'd want to kill middle-aged ladies who were misguided in their youth,' Sergeant Hill said as he and I settled down to a smoke and a cuppa after Nancy had gone back to the shop.

'I can,' I said, which I could see from the expression on Sergeant Hill's face shocked him. 'I hated those bloody women,' I carried on. 'If I'd known my own sister was part of all that . . .'

'That she kept it dark for so long shows that she knew she'd done wrong,' Sergeant Hill said.

'Our dad would've gone mad if he'd found out,' I said.

Sergeant Hill cleared his throat. 'But you know, Mr H, much as it's always useful to find out as much as we can about murder victims, I'm not sure that this white feather connection between these women will come to anything. I mean, the Great War finished over twenty years ago.' His face dropped then into a frown. 'The world's moved on, not for the better, but . . . Why, if someone had problems with these women, would he leave it until now to take his revenge? I mean, I'm assuming we have to be talking about some poor chap who had a bad time out in the trenches.'

'If these women pushed this bloke to go to war when he wasn't really up to it and he perhaps lost a leg or in some way couldn't work again . . .'

'I repeat, Mr H, why now?'

'I don't know,' I said. 'Maybe he's got worse in health as he's got older? Maybe he's been told he'll die soon? Sergeant Hill, it's a connection I found because my sister told me about it. She and I have passed it on.'

'As you should,' Sergeant Hill said as he took a drag on his fag and then breathed out slowly. 'But you know, Mr H, the big problem we have in all this, apart from the fact that we're still being bombed by the Jerries, albeit not all the time now, is that no one has seen anything.'

'I heard,' I said, 'that the father of that Jewish lady up Plashet was in the house when she died, or so it's thought.'

'Yes, he was,' Sergeant Hill said. 'But that's for the boys up East Ham, Mr H, and no concern to us down here.'

The trouble is that the coppers work for their own manors.

Someone was killing, skinning and eviscerating women across several different police divisions, but each of them was only dealing with whatever happened on their local patch. Can't blame them for that, it's the way they are required to work and the coppers are very overworked these days. But I was looking at a bigger picture that at the time I wasn't sure was right or not. All I knew then was that several of the dead women had been to school together but all of them, so far, had been White Feather girls. And underneath my fury at her, I was worried about my sister.

'Of course, as your Nancy said, Mr H,' Sergeant Hill continued, 'a lot of people didn't like what her and the other girls did when they roamed the streets to look for un-uniformed blokes. To my way of thinking, well, like you, Mr H, I never approved of such women, but . . . Quite a lot of people thought they did a good job. See them as heroines some people do, even now.'

He wasn't lying. Some people I know still think the White Feather movement was a good thing and wish it was still in operation now. But I think they're the minority. Now that war has come to us, as it were, most people want as little as possible to do with dying and killing. Most people can at least appreciate why someone might not want to fight even if they can't actually approve of it.

Sergeant Hill leaned across his table and beckoned me in towards him. I too leaned over the desk. 'Between you and me,' he whispered, 'Marie Abrahams's old man says the night she died, only a woman come to their house.'

'A woman?'

'Didn't stay, so the old man said,' Sergeant Hill continued. 'Left well before what he said was Marie's bedtime. But then what's he know? Barmy, so East Ham say. Marie had been looking after him for years while he had conversations with the wall, so it's said. So whether he saw a woman, a bloke or a dog is probably open to all sorts of questioning.' He sat up again and raised his voice above a whisper. 'Took him up Claybury, poor old bugger.'

Although I didn't exactly shudder, I did feel as if someone had just walked over my grave. Claybury is a lunatic asylum in Woodford and is a place I've often imagined I'll end my days. Once confined, the mad never come back, or if they do, they aren't themselves or anyone else for that matter.

'People have this barmy idea that Jack the Ripper has somehow come back to life,' Sergeant Hill said.

'Yes, but that's ridiculous.'

He shrugged. 'You know it, I know it . . . But the fact remains, Mr H, that no one – no one sensible at least – has seen anything or anyone around and about the places where these women was murdered.'

'There were those flowers with those horrible messages left on Violet Dickens's grave,' I said.

'Violet was a drinker . . .'

'Yes, I know, but . . .'

'Look, Mr H,' Sergeant Hill said, 'I'll keep what you and your sister have told us about the White Feather girls in mind. I'll let me opposite number at East Ham know. These crimes are horrible, truly horrific, but we've got other corpses we can't account for too. We get them every day. Our boys and the wardens find them all over the place.'

'Not skinned!'

'Not generally, no,' he said. 'But Mr H, you know that the more things like this are talked about the more worried people get, and that ain't good for no one. We're doing our best, but . . .' He shrugged again. 'Keep your sister close and soldier on is what I say.'

In other words I was to try and think no more about it. That was going to be hard, considering the fact that the following day was Dolly O'Dowd's funeral.

Chapter Seven

Aggie is a better person than I am. Come the following morning she was helping Nancy get herself dressed for Dolly O'Dowd's funeral. I did my job with the horses and the carriage and making sure that all my lads were as clean and tidy and respectful as they could be. But I couldn't comfort Nan. Later, down in the yard, Aggie watched the boys load the coffin into the hearse with me and then she said, 'Frank, Nancy's a silly bitch, but she knows it and . . .'

'Ag, I need time,' I said to my younger sister as I climbed up on to the box.

Aggie sighed and then went inside the shop with Arthur and Walter to retrieve the few bunches of flowers that had arrived for Dolly O'Dowd. I noticed when she came out that she was reading the cards on the flowers she was carrying, but I was still shocked when I heard her swear.

'Christ!'

I looked down from my perch on top of the hearse and saw that my sister's face had turned a very pale shade of grey.

Arthur, looking over her shoulder, was wrinkling his nose in what looked like disgust.

'Aggie?'

She looked up at me and said, 'God help us, Frank, someone didn't like poor old Dolly!'

I jumped down off the hearse and joined Arthur in looking over Aggie's shoulder. In one hand she had a small bunch of daffodils, in the other a rather larger posy of violets. It was in the middle of the violets that my sister had found a card that simply said, *Jealous cat*.

'Jealous cat? What does that mean?' Arthur said.

Aggie, who is accustomed to various run-ins with Arthur's less than quick interpretation of things, said, 'It means that she is or was jealous of somebody and she was a cat, meaning she was vicious with it.'

'Oh.' Arthur was silent for a few seconds before he said, 'I always thought that Miss O'Dowd was a nice quiet lady.'

'Well, she was,' Aggie said. 'To us and to my sister, but . . .'

I didn't hear anything more of what Aggie was saying, because by that time I was running back inside the shop. In spite of the fact that Dolly's sister, Nan and what looked like another couple of old spinsters were sitting down in the office, I went up to Doris at the desk and said, 'Where did all the flowers come from?'

Alarmed at my sudden and I have to admit probably red-faced appearance, Doris tipped her head towards the mourners and said, 'Mr H!'

'Doris, where did the flowers come from?' I said. 'I need to know! It's important!'

Nan, who was giving me a funny look by this time, said, 'Frank . . .'

'Well, Mrs Bentham of course brought the big bunch,' Doris said to me as she simultaneously smiled at Dolly's sister. 'Miss Nancy had the daffs and . . .'

'What about the bunch of violets?' I said as I looked, I knew in vain, at the other women in the room. 'Where did they come from?'

'Well, I certainly wouldn't have brought violets,' the older of the two said, while the other one just looked at me with undisguised fear in her eyes.

'The violets?'

I turned back towards Doris and looked her in the eye.

'Oh, they come early this morning,' she said. 'A well-wisher must've slipped them in through the front door just after I opened up. I come back from making myself a cuppa and there they was on the floor beside Miss Nancy's daffs. Lovely little things. So pretty.'

It was cold over at the East London Cemetery. But it wasn't *that* cold. I shook because someone who hated Dolly O'Dowd had been in my shop. Not content to leave his hateful bouquet on my doorstep, he'd been in my shop – where my sister Nan, for all her faults, lived. Standing now over the rough cross that marked the grave of that other 'Ripper' victim, Violet Dickens, I thought about the hateful posy that Albert Cox had discovered on her plot.

My lads and I had lowered Dolly's coffin into the ground by this time and I was out of the way having a smoke while Father Burton said his piece. I'm not a religious man. Not many of us who came through the Great War are. As the priest droned on, I began to think about those other figures of authority, the police. Sergeant Hill wasn't a bad bloke, but he'd made it plain to me that the Ripper murders were no one's top priority. With enormous bombs capable of killing thousands of Londoners on the cards almost every night, I couldn't blame them for not putting the Ripper and his doings first in their thoughts. But that hadn't helped the women who'd already died or was of any use to those who might yet become victims of this killer. I looked over at the small group of women over by Dolly O'Dowd's graveside, my eyes focusing on my sister, Nan.

To say that the sight of my poor weeping sister made my heart melt would be a lie. I was still too disgusted with her and what she'd done all those years ago for that. But I had promised her, when Dolly had been found murdered, that I would try to find out who was killing these women. At the time, of course, I hadn't realised that the victims were connected in the way that I had subsequently discovered they were. And of course there were others too, women still alive and possibly in danger – including Nancy.

From what Sergeant Hill had said, it was doubtful whether the other women who'd been White Feather girls with Nancy would be found and warned about the possibility that they could be in danger. That would not be good for morale. It could spread fear and discord. I felt, however, that if I could just find these women I might be able to make them more careful while at the same time not frightening the poor things to death. How I was going to do this, I didn't know. But it was going to mean talking to Nancy in as reasonable a way as I could manage. After all, the Great War and everything that had happened around it was a long way in the past. I had almost convinced myself that that was true when I turned away and looked at the trees on the eastern side of the cemetery. On top of a tall monument, a stone-draped vase it was, the severed head of one of our poor young officers burbled blood from its smashed mouth on to the ground. Mocking my stupidity. One thing about being in and surviving the Great War is certain, and that is that it is never, ever over. I will not and cannot ever be free.

There was no wake following Dolly O'Dowd's funeral. The Duchess had offered our parlour to Rita Bentham for a small gathering, but she'd turned it down. Dolly's house, the one where she and Rita had lived with their parents, had been emptied out and shut up only two days after she died. What remained of Dolly O'Dowd and her world was being put away as quickly as her sister could manage. She only came back to the shop briefly, and that was just to pay her bill. Aggie, who was still at home and who had made herself ready to look after Nan when the funeral was over, said of Rita Bentham, 'Stuck-up mare! Now she's got her own place out in Essex *and* Dolly's old house. She's all right!'

Nan didn't say much. While the lads washed down the hearse and stabled the horses, I took the card that had been on those violets over to the police station. The Duchess, meanwhile, made tea and went and sat with my older sister until, just as the light was going in the afternoon, I went into the parlour to see her myself. All in black and wearing for some reason a skirt that reached down to the floor, Nancy looked like one of those drawings of Victorian widows you sometimes find in old books. There was even some sort of bonnet on her head which was fastened with a very old-fashioned black crepe bow. I thought then that she looked rather striking. She didn't look up at me and I, though observing her closely, didn't speak for some time.

At the end of the Great War there were near enough two million what they called then 'surplus' women. These were ladies who would never marry due to lack of eligible men. Some had lost their sweethearts in the trenches; others, like my sister, had never and would never have a gentleman caller or a beau. Of course, not all women of Nan's age were left on the shelf at the end of the war. Some, like Nellie Martin, married and had a normal life. But the women who did marry were of a much more sociable type than my sister. They were also, and there's no getting away from it, far more obviously attractive than either Nancy or our cousin Stella. It is a fact of life that when men are in short supply, it is the pretty girls who will get them. Maybe my sister could have found comfort with a wounded man, but Nancy, for all her patience and care with the Duchess and her illness, is a squeamish soul. She could never have dressed a leg stump or taken a crippled man out to the privy – or so I'd always thought. I sat down beside her, feeling her cringe beside me as I did so.

'Nancy,' I said, 'do you know where any of the other White Feather girls are?'

She looked up at me with huge, tear-filled eyes. 'I told the coppers . . .'

'Coppers are not going to have time to go and find these women,' I said. 'Nancy . . .'

'You don't care about them!' she said bitterly. 'They was what I was and you hate me!'

I looked down at the Turkey rug beneath my feet. The Duchess has always tried to have something nice on the floor of the parlour at the very least. Bloody Nancy! I didn't hate her as such. I didn't like her at that time and I told her honestly that I didn't know when I'd be able to really like her again. I also told her that what I was doing, what she'd originally wanted me to do, was far more important than anyone's feelings anyway.

'Those twins you were friendly with and the others might be in danger,' I said. I then added a little more softly, 'You might be too, Nan, but then you have me to . . . I'll take care of you . . .'

She looked over at me and then she said, 'Frank, I only really kept in with Dolly. Through her I knew where Nellie was, and Violet I still saw about sometimes, although she and me never spoke. But we was all at school together. Marie, Fernanda and Margaret were outsiders to me and I didn't know them well. But the Harper girls are Nellie Martin's cousins. Nellie's mum still has their greengrocer's shop on Prince Regent Lane . . .'

I'd forgotten all about the fact that three of the girls had actually been related.

'Mind you,' Nan said, 'Nellie's mum don't talk to that side of the family. Esme and Rosemary's dad, Nellie's mum's brother, took everything for himself when Nellie's grandad died, and he left their church too, apparently. Nellie's mum and her sister got nothing and so they don't speak to him.'

'She may still know where they are.'

Nancy nodded slightly. 'They come from Forest Gate.'

'Do you know where?'

'No. Esme I know got married.' Nancy went very quiet for a few moments after that and then she said, 'She was pretty, Esme. Like Nellie and Violet.'

Esme, Nellie and Violet had married. Nan herself, Dolly O'Dowd and Marie Abrahams most certainly had not. As for the others, it seemed that Nan at least didn't know what had become of them. The White Feather group that she had belonged to hadn't, like so many of them, survived the Great War. Existing friendships had carried on, but that fervour, that barmy soldier worship, had broken down underneath the reality of a world dominated by dead men.

The sirens went off then and I, for once, left my sister on her own to get herself down to the shelter. As soon as I'd settled the Duchess, I took off. Maybe consciously, maybe not, I headed down towards Prince Regent Lane that night. And even though I was terrified and the voices in my head were babbling and chattering fit to deafen me, I could see that the street was flat almost as far as the eye could see. Where Martin's the greengrocer's had once been there was just a shallow pile of bricks and wood and odd bits of torn-up newspaper.

Chapter Eight

'Our Nellie took her husband's name when she got married,' old Mrs Martin told me as she sat on the doorstep of her house in Iniskilling Road. 'But then when he died she went back to Martin. 'Cause of the shop, see. She worked there.' Then she frowned. 'Not that there's any such thing as a Martin's shop since last Tuesday, but . . .'

Fortunately for the Martin family, no one had been in the shop or its shelter when it took the direct hit that obliterated it. But the fact that the shop had gone in such a dramatic fashion had left Mrs Martin with a deep distrust of any sort of shelter. Sitting on her doorstep was what she did during raids these days. I came across her just after the all-clear had sounded. She'd been where she was, so she told me, for hours.

'It's only me and our Sylvie now,' she continued. Then, looking up at me, she said, 'That's Nellie's younger sister. Our George got took with TB back in twenty-eight and my old Stan was called to the Lord on the last day of nineteen nineteen. Nellie's daughter, our Linda, is evacuated out to Loughton.'

Although she had only just lost Nellie, Mrs Martin was dry-eyed in the face of her recent and past bereavements. But then she was evidently, as I had been told, a religious woman. Her loved ones had gone to the Lord and so were safe in His care. Nan hadn't known exactly where on Iniskilling Road Nellie Martin had lived. But I knew I'd soon find out. Even when it's freezing cold, people still live largely on their doorsteps when there isn't a raid on around our manor. Some houses are half in ruins and so only one or two rooms are still fit to be lived in. Some of the streets only contain one or two families now, the rest of the population having been bombed out. Folk stay on their doorsteps so they can have someone to talk to. That Mrs Martin sat on hers irrespective of what was happening up above was fortunate for me.

But even after I'd found her, I didn't know how I was going to find out where her nieces might be. I didn't want to alarm the old woman. I'd come, after all, in good faith, as she, I hoped, could feel. As the brother of one of her late daughter's old friends and as the person who had found Nellie's body.

Mrs Martin looked up at me and smiled. 'I do remember your sister,' she said. 'I don't think Nellie was always very nice to her when they was at school together.'

I didn't say anything but just kept on looking at her, smiling.

'That poor Dolly should die in the same way as Nellie is a terrible thing,' Mrs Martin said. 'You know, Mr Hancock, that during the Great War, Nellie and my brother's two girls used to go around with Dolly and your Nancy and some other girls. They were keen to encourage the young men to join the forces.'

She didn't say the words 'White Feather girl', and to be fair to the old woman, I don't think she probably even imagined that that was what Nellie and the others had been doing. What she said next, however, did shock me, because it meant that all of a sudden I could be open with her.

'Do you think, Mr Hancock, that this person who killed my Nellie and then Violet and poor Dolly is murdering the girls in that old group of theirs for some reason?' she said. 'They only ever meant to do good, you know.'

I hunkered down so that I was on the same level as her and I said, 'Mrs Martin, I don't know and that's the truth. But that thought has occurred to me, and so if you know where your nieces live . . .'

'Canada,' Mrs Martin said matter-of-factly. 'Or rather that's where my brother and Rosemary went.' She shook her head sadly. 'Terence, that's my brother, he and me fell out. He gave up the church and . . . well, anyway, he went to live in Canada with his wife and with Rosemary back in the twenties. I don't think she married, Rosemary.'

'And . . .'

'Esme? Well, she got married,' Mrs Martin said. 'Some fella from up north London somewhere, I believe it was.'

'Do you know if Esme went to live in north London?' I asked.

'No.' She shook her head slowly once again. 'After I fell out with Terry . . .' Then suddenly she frowned and said, 'Mind you, I did hear a rumour that Esme and her husband had a flat over Leyton way just after she got married. But that has to be fifteen years ago. She could be anywhere now.'

But Leyton was something and so I asked her where in that manor Esme might have lived. But she didn't know.

'We'd all fallen out by the time Esme got married,' she said to me as I made my way back down her little shattered front garden path once again. 'When Terry took up with them unnatural types and then went and got June and the girls involved in it too . . .'

'Unnatural types?' I asked. 'What . . .'

'Them as raise the dead,' Mrs Martin said with a visible shudder. 'Spiritualists.'

'Your brother joined the Spiritualist Church?' I said.

Mrs Martin shuffled herself in an agitated fashion. 'Church, they call it!' she said. 'More like a bunch of devil-worshippers if you ask me! I wouldn't have nothing to do with it or Terry after he got involved with it.'

Violet Dickens had been interested in spiritualism. A woman calling herself a medium, a Mrs Darling, had been close enough to Violet to want to pay for her funeral. I knew that my Nancy would never get involved in anything so far away from the teachings of the Catholic Church, but what about the other White Feather girls?

'What about Nellie?' I asked. 'Was she interested in spiritualism?'

'My Nellie?' Mrs Martin shook her head vigorously. 'No, no, no, no, no! No, I told her it was the devil's work and that to go anywhere near it was putting your soul in great danger.'

'She believed you?'

'Well of course she did! Dr Stansfield, that's our minister, he told her too. Nellie weren't taken in by their evil ways!'

But as I walked back to the shop, I wondered. Two of the White Feather girls, Violet and Esme, had apparently become spiritualists. How had that come about? And if Nellie Martin had been so convinced that talking to the dead was an evil, dangerous practice, why had the minister of her church had to tell her that as well as her mother? I was going to have to go and see the medium who had paid for Violet Dickens's funeral, Mrs Darling.

Albert Cox shouldn't strictly have given me the address of one of his customers. But once I'd explained what it was for, he was only too happy to help me out. Mrs Darling lived in a house at the end of a terrace on Keppel Road, East Ham. Because it is that bit north of Plaistow and the docks, which are Hitler's main targets, East Ham hasn't been hit nearly as much. Life there, though by no means easy, is a bit more normal and quite a lot less dusty than it is down our way. Though not that much different in style from our houses in Plaistow – Victorian and Edwardian terraces most of them – the houses in East Ham were and always have been that little bit better. As I walked down Caulfield Road to get to Mrs Darling's house, I saw that quite a few net curtains twitched as I passed. But then this was not Canning Town, where Lascars are common. You don't often see people like me in East Ham. Not that it bothered me. I was too busy thinking about how I was going to approach Mrs Darling to be bothered with what people might think of me. I didn't, after all, know the woman, and to ask her about the where- abouts of one of her sitters was something she might take very badly. But then I'd already decided to approach the subject of the remaining White Feather girls by referring back to Violet Dickens. Violet had definitely been a sitter and I was going to have to say that I'd discovered where Mrs Darling lived through the Dickens family. I don't like lying, but I doubted very much whether Mrs Darling would ever see Fred Dickens again – if she did he'd probably be incoherent – and besides, I had to protect Albert Cox. I owed him.

I don't know what I thought a medium's house might be like. I think I had some sort of notion that it might look as if it were still stuck in the Victorian age. Not unlike my own flat, if I'm honest. But when the door that I knocked on opened, I saw that the hall inside, though dark in colour, was lit by what to me was a bright, modern electric light bulb. It looked clean, as did the woman who opened the door.

'Yes?'

She could have been anything from forty to sixty. Slim and dressed quite dramatically in black, she was nevertheless a plain, fair woman who trembled just a little as I spoke to her.

'Mrs Darling?'

'Who wants to know?' she asked in a voice that now it had taken on a challenging tone was a little rough around the edges in places.

'Um, my name is . . .' Then, realising that I wasn't really comfortable not knowing who I was talking to, I said, 'Are you Mrs Darling?'

The woman swallowed hard and then pulled herself up to her full height. 'I help her out,' she said. 'I . . .'

'I'd like to speak to Mrs Darling,' I continued. 'Would it be possible to . . .'

'Who is it?' A voice from deep inside the house rumbled out to me at the front door. 'Cissy?'

The woman in front of me stared and then licked what were very dry lips. It was unnerving. She had the kind of ice-blue eyes that can look almost luminous in certain lights. Very pale, almost I'd say otherworldly. Good eyes for a medium, even though she quite clearly wasn't *the* medium. She it was who was lumbering up the hall towards the front door now.

'Cissy?' she said to the pale-eyed woman once again. 'Cissy, what's going on?'

In the absence of anything so much as a squeak from Cissy, I said, 'Are you Mrs Darling?'

The woman, who was twenty stone if she was an ounce, pushed past Cissy and stood in front of me, frowning. Almost as dark as me, she sported a massive black twist of hair on the top of her head which, just like the full-length dress she was wearing, was decorated with large emerald-green bows.

'Yes, I am Mrs Darling,' she said in a voice that was clearly trying not to sound too common. 'Who are you?'

I took my hat off and smiled in a way I hoped was pleasant. 'My name is Francis Hancock,' I said.

'Oh.' Pale Cissy put a hand up to her mouth.

Mrs Darling looked at her and then she looked at me. 'Hancock?'

'He's an undertaker,' Cissy said in almost a whisper. There was real fear in her eyes, but then there wasn't really anything strange about that. People are rarely pleased to see people in my profession.

'Hancock?' Mrs Darling furrowed her great ox-like brows and then said, 'I used to know a Hancock years ago. A girl.'

'Did you?' I said. By the look of her Mrs Darling had to be at least in her fifties. She must have known Nan. 'That's probably my sister. It's my sister, indirectly, I've come to see you about, Mrs Darling.'

Suddenly she lost her aggression and looked very obviously sympathetic. 'Oh well, love,' she said as she lost her battle with being posh and reverted to her real accent, 'you'd better come in. If I can't put you in touch with your sister then I don't know who can.'

She obviously thought that Nan was dead. I didn't disabuse her of this notion until we were alone in her parlour.

'I'd like to say that Cissy has a gift, but in all truth, I can't do that,' Mrs Darling said after Cissy had brought our tea in and then left the room. 'Bereaved six months ago – her husband. She come to me, like yourself, wanting to make contact. And, well, we're getting there. But she wants more, God love her. Feels she has a gift . . .'

'You don't think that she has?' I asked.

'Love, the spirits choose, not us,' Mrs Darling said. 'And they ain't chose Cissy Hoskin. Not yet. But she wants to be here and so . . .' She shrugged her meaty shoulders. 'But now you, my love, what can I do for you?'

I took a sip of my tea before I launched into my story. At first she was angry at what she saw, quite rightly really, as my having gained entry into her house by false means. That Nan wasn't dead appeared to annoy her. But when I mentioned that why I'd really come was in connection with Violet Dickens, Mrs Darling calmed down.

'Poor Vi,' she said as she dabbed a moist eye. 'Now the spirits absolutely loved her. I have to say, I have wondered whether that was why she was took.' Then she looked hard at me again and said, 'So what you got to do with Violet, then?'

I told her about the White Feather girls, then asked her about a lady called Esme who had been known by the name Harper before her marriage.

'I don't know what her surname is now or even really where she might live,' I said as I watched Mrs Darling's pallor turn very quickly to ash. 'But it's possible she started coming to you when Violet Dickens did. They were White Feather girls together, you . . .'

'I know.' Her great head nodded backwards and forwards. 'You know.'

She looked across at me through dull black eyes. 'You think this killer may be going after the girls in . . . in the White Feather group? From all that time ago?'

'It's the only thing that has connected all the victims so far,' I said. 'Nellie Martin, Violet Dickens, Dolly O'Dowd, Marie Abrahams . . .'

'Marie Abrahams is dead?'

'Yes,' I said. 'Didn't you know? It's been all over the manor.'

She puffed her big cheeks out and then wiped a runnel of sweat from her brow. 'When you live your life with spirit . . .' She shrugged.

'Mrs Darling, you said that you knew . . .'

'Violet Dickens was a White Feather girl, as was Esme Harper as was,' she said. 'Nellie Martin was Esme and her twin Rosemary's cousin. Caused all sorts of trouble with the Martin side of the family when Esme and her sister and parents started coming to sit here.' She leaned forward and whispered, 'Baptists! But Esme came, she still comes. Nellie Martin come once, just to see like. But she never carried on, not her.'

'It's because Esme lost contact with her family that I'm here, Mrs Darling,' I said. 'I don't know any better than anyone else whether this killer really is singling out ex-White Feather girls. But it seems to me there could be a pattern. I'll be honest, I'm worried for my sister. She was a White Feather girl with Esme, Violet and the others too.'

'Well then why aren't the coppers talking to me? Why are they doing nothing?' Mrs Darling said.

'Well, they're looking into the murders, of course they are. But they've a lot of other things on their minds too, haven't they? And anyway, I don't *know* that the White Feather movement is the connection. But . . .' I paused a little, trying to gauge what her reaction might be to what I was about to say. But I couldn't and so I said it anyway. 'A lot of men were upset by those girls in the Great War,' I said. 'I'll be honest, Mrs Darling, I was and remain one of them. Don't get me wrong, I'm not excusing murder, but if some poor chap who maybe lost an arm or an eye or maybe just his hope in the future because he got so badly wounded in the First Lot is doing this, I can understand it. A lot of men went out to the trenches who shouldn't have been there. Men who were not A1 or men who were not right in their minds. We all suffered, but they suffered more than most. And all for nothing! If they hadn't lied they could have missed the whole thing! And all for not wanting other people to call you a coward.'

She looked down at the floor and said, 'I know.'

'My own sister was one of them,' I said. 'My own sister! I've only just found that out, and Mrs Darling, I still feel shocked and horrified by it. And I will be honest with you and tell you that as much as I fear for these women, I also feel resentful of them too.' I felt my eyes sting as I attempted to hold back tears of anger. 'It's cost me a lot to come here. A lot.'

It was some time before she answered, and then she said, 'Esme Robinson, as she is now, comes to sit in the circle twice a week.' She looked up. 'She's here this evening.'

'So if I can . . .'

'Oh, you're welcome to come. Not to join in the circle unless you want to, but . . .' She regarded me levelly and, I felt, with sadness in her eyes too. 'I don't see you as a man at peace with the world of spirit.'

I looked away. I didn't want her to see either the disbelief or the madness in my eyes. Ghosts are something I don't need to conjure. Ghosts live in my mind.

'But you can come and speak to Esme. Speak to me too,' she said.

I looked up at her and frowned.

'Until I married, I was called Miss Margaret Cousins,' she said.

For a moment I was literally speechless. Margaret Cousins had been one of the White Feather girls.

'I was in the movement. Never got on with your Nancy, though, like I never got on with Nellie Martin.'

'But I've spoken to Nellie's mother,' I said, 'and she never mentioned that her nieces had got into spiritualism through you!'

Margaret Darling's face darkened. 'Well she wouldn't, would she? Even if she knows!' she said. 'I'm the bloody devil incarnate to her! I only knew Nellie and your sister because of the White Feather movement. When it was over, that was that. They never even knew that I was married or that I took over my old mum's house up here in East Ham. Leastways I never told them. I've not spoken to your sister in over twenty years.'

I sat for a moment then and scratched my head. Mrs Darling offered me a fag, one of her husband's, apparently, which I took.

'So, Mrs Darling,' I said, 'if you are Margaret Cousins, that only leaves two more White Feather girls apart from my sister and Esme Robinson.'

'Yes,' she said as she leaned over to give me a small Bakelite ashtray. 'Rosemary Harper, but she went to Canada with her parents. Married a Canadian, I understand.'

'There was a Fernanda somebody too,' I said.

'Fernanda Mascarenhas,' Mrs Darling said. 'But Gawd knows what become of her.'

'Why?'

'Fernanda, pretty as a picture as she was, come from a poor

background,' she said. 'Oh, she could put on airs and graces, but there was always something desperate about her. I'll be honest, I liked her a lot, but . . . There was something very hard about her too.'

'Hard?'

Mrs Darling shook her head. 'I don't know,' she said. 'Maybe it was just me. But whenever Fernanda gave a chap a feather, it was done without any emotion, almost I'd say without any belief. Sometimes I used to wonder why she, of all of us, did it.'

'Well we'll have to find her somehow,' I said. 'Like the rest of you, she could be in danger.'

Mrs Darling looked at me with level, sad eyes and said, 'I paid for poor Violet's funeral, you know. She never had nothing. I ain't paying for no one else's, mind!'

Chapter Nine

I couldn't get back to Keppel Road until just after five that evening. Because of the risk of raids, Mrs Darling had apparently been in the habit of starting her circles early.

'Oh blimey, we're just about to go in now!' she said as she hustled me impatiently into her house. 'I thought you was coming earlier to speak to Esme.'

'I was,' I said. 'But I got caught up at work . . .'

An old girl on Haig Road had finally given in to the cancer that had caused her to scream her way from this world and into the next. I'd had to deal with the exhausted family left behind. Not any doctor. They hadn't been able to pay for one of those. Me.

'Well, Esme's gone in now,' Mrs Darling said as she waved a hand towards her blacked-out parlour. 'I can't break the ambience. You can talk to her afterwards. Now you can either join the circle or you can sit out here in the hall.'

I said I'd take the hall if it was all the same to her. As I sat down on one of the hardback chairs I looked into the room just before Mrs Darling disappeared. There wasn't enough light to be able to see any details of who was in there, but in number there were probably five plus the medium, who made six. For quite a while after Mrs Darling closed the door on her circle there seemed to be no noise coming from that quarter at all. Although quite what I had been expecting, I hadn't really known. I hadn't, with the exception of Aggie, told my family where I was going. Neither the Duchess nor Nancy would have approved. Aggie, however, I knew had been to see a couple of mediums and such like in her time.

'They don't all go on about "is anybody there",' she'd told me just before I left the flat. 'They've all got their own methods for contacting the dear departed. Some of them just sit in silence and let the spirits come to them. All Tommyrot, of course.'

'If you didn't believe it, why did you go?' I asked her.

My younger sister isn't given to tears, but I'd seen one start in her eye then. She'd swallowed hard. 'I wanted to talk to Dad again,' she said in her familiar matter-of-fact way. 'I missed him. Still do.'

Then before I could get sentimental in any way, she'd pushed me out the door and told me to 'get to your spooky meeting'. In the hall outside said spooky event, I thought about my old dad. I had no expectation that he might suddenly appear in front of me or anything like that. But what Aggie had said had made me think. I missed and miss him too. He had a keen sense of humour, Tom Hancock, or 'the Morgue', as some of the local 'erberts had it. He'd never minded. He could find the funny side of most things, old Tom Hancock. I thought about him sitting where I was, outside a seance, and I imagined how hard it would have been for him to keep a straight face. Just the thought of him busting to giggle made me want to laugh. But luckily I did manage to hold on to myself and not break into laughter even when, just over an hour and a couple of very noisy sighs later, a very odd collection of people came out of the seance room with Mrs Darling.

As well as pale Cissy there was an equally pale, if rather younger woman, called Miss Driver. A boy in a tight black suit was apparently a Mr Watkins, and then there were the Robinsons, Esme – Harper as was – and her husband, Neville.

I've always been of the opinion that opposites attract. But I know that isn't always the case. When the very similar come together, however, it is odd. Esme and Neville, from the look of them, could have been brother and sister, both tall, thin and lugubrious of both speech and movement. Looking at those two standing side by side drinking tea out of Mrs Darling's best china was a strange and disturbing thing. The medium had told everyone that I was there for a private reading I had booked for after the seance. The idea was that Mrs Darling would hold Esme Robinson back so I could talk to her once she'd shown all the others the door. But I doubted even the formidable Mrs Darling would be able to shake Neville off with any kind of ease.

And I was right. What I hadn't, however, even thought about was the possibility that all of the sitters might want to stay on in the parlour almost indefinitely.

'My late mother came through tonight,' Mr Watkins said in a voice that was so put-on posh that I honestly wanted to thump him.

'Oh.'

'Her name was Gwyneth,' he declaimed. 'From a very good Welsh family. Very educated. Very tasteful.'

'Mr Watkins's mother was very chatty tonight.'

I looked down and saw that Cissy, carrying a plate of very few, very plain biscuits, had joined us.

'Mother prefers to communicate via the planchette,' Mr Watkins said as he first looked disgustedly down at and then rejected the biscuits.

The planchette as I understood it was like a pointer on casters that spelt out words with the aid of letters of the alphabet that were arranged around the outside edge of the seance table. Use of this device meant that the messages from the dead did not have to come via the medium's mouth. Quite a relief, I imagined, for a large, weary-looking woman like Mrs Darling.

'Well now, we really must break it up as I have to give this gentleman his time,' Mrs Darling said as she addressed the room in general and smiled at me.

'Oh, but of course!' I heard the nervous voice of Esme Robinson say. 'Oh, Margaret dear, we don't want to hold you up.'

'No indeed,' Neville agreed.

They began to drink up their tea rather more quickly than either Mrs Darling or myself had wanted. If only Mr Watkins, Miss Driver and Cissy had done likewise. About fifteen minutes passed before Mrs Darling finally said, 'Oh, for

Gawd's sake, this man's been waiting for over an hour! Don't you people have shelters to go to?'

Neville and Esme Robinson headed for the door immediately. Mr Watkins, Miss Driver and Cissy followed reluctantly. In the hall, Cissy said, 'But don't you need me, Mrs Darling? On the door or . . .'

'You get yourself home, Cissy,' Mrs Darling replied. 'A raid could start at any minute and I don't want you walking the streets when the Jerries come.' Then, turning to Mr Watkins, she added, 'Will you walk Cissy and Miss Driver home, Mr Watkins?'

The boy mouthed a reluctant yes. But his heart wasn't in it. Cissy looked more like the pale, dried-up image of the spinster that since the Great War we've come to see as an object of pity, rather than the widow she said she was. Miss Driver, though young, was so washed out she was almost grey. They all shuffled forwards just as Mrs Darling reached out and grabbed Esme Robinson's hand before she could reach the front path.

'Oh, Esme,' she said, 'I need a word . . .'

True to form, when Esme Robinson was called back by the medium, so, by extension, was her husband Neville. Cissy, Miss Driver and Mr Watkins I noticed were still talking in the hall when Mrs Darling finally shut the door on them.

'I haven't seen Nancy Hancock for years,' Esme Robinson said when Mrs Darling told her who I was.

Neville, frowning, said, 'I have heard of your firm, Mr Hancock. But living in Forest Gate as we now do . . .'

'Esme, dear,' Mrs Darling cut in, 'Mr Hancock needs to talk to you about Nancy before,' she stole a quick glance at Neville, 'before he has his private sitting. It's about, er, it's about when we knew Nancy, years ago. He'd like a word, in private . . .'

Neville cleared his throat and then his wife said, 'Oh, there's nothing I can't talk about in front of my husband. I wouldn't want to.'

The medium looked at me, I looked at the medium and the Robinsons looked at both of us.

'Mrs Robinson,' I said to Esme, 'you, Mrs Darling, my sister Nancy and some other women were . . . well, you got together in the Great War . . .'

'Oh, we were White Feather girls together,' Esme Robinson said with a smile.

I looked across at Neville Robinson, who was by this time beaming with something that looked like pride.

'Sterling job they all did too!' he said. 'Sterling job!'

I felt rather than saw Mrs Darling's shock. I was too fixated on Neville. Two or three years at the most older than me, he must have been involved in the First Lot in some capacity.

'Are you interested in what we did when we were White Feather girls, then, Mr Hancock?' I heard Esme Robinson say so breezily I swear I could have slapped her face.

Tearing my gaze away from Neville's grinning features, I said, 'No. Not exactly.'

I clammed up then. I do sometimes when I'm angry. The medium looked at me again and then she said, 'Esme love, you know that poor Violet passed on a while ago. Like her, your cousin Nellie died a horrible, violent death. Then there was Dolly O'Dowd, and now this latest, Marie Abrahams . . .'

'All spinsters or widowed or living with terrible drunks,' Esme Robinson said. Then, suddenly becoming excited, she went on, 'Margaret, you know that Marie was getting interested in the spirit world just before her own passing. I reckon if we tried to contact . . .'

'Esme, Mr Hancock thinks that the person killing our old friends is doing so because they was White Feather girls.'

'It is the only thing all the victims have in common,' I said.

There was a silence. For just a moment the relentless good humour of the Robinsons came to a halt. But only for a moment.

'Well, Esme has me, doesn't she?' Neville said with a smile. 'I mean, as you said, Esme dear, the rest of the women have been on their own, or as good as.'

His wife smiled adoringly. 'I'll be quite safe,' she said.

Coldly and without shouting, I lost my rag. 'Oh, so that makes everything all right, does it?' I said.

The Robinsons looked at me as if I was speaking in a foreign language. I felt one of Mrs Darling's plump hands on my arm.

'There's still a lady out there called Fernanda Mascarenhas,' I said. 'Don't know what her situation is. My sister Nancy is a spinster. I know that your sister, Mrs Robinson, is away in Canada. But then there's Mrs Darling . . .'

'Oh, there's always people in and out of this house,' Esme Robinson replied with her now completely fixed smile.

Mrs Darling's broad face took on a cynical look. 'Esme,' she said, 'apart from sitters, there's my old man, but he's either at work or fire-watching. He's never in! Then there's my son's missus over once a week to help with the polishing, if I'm lucky. Cissy's in and out as takes her mood, but she ain't exactly Kid Berg, is she?'

'Oh, no one would want to hurt you Margaret!'

'I was a White Feather girl, Esme! That's what we're trying to tell you! And if Mr Hancock here is right, then someone may very well want to hurt me!' She sat down, taking her considerable weight off her feet. 'Some of them men what we gave white feathers to was sick or on leave or . . . None of them boys deserved to be called cowards by little bits of girls like us! We could've made any number of poor souls go out to the trenches and get theirselves horribly injured or made sick in their heads.'

'Yes, but you don't . . .'

'Oh, come on, Mrs Darling, you girls were only doing what was right.' Neville Robinson cut across his wife's words with a smile upon his face. 'The Great War was not a time for cowards. Couldn't afford them. We needed heroes, and in the main we got them too.'

I wanted to hit him so hard that his head would come off. But I don't do things like that, not now, and so I said, 'And what did you do in the war, Mr Robinson?'

No one who was there ever talks about heroes. No one.

'I served my country,' Neville said, even then still wearing his bloody irritating smile.

'What service were you in?' I asked. 'Where did you see action?'

But I knew before the smile finally died on his face and

Neville turned away. No one who had even been in a trench for a day could talk in the way that he had!

'Oh, Neville wasn't fit enough to fight,' Esme Robinson said. 'He's a delicate chest . . .'

'I served King and country in the police force,' Neville said, grave now, but his head held high in the air. 'Islington. On the home front.'

'Yes.' I looked into his eyes and saw them shift away quickly to anywhere that was not near me in that room. 'Want to know what I did in the First Lot, Mr Robinson?' I said. 'Want to know about when I came home on leave and got a handful of white feathers?'

A copper! He knew nothing! Coppers after all hadn't been given white feathers. Coppers had been serving 'King and country'. They'd had the uniforms to prove it. And deep down Neville Robinson knew it. He didn't say another word.

'Mr Robinson,' I said, 'I joined Kitchener's New Army to fight the Hun with my pals. I swallowed it all, the glory and the patriotism and all that business! All my pals went – I had a lot of pals, Mr Robinson – but only me and my mate Ken came home. Two of us!'

Neville Robinson looked down at the floor. I was not, however, prepared to let him off yet. I was in my stride. It happens rarely, but when it does, it really does.

'Do you know,' I said, 'how many British casualties there were on the first day of the Battle of the Somme?' No one answered and so I just carried on. 'Fifty-seven thousand, four hundred,' I said. 'Imagine. All that death. I don't have to imagine of course, because I was there. I went over the top at Gommecourt. Half past seven in the morning, me and a load of my mates walked – *walked* – into no-man's-land. Through smoke and into the German guns we walked shoulder to shoulder because our idiot generals didn't trust us, amateur soldiers, men they had encouraged to join up and fight, to do anything more intelligent. And we didn't! Three of my mates died before the battle was even five minutes old. The bloke next to me, a grenadier, trained to throw Mills bombs into the enemy trenches, just froze. Mid-throw!' I could feel the tears that always come into my eyes when I tell this tale, and I waited for the shocked expressions on the faces of my listeners it would later elicit. 'He stood there and then . . . then he disappeared. There was a . . .'

Mrs Darling looked at me, puzzled, and then said, 'Disappeared?'

'There was an explosion and then he was gone!' Because that was how it had been. That was exactly what I had seen. No agonised last words on the bloke's lips, no bits of arms and legs and head flying about in all directions. 'He vaporised,' I said. I looked at Neville Robinson, who was still staring down at the floor, as now was his wife. But Mrs Darling looked shocked, genuinely horrified.

'God help us!'

'I hadn't realised that bodies did that,' I said. 'What did I know?'

'And so . . .'

'And so I was supposed to carry on walking,' I said. 'Captain Southern, our officer, came over and shouted at me and told me I was to keep walking. But . . . I couldn't move. The

Germans hadn't stopped firing, there was smoke and blood and screams everywhere and me and Captain Southern could have been hit at any time. But I just couldn't move!'

I couldn't cry in front of someone like Neville Robinson. I couldn't cry in front of his White Feather girl wife – and I didn't. I became bitter and my voice I knew twisted with my hatred, because now was the part of the story where that really began. 'He could see that every part of me was shaking in terror, but Captain Southern still shouted at me to get on and walk forwards,' I said. 'He told me that if I didn't I would be shot.'

There was a silence. I obviously hadn't been shot but I had disobeyed an order.

'I hit him,' I said. 'Punched him straight in the face.'

The silence became a room holding its breath.

'Mr Hancock . . .'

'No one saw, or if they did, they didn't take any notice. Who cares what goes on when death is looking you in the face? Captain Southern could have shot me then and there, but to his credit he didn't. What he did do was probably worse,' I said, 'because he dragged me forwards into the guns, screaming at me, telling me I was a worthless wog who didn't know his duty. Somehow I began to function again. If you can call what I did functioning. But I shot Germans, which was what I was supposed to do. With Captain Southern beside me, I shot two in the face and God knows how many more in other parts of their bodies. I still see the heads of those I shot in the face. I . . .' Suddenly aware of the fact that I had probably gone too far, that people don't want or need to know what I see in my waking nightmares, I paused, and then I took a breath and said, 'I don't know when Captain Southern died. But suddenly he wasn't pulling at me any more, suddenly he was just gone. Vaporised maybe, like that grenadier. I don't know. But I never saw him again. You, Mr Robinson, probably feel I should have handed myself in to my superiors. You maybe consider me a coward.'

Neville Robinson said nothing.

'But we captured the German positions we had been told to fight for, us, a load of rank amateurs. It was considered one of the few victories of that day,' I said. 'Not that I consider it so even now. The whole thing was a farce, from beginning to end. The Great War! What a waste of life and time and sanity!'

Still Neville Robinson said nothing. But then what could someone like him say? I feel different from most people, but from him – it was almost as if he was from an alien planet.

'So when a young lady tried to give me a white feather when I came home on leave after all that, I just ran away,' I said. 'I ran and I ran and I've been running ever since. Not because I was afraid of her and her feather, but because I was afraid of myself, what I might do.'

Exhausted, I stopped speaking and panted to catch my breath. Everyone looked at me.

Then, in a burst of what felt like spite, Esme Robinson said, 'Well, if you're so angry about all of that, then maybe it's you who's been killing all our old friends, Mr Hancock.'

Mrs Darling shot me a warning look. I think she thought that I might just explode, but I was too tired by that time, so I said, 'Well maybe I am, Mrs Robinson. But then if that's the case I'm a bit of a bloody fool, aren't I, warning you? Why should I warn you in particular? What is so special about you?'

'Well, nothing. Myself and Neville are modest people. We . . .'

'Mrs Robinson, you and your husband can heed my warning or not, but apart from your sister in Canada, we still have to find one more White Feather girl,' I said. 'Now, do you know where Fernanda Mascarenhas might be?'

I didn't stay long with Mrs Darling after the Robinsons had gone. I hadn't wanted to go into my history at the Battle of the Somme and was still cross that the way Neville and Esme – self-satisfied and blindly patriotic – had in effect forced me to do so. I also didn't feel as if they had really taken my warning about the possibility of Esme being in danger seriously. But Mrs Darling assured me that she, at least, would take care and would also look out for any sign of the elusive Fernanda Mascarenhas.

'Portuguese her people was,' she said. 'From down Canning Town somewhere. Not that none of us ever saw her place, I don't think. She was a proud girl, she wouldn't have wanted us to. As I told you before, poor they was, her family.'

Lascars or sailors originally from India have lived in Canning Town for years. Mostly Hindus, some of them were also natives of the old Portuguese colony of Goa. They were Christians to a man and tended to have taken Portuguese names too. I wondered if Fernanda's family had been one of those. Not that Mrs Darling or anyone else who'd known her had ever mentioned that Fernanda was anything other than a white girl.

Although we didn't have a raid that night, I nevertheless walked home, to be immediately presented with a bombshell.

'Arthur's been called up,' Aggie said to me as I walked into the kitchen. 'Air force. Gonna be a fly boy.'

She said it lightly but she didn't smile as she did so. Aggie is no fool; she knows as well as I do that no one in air crew, be he pilot, rear gunner or navigator, lasts very long up there. Not usually.

I sighed. Much as I liked the boy, much as I feared for him, there was little I could do about his call-up. And besides, Arthur was by his own admission champing at the bit to get out and have a go at Adolf.

'You'll have to find another bearer,' Aggie said. 'Another old codger to go along with Walter.'

I rolled my eyes and then sat down at the kitchen table. Walter Bridges, my elderly pall-bearer, is also a not inconsiderable lover of pubs and their products.

'Well, you can't have another boy, Frank,' Aggie said as she came over with a cup of tea and put it down on the table in front of me. 'Whoever you get'll just end up going off to the Forces.'

'Unless I do it,' said another voice from the corner of the kitchen over by the range. I hadn't noticed Nan sitting by the stove, warming her hands.

'You?'

'Why not?' Her face was almost completely unlit by the one weak gas lamp beside the larder. This had the effect of making it look as if Aggie and I were having a conversation with a skirt and a pair of shoes.

'Why not?' Aggie said. 'Well, Nan, what can I say? I mean, apart from the fact that I don't really see you carrying a heavy coffin alongside a drunk and any other odds and sods Frank can get together, who's going to look after the Duchess while you're off doing your new job?'

'Mum says she can do most things for herself these days,' Nan said.

'Oh, so you've already discussed it with her, have you?' Ever since Nancy had announced that she'd once been a member of a White Feather group, Aggie had been far more harsh than she usually was with her. But then so had I.

'I don't see why I can't do it!' Nancy said as she leaned forward in her chair so that now I could see her face. 'Anyway, it's up to Frank.'

'I worry about the Duchess,' I said. My mother is old, she has arthritis and I know that on bad days she can neither walk nor feed herself with ease.

'Mum says that she can manage,' Nan said. There was some determination in her voice. I knew she'd always harboured a faint hope that she might help out with the business, but it had never come to anything before. Maybe she felt that in light of what she'd done back in the Great War, she had to try and prove herself to us all in some way.

'Well, Mum can't manage!' Aggie snapped back angrily. 'You know that!'

'She said she can!' Nancy said. 'I told her that Arthur was leaving and I said that maybe I could help out our Frank, and Mum said she thought it was a good idea. I can sort her out before I go to work, and anyway, it ain't like we're going to be out all day or . . .'

'Look,' I interrupted, 'the Duchess is asleep now. How do I know what she may or may not have said? Why don't I ask her tomorrow?'

'Because it's bloody ridiculous!' Aggie said. She pointed to Nan. 'She can't carry a coffin! Look at her! Five stone wet through!'

'I am not five stone!'

Aggie, annoyed at being taken so literally, dived into her handbag, took out her fags, lit up and said, 'Oh, you know what I mean, Nan! You're skinny, aren't you? You know you are! More strength in a fag paper than in your arms!'

'I can work,' Nan said bitterly. 'I'd like to see you lift Mum in and out of bed when she's bad!'

In that she wasn't wrong. Thin but strong is our Nan, always has been. But to have her as one of my bearers? That was quite another thing. For starters, I had to decide whether I wanted to work with Nan or not, and further, whether she would be able to put up with being around Walter and myself. My language can be a bit rough at times, while Walter's is more often than not ripe, to say the least. Not that I was really worried about what sort of effect that might have on Nan. I was still too angry at her to be that bothered. But I did have to consider the Duchess, whatever she may or may not have said to Nan, and also our customers. After all, war or no war, not many females had entered the undertaking profession. I couldn't think of one.

'I'll speak to Mum about it in the morning,' I said finally. 'See what she says.'

'So you're not saying no, then?'

Nan's eyes shone for the first time in a long time. I didn't know, under the circumstances, whether to be happy or sad. Aggie left the kitchen in either disgust or irritation and I changed the subject.

'Nan,' I said, 'can you tell me anything about your old mate Fernanda Mascarenhas?'

She looked a little taken aback for a bit, and then she said, 'What do you want to know?'

'She lived in Canning Town,' I said. 'Do you know where? Did you ever go to her house?'

Nan shrugged. 'No. They was very poor, Frank, her people.' And then all of a sudden I saw something occur to her and she said, 'But I think Marie might have gone there. I'm sure she did. Marie and Fernanda became really firm pals at that time.'

'Nan,' I said, 'was Fernanda Mascarenhas white?'

She looked at me steadily for a few moments, probably with more confidence than she had done for a while, and then she said bitterly, 'Whiter than either of us, Frank.'

Chapter Ten

I n spite of the fact that no raids had taken place the previous
night, I'd slept little by the time I got up the following
morning. Because I'd slept so badly, I got up early and
took myself off for a while before the business of the day began.
I headed west, towards Canning Town and Hannah. Whether
she'd be awake at half past four in the morning, I didn't know.
That she'd be alone I could be sure of, however. Hannah doesn't
have men staying over, as it were; only I can ever do that. I
don't do it often.

I walked down the Barking Road towards Canning Town,
past houses – some empty, some not – shops, churches and
great pyramids of rubble. They were everywhere, lurking in
the darkness like misshapen thoughts. Like the smell of the
sewers, rubble that was once someone's business or home
dominates life in the East End. Scrambling my way to
Hannah's house on Rathbone Street, I did see a few people
– wardens and one solitary copper. But most had taken advan-
tage of the quiet night, and beds were, for once, full of the
sleeping.

Rathbone Street gives its name to a market which, at one time, was a lively and thriving thing. Now business still goes on, amongst the dust and the rubble, but it's of a poor, half-starved variety. Of course certain elements on Rathbone Street have always had a hard time making a penny or two. Where my Hannah lives is not the only house that numbers prostitutes amongst its tenants. The street has always had them and, if it survives the bombing, probably always will. Not that any of the 'girls' down there will ever make her fortune. In general they're too old for that, and their customers don't have deep pockets. Foreign sailors and dark-skinned local lascars – men who look like me – tend to be their regulars. No lusty aristocrats out for some cheap fun in Canning Town. There's poor and then there's *really* poor, with the latter not much appealing to the British upper crust. That said, Hannah doesn't do too bad. I give her whatever help I can, financial and otherwise, and where she lives isn't a terrible place. She has her room in the house of the old abortionist Dot Harris – it suits her. Dot has to be eighty if she's a day, and is full of aches and pains and complaints. I was surprised to see her standing outside her street door so early in the morning.

'Mrs Harris?' I said as I walked towards the house.

Dot, who had obviously been in the middle of some sort of trance when I came upon her, put one pudgy hand up to her chest and said, 'Bloody hell!' Then, finally focusing in on my face, she said, 'Blimey, Mr H, you give me a turn! What you doing out and about at this time in the morning?'

'I couldn't sleep,' I said. 'Wanted to walk . . .'

Like everyone else in the East End, Dot knows my reputation. She rolled her faded blue eyes and then she said, 'You know, Mr H, you should try to sleep when you can, given the state of your nerves.'

'You too should try to sleep, Mrs Harris.'

Dot smiled. Like me she sleeps little and never ever goes down into any air raid shelter. There's one in the back yard of her house for the use of her girls. But Dot, like me, is no lover of confined spaces.

'I was looking at the houses round here,' she said as she pulled the corners of her shawl a little bit more tightly around her neck. 'I like looking at them when it's quiet. Some of them are empty now, of course, gutted out, many of them. But some have got people in, and it's them I think about when I look around in the early hours, when it's quiet. Makes me smile thinking about them all tucked up and sleeping away. Makes me think about the old days.'

'Before the war?'

'Yes. You come to see my Hannah, have you?'

'Well . . .'

'She's soundo,' Dot said. 'Her and Bella was busy last night. But then I don't suppose you want to hear that, do you?'

I looked away, my mind searching desperately for a subject to which I could change the conversation quickly. I don't like what Hannah does. I offered to marry her and change her life for ever, but, as well as being independent, Hannah doesn't trust anyone, not even me, not really.

'Mrs Harris,' I said as something did finally come to me, 'does the name Mascarenhas mean anything to you?'

'Why?'

Even with me, her eyes narrowed into lines of suspicion. They don't give anyone information without a fight in places like Canning Town.

'My sister had a friend with the surname Mascarenhas,' I said. 'Years ago.'

'You mean your older sister?' Dot said.

'Yes, Nancy,' I said. 'She . . .'

'Ronaldo Mascarenhas worked as a steward on ships as went all over the world,' Dot said. 'Brought his wife over here with him who never spoke a word of English. But they had three daughters who I suppose must be around about your age or your sister's. I remember their names to this day because they was so unusual.' She smiled. 'Isaura, Piodard and Fernanda.'

At the last name I felt my heart jump. 'Fernanda!' I said. 'Yes, that was Nancy's old friend, Fernanda! Do you know where they live?'

Dot Harris frowned. 'Oh, Ronaldo and his missus went back home years ago,' she said. 'I think the girls stayed here, you know, in England.'

'Including Fernanda?'

'Yes, although I don't know where any of them are. You sure your Nancy went around with Fernanda?' Dot asked. 'You sure it weren't one of the other girls?'

'No.' Dot looked troubled and so I leaned in closer towards her and said, 'Why?'

Dot Harris did what she didn't often do and looked embarrassed. 'Well, Mr H, it's, well . . . it's . . .'

'Dot?'

She took a deep breath and then she said, 'Your older sister, Mr H, is a very dark lady, ain't she? Like you and . . .'

Frowning now, I said, 'Yes.'

'Ronaldo Mascarenhas and his missus was from India, like your mum,' Dot said. 'Portuguese India some people call where they come from. That's where they went back to. But anyway, they had three kids. Two of them was brown, like both of them, and one was white – like your younger sister. She's a very light lady, ain't she?'

'Fernanda Mascarenhas was white.' I knew that, I'd been told it, but no one had until then let me know that her parents were black. But then maybe no one else I had spoken to had known. Maybe that was why no one except apparently the late Marie Abrahams had ever been to Fernanda's house. I was just thinking "why Marie?" when Dot, entirely off her own bat, possibly supplied me with the answer.

"Course, Fernanda stayed on because she got married here,' she said. 'Fixed up with some Jewish bloke, relative of a friend of hers, I heard. But anyway, Ronaldo was wild. Strict Catholics the Mascarenhas family. Cut the girl right out, they did. Right out!'

As far as I knew, Marie Abrahams had been an only child. Her and her father had lived together for years before her untimely death. But then maybe it was another relative of hers who had married Fernanda? Doris knew the family somewhat. I would have to speak to her about it.

'Dot, how do you know all this about the Mascarenhas family?' I said.

'Oh, well, Mr H, Ronaldo was one of me regulars back

when I used to do a job of work on the street,' Dot said. 'Old bag as I am now, there was a time when I was too busy getting in trouble meself to have time to help other girls get theirselves out of the family way.'

And then she laughed really loudly. It was enough to wake a very angry and sleep-sodden Hannah, who stuck her head out of the window of her room and said, 'Dot, what the fucking hell are you doing?'

My mother knew all about Nancy and her involvement with the White Feather movement by this time, and although she still of course loved her daughter, things were a little frosty between the two of them.

'I have told Nancy that if you will accept her, I have no problem with her working in the business,' she said later on that morning when I joined her for breakfast in the kitchen. Aggie had gone to work and Nan was out shopping, so we were alone.

'She wants to replace Arthur,' I said.

'I know,' the Duchess said. 'Bearing.' She shrugged. 'It's heavy work.'

'I know.' I'd done it myself for years, when my dad was still running the business. 'But are you going to be able to manage sometimes without her?'

The Duchess shrugged. 'What would I do if Nancy did not live with us? If she were married? I would cope.'

'Yes, well . . .'

'She wants to feel useful,' my mother continued. 'Also . . .' She looked up at me with wet eyes. She wasn't exactly crying but she was close. 'Also, Francis, I think that your sister may wish to do penance maybe, for what she did during the Great War. I think that maybe this could be some kind of mortification.'

That hadn't occurred to me, but of course with Nan being so religious it did make sense. I didn't reply to that specifically but said instead, 'Arthur has a lot to do before he leaves and so I've told him to take next week off.'

Arthur's only family, apart from some elderly aunts, is his mother. I knew she would be devastated at the thought of being left on her own, and would appreciate some time with her boy before he headed off to the rigours of basic training and then God alone knew where.

'You'll try your sister out?'

'Next week, yes,' I said.

'I've lent her one of my long black skirts,' the Duchess said. 'And a jacket.'

'I think you should have her wear a topper,' Doris cut in as she bustled into the kitchen to make herself a cup of tea. 'I think Miss Nancy'd look lovely in one of them. She's a good looking lady. Do you know, Mr H, I think your sister is going to be the first lady undertaker in London!'

'Well . . .'

'I mean, I know we don't know all that goes on up west or in south London or . . .'

'Doris,' I said, 'you know Marie Abrahams?'

'The woman murdered up Plashet?'

'Yes. You don't,' I asked, 'know whether any of her male relatives married out, do you?'

Hannah hadn't known anything about the Abrahams

137

family. She had, however, accepted the fact that Dot Harris could be right about a possible marriage between one of Marie's relatives and the daughter of a black ship's steward from old Portuguese India – albeit a very pale daughter. Not that she personally had heard of such a thing.

Doris frowned. 'Oh, I don't know about that,' she said doubtfully. 'I don't *know* that family, if you know what I mean, Mr H. I just heard that the old man was a bit simple and that he and Marie had moved to Plashet before the Great War. Do you know who this relative of theirs is supposed to have married out with?'

'A woman from a Portuguese Indian family . . .'

'Goa,' my mother put in. 'That is the Portuguese part of India. Goa.'

'Oh.' Doris smiled. 'You been there, have you, Mrs H?'

My mother smiled. 'My father was Goan, Doris,' she said.

I sometimes forgot that. Of course my grandfather had been a Portuguese Indian. Not that my mother had spent any time I knew about mixing with Portuguese Indians since she'd been in England. The Duchess had been born and brought up in Calcutta and so most of the Indian friends she did have were Hindus.

'Doris, it's possible,' I said, 'that someone in Marie's family may well have married into a family called Mascarenhas.'

'That is a Portuguese name,' my mother said.

Doris shrugged. 'I've never heard of such a thing before,' she said. 'But I can ask around.' Then, frowning, she added, 'You know, Mr H, you could go and ask Marie's father.'

Albeit inside, I shuddered. Marie Abraham's father was in

Claybury mental asylum. What if I went up there to talk to him and lost my mind? What if they saw what I was up there and kept me in?

'I could . . .'

Doris picked up the kettle, filled it with water and then lit the gas on the range underneath it. 'He was a tailor, her old man,' she said. 'Simple, as I've told you before, Mr H. But he could make a jacket and trousers, provided you wasn't expecting Savile Row. I expect they've taken him up Claybury because of what's happened to Marie. You should go and see him.'

It was all so easy for her! She could go into a lunatic asylum and know that she wouldn't see talking severed heads lying all over the floors of the corridors. But then my mother said something that made me think that perhaps I didn't have to face such a thing entirely on my own. 'Francis,' she said, 'didn't Nancy know this lady, Marie Abrahams? Surely if she did, then at some point she must have come across her father too?'

That afternoon, Arthur and I saddled up the horses in the back yard and then rode them out on to the Barking Road. It was a dark, foggy afternoon but Rama and Sita hadn't had a good gallop for some weeks, and besides, I wanted to get away for a bit. For years Hancock's have taken their horses for exercise to the marshes down by the gasworks at Beckton. It's a strange, half-wild sort of place where poor kids scour the boggy land for any coal that may have dropped off from trucks making delivery to the gasworks. Some people grow vegetables down there too, and then there are the gypsies. They are good horsemen, and like my father, I've always had my horses shod by a Beckton gypsy family called Smith. Time was when Horatio Smith used to go for gallops with me, but since his death, his brother, George Gordon, hasn't had the same interest in it. So now it was just Arthur and me, the swirling fog and my own thoughts. Not that I really thought that much about anything really. That's the good thing about exercising a horse in open country, it frees your mind to be a blank slate, and that, for a man like me, is a very soothing experience. For a mind that constantly jibbers, jabbers and hums, silence is truly the best and most soothing medicine.

But the gallop was only to be a short respite from the real world. As Arthur and myself walked the horses past Plaistow police station, Sergeant Hill, who had been just going back into the building, came over and said, 'Have you heard about Fred Dickens?'

'Fred Dickens?' I said. 'You mean husband of the late Violet Dickens?'

'The so-called Ripper's second victim, yes,' Sergeant Hill said.

I recalled Fred and his lodger Ronnie Arnold sitting outside the Tidal Basin pub as drunk as lords.

'Turns out,' the copper continued, 'that Fred's been having a bit of a romance, like, with some barmaid called Matilda.'

Matilda – Tilly. That must have been the woman Fred and Ronnie had told me about when I found them outside the Tidal Basin after I'd been to visit the landlord. I told Arthur to ride Sita home and then I dismounted and held on to Rama's reins while I had a confab with Sergeant Hill.

'So what . . .'

'Does it mean?' Sergeant Hill moved in closer towards me and said, 'It means, Mr Hancock, that Fred Dickens lied. When Violet was found, we asked him all sorts of questions about his relationship with his wife, including whether or not anyone else was involved, if you know what I mean. He told us categorically that there was no one else.'

I looked into the fog around and about us, making sure as far as I could that no one else was there. Not that I could in any way be sure. 'Sergeant Hill,' I said, 'just because Fred was having a fling doesn't make him a killer. It certainly doesn't mean that he's the killer of any of the other women, does it?'

'No.' Sergeant Hill puffed heavily on his pipe and then he said, 'But if he was seeing this Matilda, he could have got rid of his missus, couldn't he?'

'I'm not saying it's not possible,' I said, 'but . . .'

'But you think it's to do with the old White Feather lark, don't you?' the copper replied. 'Not that I'm saying that it ain't . . .'

'Sergeant Hill,' I said, 'I think that Marie Abrahams's father might know where one of the other White Feather girls might be.'

'Coppers at East Ham took him up to Claybury,' Sergeant Hill said. 'Mute he was, so they had it.'

'So East Ham didn't talk . . .'

'Oh, I think the coppers spoke. It was Nathan Abrahams who didn't – leastways not once the initial shock had passed,'

Sergeant Hill said. 'Why, you planning to go and see him, are you, Mr H?'

'Yes.' Instinctively I put my head down a little. Sergeant Hill knows how I am. He knows that going to a place like Claybury isn't easy. What I knew, however, was that there was nothing he could do to help me with that. The coppers are stretched with regard to manpower and I knew as well as he did that my theory about the White Feather girls was not one that the police shared. As far as they were concerned, they were looking for some sort of nutter who killed for mad reasons they didn't even want to understand. To be fair to them, in the situation we're all in – at war – there isn't time.

'Well, you're more than likely to get nothing out of the old man,' Sergeant Hill said. 'Always been a bit funny, like, apparently.'

'Yes, I know.'

'Well, Mr Hancock, as long as you know what's what,' Sergeant Hill said as he began to move back through the mist towards the police station.

'Oh, Sergeant Hill . . .'

He turned.

'What about Fred Dickens?' I said. 'What's happening about him?'

'Well, he's in custody at the moment,' Sergeant Hill said.

That seemed very serious given that Fred Dickens had only apparently owned up to having an affair.

'But . . .'

The sergeant came closer towards me again, through the thickening mist.

'The person what tipped us off about Fred also had thoughts about what he might have done to Violet,' he said in a low voice.

'What, that he might have killed Violet?' I said. When I'd seen Fred Dickens, he had been far too drunk to do anything except roll about and swear. A proper alcoholic, he probably wasn't too far away from death himself. 'How would anyone know such a thing?'

'Depends whether that person lived with the people involved,' Sergeant Hill replied.

The name in question came to me quickly. 'You mean . . .'

Sergeant Hill moved back away from me again, through the fog. 'Good afternoon, Mr Hancock,' he said, and then he disappeared into the police station.

Apparently alone in a sea of silent fog, I wondered why Ronnie Arnold had gone to the police about his very convivial landlord, Fred Dickens. At that moment I couldn't accept that Fred had killed his missus. I certainly couldn't even begin to think about the alcoholic man I'd seen at the Tidal Basin in relation to the deaths of the other women. But Ronnie Arnold must have had a reason for doing what he had, even if that reason involved his having killed or at least harmed Violet Dickens himself.

Chapter Eleven

Even if I hadn't wanted Nan to come with me to Claybury Hospital, I couldn't have done much without her.

'If you're not a relative or a friend then you can't come in,' the nurse at the entrance to the men's wards said.

Of course I'd started to stutter almost as soon as we'd walked through the front gate and so I hadn't sounded exactly competent or even probably very sane. But then asylums, loony bins, nut houses, whatever you choose to call such places, don't sit well with me. I know there are times when I should be in a place like Claybury myself. In fact when I came out of the army in 1918, I was threatened with it. Not by my family but my old sergeant major. Just before demob, it was.

'If you carry on like this, Hancock, we'll have you put away,' he'd said to me on the day when the violence in my mind had made me tear the skin from my arms and hands in sheer rage. 'And we all know what happens to nutters in them places, don't we?'

Slowly at first his threat had filtered into my brain, bringing with it the horror stories that exist about such institutions. We've all had a relative or a friend in such places and we've all heard the rumours that gather around them too. In the nut house you lose your liberty; they lock you up, clean and feed you by force if necessary, and when you cannot sleep on account of the demons in your head, they tie you to your bed with leather straps. There are lots of tales about violence, but for me probably the greatest fear I possess about asylums is the way they want to treat all the patients the same. My running, for instance, which is essential to my sanity when the bombs begin to fall, would never be allowed in a place like Claybury. I would be one of those tied to his bed, screaming.

Quite how I straightened myself out after what the sergeant major had said to me, I don't know. But I did. Or rather I learned to hide my madness and my misery a bit better than I had done before. Now, of course, many of the loony bins are used as ordinary hospitals too. The central London hospitals are too vulnerable to German attack. In Claybury, not all the patients were mad.

'Now look, I know Nathan Abrahams,' Nan told the nurse. 'I'm a friend of his family. His late daughter specifically, like.'

'Mr Abrahams has been very distressed by the death of his daughter,' the nurse responded loftily.

'Yes, I know, which is why we've come to give him some comfort,' Nan said in a tone that was very bold for her. She's usually not good with strangers. But I thought at the time that maybe her desire to be seen to be doing her bit in my eyes was what was driving her. Nan was, after all, still trying to make up for what she'd done with the White Feather girls back in the Great War. We both of us knew it.

The nurse considered this for some time before she spoke again. Her eyes, if not her voice, were still full of suspicion, but she said, 'You wait here and I'll bring Mr Abrahams out. You can have five minutes.'

There was a bench by the side of the wall just before the locked entrance to the men's wards, and so Nan and I sat down on it while we waited.

'He was a little man, Mr Abrahams, as I recall,' Nan whispered to me once we had settled ourselves down. Somewhere in the building, someone screamed. 'Fair-haired. But then Marie was fair. Lovely blonde hair she always had.'

'Nan,' I said as I suppressed a shudder, 'h-how did you keep your . . . well, your being a W-White F-Feather girl, how did you keep it from Dad and the Duchess?'

Looking down at the brown lino floor, she didn't say anything, just cast her head from side to side as if she were in pain.

'Nan?'

'We was just girls!' she blurted. 'Just friends. And then . . .' She looked up at me and said, 'It never started like how it became. We were young women going for walks together, shopping, meeting friends and friends of friends. Of course we talked about the war, about our boys. I talked about you, Frank. I was very proud of what you were doing.'

'S-s-so how . . .'

'It was the Harper girls who suggested the White Feather

thing,' Nan said. 'They'd read about it in the newspapers and their parents were the type who thought that such a movement was a good idea.'

Having met Esme Harper as was, I knew that she at least was still very much of the same mind. Nan knew that I'd met Esme and the medium once known as Margaret Cousins.

'Was Esme still . . .' she began.

'She's ashamed of nothing,' I said. 'But your old mate Margaret is. I know you don't approve of spiritualism, Nan, but Margaret Darling is, I believe, a good woman.'

'To be fair, Margaret was one of those who was never really comfortable giving out white feathers,' Nan said. 'She did it, but she felt sorry for the blokes she did it to.'

There was a jangle of keys in a lock and the door to the men's wards opened. The nurse we'd spoken to earlier appeared. Behind her she dragged an ancient wicker bath chair. Once through the door, she turned the chair around and I saw a tiny, pale man covered in thick grey blankets sitting in it. His eyes were so fixed and blank he could have been a blind man.

'Well, here is Mr Abrahams,' the nurse said to us as she parked his chair in front of where we were sitting. 'You may have five minutes, and please do not upset him.'

She looked down at the watch pinned to her uniform and then went back to her desk to one side of the locked door.

Nan leaned towards the Bath chair and smiled. 'Hello, Mr Abrahams,' she said. 'Remember me? Nancy Hancock? I was friends with your Marie, remember?'

There wasn't so much as a flicker of recognition, or anything else for that matter. Nathan Abrahams just breathed. Slumped like a doll without its stuffing, he sat in that chair and did nothing except live. Not even yet another scream, which this time was followed by a furious altercation of some sort, roused him from whatever had silenced him.

But my sister, to her credit, persisted. 'I was so sorry to hear about Marie,' she said. 'I know I hadn't seen her for years, but . . . My mother's been ill and looking after her has . . . has taken time. But your daughter was a good woman, Mr Abrahams. She was a good daughter to you, I know.'

Still nothing. I looked around as a way of distracting myself from where I was. I couldn't speak to the old man; I couldn't easily form any words. In my mind I was with the people beyond the nurse's desk, beyond that locked door that led into a world of pain and madness and lack of comprehension.

'We used to go around with a lot of other girls back in the old days, Marie and me,' Nan said to the old man. 'Do you remember? There was Violet and Dolly, Esme and her sister Rosemary, Nellie Martin of the greengrocer's family down Prince Regent Lane, Margaret Cousins . . .'

She paused then. Of course I'd asked her to ask the old man about the Goan girl from Canning Town. There'd been not a flicker from Nathan Abrahams as yet.

'Fernanda Mascarenhas?'

Still nothing.

'You remember Fernanda, Mr Abrahams,' Nan persisted. 'She was very pretty, like your Marie, very fair.' She looked up at me and said, 'Not like me and my brother, you know.'

But nothing happened on Mr Abrahams's face. Still the

same blank expression signifying, to me, a complete and utter absence. I would have gone then. I wanted to go. I wanted the noises that were starting up in my own head, and joining in with the mad noises around me, to stop. But Nan took one of the old man's hands in hers and said, 'Well look, Mr Abrahams, I am truly sorry about your Marie. And sir, I do wish you well, honestly I do. I'll never forget them lovely bread and butter puddings you used to make for all of us girls years ago. They was the best bread and butter puddings in the world.'

The nurse, who had been watching us all along, stood up. Nan, still holding the old man's hand, picked up her handbag and began to get up from the bench. But then suddenly she stopped. Turning to me she said, 'Mr Abrahams just squeezed my hand.'

'What?'

'You've got to go now,' the nurse said. 'That's enough.' She put a hand on the back of the Bath chair.

Nan bent down towards Mr Abrahams and said, 'Is there something you want to tell me?'

It was only then that his face came to life. Not dramatically, or even particularly obviously. But something changed and it was something that was easy to see. The nurse began to pull the chair away from Nan. Mr Abrahams, however, dug his fingers into her hand, hard.

'Ow!'

'You've got to leave!'

'Ow, he's . . .'

'Come back again!' His voice wasn't that much more than a whisper, dry and heavily cracked around its edges.

'Mr Abrahams!'

He held on to Nan's hand like a limpet.

'Please . . .'

Nan, looking daggers at the nurse now, said to the old man, 'Yes, of course I will, Mr Abrahams. I'll come tomorrow.'

The nurse, peeling Abrahams's fingers from my sister's hand said, 'Come on! Let go now!'

'Please . . .'

'I'll . . .'

'The lady will come back and see you tomorrow,' the nurse said. 'Now let go, please, Mr Abrahams.'

A second passed and then he let go. At the same time his face slackened and went vacant once again. Nan, nursing her lightly scratched hand repeated, 'I will come and see you tomorrow, Mr Abrahams. I promise.'

The nurse unlocked the door to the wards and then turned to look at us once again. 'Yes, come,' she said, albeit with her apparently customary grumpiness. 'That's the first time he's spoken since just after his daughter died. But don't upset him. Don't make him agitated.'

That night the raid, when it did come, was short and to the west of our manor. The girls, Stella and the Duchess all went down the shelter. For once I didn't go out running as I usually do when a raid is on. Maybe because the bombing was so far away I didn't feel as threatened as I usually do. Instead I stood in the alleyway behind the stables, smoking and looking at the searchlights light up the sky, listening to the sound of our anti-aircraft batteries. There is often a terrible beauty in the colours and shapes of the flames that leap up once a bomb has hit the ground. The colours change depending upon what is being burnt and the shapes of the flames can come to resemble things that are sometimes either familiar or just strange. I've seen a lot of devils in the fires since the bombing began, but then I saw a lot of those back in the trenches. I saw them there when nothing was burning.

As I watched the sky light up in red and yellow and then turn green, I thought about what Sergeant Hill had told me about Fred Dickens back in the afternoon. He was in custody because Ronnie Arnold had told the coppers that Fred was or had been having an affair with the Tidal Basin's barmaid, Tilly. When the police had asked Fred about his marriage and relationships just after they'd found Violet, he had apparently lied. Everything had been sweet between him and his missus, according to Fred. But then what bloke, particularly a drinker, wouldn't say that to anyone prying into his private life, especially coppers? And besides, even if Fred had killed Violet, I was pretty sure he hadn't killed all of the other women. Why would he? Apart from probably being too drunk most of the time to do such a thing, what could possibly be his motive?

And yet questions remained. Violet, like the other victims, had been disembowelled. Unlike them, however, she had lain undiscovered for weeks, and given the amount of blood that must have come out of her, surely Fred or Ronnie must have seen or heard something. But then maybe Ronnie had. Maybe he'd finally broken through the booze and decided to act? Unless of course he was covering his own tracks by grassing on Fred. But why would Ronnie have killed Violet? The three of them by all accounts had lived together in Freemasons Road reasonably peaceably.

The next morning I had to bury the mother of the land-lord of the Tidal Basin. She was due to be interred in the East London Cemetery at eleven. The wake was going to be at the pub afterwards and I wondered whether Tilly the barmaid would be there. Myself and my lads, which on this occasion was going to include my sister Nancy, had been invited to the do, and it wasn't as if we had any other funerals booked for that day. If she was there, would or should I even try to speak to Tilly about Fred? I didn't know whether the woman was married or had a boyfriend or anything. The coppers, I imagined, had spoken to or were about to speak to Tilly. Not that in my heart of hearts I felt there was very much she could tell me. There was more to these women's deaths than just the desire of one of their husbands for a barmaid.

On the way back from Claybury, Nan had told me that one of the theories about the old Jack the Ripper murders was that Jack was hiding his real intended victim within a series of other gruesome killings. Was only one of these modern-day women really meant to die?

The ground shook a little as something exploded over, I reckoned, Poplar way. I thought about my family down in the Anderson shelter, about how my mother would be point-edly ignoring the explosions while cousin Stella shook like a leaf. My sisters, in their own ways, wouldn't be afraid. Aggie for her part would curse the Jerries, which the Duchess would pretend not to hear. Nan, generally hunkered down in a corner, would say her rosary over and over and over again. She is a strange creature, my older sister. Bitter and yet in certain lights oddly beautiful, Nan is not someone I'd have imagined would ever have had the stomach or the strength for undertaking – if indeed she proved to do so. But according to Aggie, ever since I'd said that she could try out to take Arthur's place, Nan had talked of little else. It was a strange turnaround in a woman who had always seemed to be settled in the home. But then something else Aggie had told me was that Dolly O'Dowd's death had apparently made Nan think. Never before had she spoken of actually using her life in some way. But as Aggie told me, Dolly's death had placed the hand of time, as it were, on Nan's shoulder. As it went, she had actually taken the initiative with Marie Abrahams's father earlier on at Claybury. She had certainly taken over from my stuttering efforts very confidently. Nan it was who had eventually got the old man to speak. Nan it was too who had promised Nathan Abrahams that she would return.

Chapter Twelve

'Oh, Mr H, there's a note for you!' Doris said as she pushed a scrap of paper into my hands.

'What?' Arthur had just climbed up on to the hearse and taken the reins of the horses in his hands when Doris came shooting out with her little piece of paper. 'What's this?'

'I dunno,' Doris said. 'It was on the mat when I come in this morning. It's got your name on it.'

I started to unfold the small piece of lined paper whilst also calling out, 'Nancy!'

We should have been on our way down to the Tidal Basin pub five minutes before, but Nan was still nowhere to be seen. Walter Bridges, who was perched up on one of the back wheels of the carriage, muttered, 'Women!'

I read the note, which was signed *Margaret Darling*. It said: *Mr Hancock, I need to speak to you. If you come after seven this evening, I'll be waiting.* The medium didn't say why she wanted to see me or whether it was connected to anything she and I had spoken about before. But I resolved there and then to go and I put the note into the pocket of my waistcoat. 'Nancy!'

But as I looked up, I saw that she was in front of me. Dressed in one of the Duchess's long black skirts, Nan also wore a tightly fitted black jacket. Her long, thick hair was tied in a bun which nestled at the nape of her neck. On her head she wore a top hat, the same as the rest of us. Unlike the rest of us, however, she looked absolutely stunning. Not that I told her that. I didn't even help her get up on to the hearse beside Arthur. Amazing though she had proved to be in the looks department, Arthur, Walter and myself knew that we had to treat my sister just like any other member of the firm. Soon her thin shoulders would have to be bearing much of the weight of a coffin. There was no way that blow could be softened for her, and if she couldn't do it, her career as one of my assistants could come to a very abrupt close.

'All right,' I said, once Nan had settled down beside Arthur, 'let's go.'

Terry Oldroyd, the landlord of the Tidal Basin pub, gave me a half-pint mug filled to the brim with malt whisky.

'Mum would've loved what you done today, Mr Hancock,' he said as he clinked his own glass against the side of mine. 'My dad always said that we could trust your firm to do a proper dignified job, and he was right.'

'Reverend Sutton performed a very nice service,' I said as I raised my glass to my old friend Ernest Sutton, vicar of St Andrew's Church, Plaistow. Elsie Oldroyd had been one of his most stalwart parishioners. Now, after his job was over,

Ernie was leaning against the Tidal Basin's bar, partaking of the generous hospitality of old Elsie's son.

'Oh yes,' the landlord said, 'but Mr Hancock, the way you led Mum to her grave, that stick thing in your hand . . .'

The 'stick thing', or wand as we call it, is something that many undertakers use when they conduct a funeral. Back in the nineteenth century, when grave robbing was rife, it was used as a weapon to keep prospective thieves away from the body of the dear departed. Before that, the wand was said to have been used more magically, to beat evil spirits away from the last resting place of the dead. Although it was very recently quite badly damaged, I am very fond of my wand and in fact would feel very unhappy to be without it.

'And your bearers didn't so much as hesitate,' Mr Oldroyd continued. 'Rock solid. And your sister a bearer too! Blimey, Mr H, what a lady your Nancy is! Your dad would have been so proud!'

He was right there. Together with Arthur and Walter, Nancy had hefted Elsie Oldroyd's coffin as if she had been doing it all her life. Only once did a little bit of strain show on her face and that was when the three of them, plus myself, lowered the coffin on to the ground beside the grave. Then the effort of it had made her wince. But she'd covered it up well and now I was pleased to see that she was having a drink, albeit small, together with Ernie Sutton at the end of the bar. For the first time since she'd revealed her, to me, shameful past, I actually felt as if I was beginning to like my sister again. Arthur and Walter came into the pub then, and Mr Oldroyd, when he saw them, called out to a fat red-headed woman who was behind the bar, 'Oi! Tilly! Drinks for Mr Hancock's boys, girl! Give his young lad a good drop, he's just been called up to the air force.'

I saw Arthur smile, but Tilly didn't so much as crack her mouth. Youngish, probably in her early thirties, she wasn't an attractive woman. True, she had rather pretty long red hair, but as well as being a big woman, she was also a very flabby one, flabby, and by the look of her, bad-tempered too. From my point of view she didn't look exactly approachable. She slammed the pints of bitter she drew down in front of my boys and then immediately walked away from them with a sour expression on her face. How I was going to talk to her about Fred Dickens I couldn't imagine. How I was going to fool Terry Oldroyd into believing I could drink a half a pint of whisky and still stand up was another mystery I had to solve.

'Drink up, Mr H!' the landlord said as if reading the thoughts in my mind. 'There's more where that come from!' He tapped the side of his nose conspiratorially. Not that black-market booze is any great secret in a place like Canning Town. But the landlord was drunk.

About half an hour passed before I asked Walter to go outside and check on the horses. He wasn't keen to do this, but he unlocked the door of the snug and went to go out anyway. Unfortunately, as he left, someone else came in. Ronnie Arnold burst through the door as drunk as a lord and weeping.

'Tilly!' he shouted as he looked across the bar at the startled woman behind the beer pumps. 'Tilly, Fred's in prison! He done a terrible thing! A terrible fucking thing!'

'Bloody hell!' Terry Oldroyd got up off his bar stool and

pushed his way through the crowds towards the man at the door. 'Ronnie Arnold, how dare you come here!' he roared. 'My poor bleedin' mother not a day under the earth and here you are, drunk as fuck!'

'But Mr Oldroyd, Fred's not gonna come for Tilly no more,' Ronnie Arnold spluttered by way of a reply. 'He done his missus and now he's gonna hang!'

For once, Tilly's face showed some emotion. It was horror and shock. 'Fred . . .'

None of them obviously knew what I, and Ronnie Arnold, did – namely that Fred had been in police custody.

'Fred Dickens killed his missus so he could be with Tilly!' Ronnie Arnold said to what had now become a completely silent pub. People looked at each other; the landlord looked at me with a very puzzled expression on his face. But not a word was spoken until Terry Oldroyd took Ronnie by his collar and said, 'Ronnie, you weren't invited to this wake.'

'Yes, but . . .'

'My mother's died, and coming here like this, it ain't on,' Oldroyd said. 'I don't care what Fred Dickens may or may not have done, this is my mother's big day and you ain't going to spoil it!'

He told one of his sons to open up the door to the snug once again and he threw Ronnie Arnold through it and into the street. The boy then locked the door behind the drunk and people began slowly to talk once again. No mention was made of the incident, until some time later I heard Mr Oldroyd call his barmaid over and say, 'You know anything about Fred Dickens doing his missus in, do you?'

'No, Mr Oldroyd,' Tilly replied. 'No, I don't.'

'Because I know you and he was close,' Terry Oldroyd said to her with more than a little edge to his voice. 'I never liked it, and if you ever get close to either him or that fucking Ronnie Arnold you can have your cards.'

Tilly looked down at the floor and didn't say anything. I used the fact that Oldroyd was distracted to give my whisky to one of the Tidal Basin's older residents, and then I went and talked to my sister. Although she hadn't enjoyed doing Elsie Oldroyd's funeral, she said that it had made her feel useful. I just hoped that she wasn't mortifying herself too much.

The wake was breaking up, with Terry Oldroyd passed out in the public bar, by the time I had a chance to speak to Tilly. I leaned over the bar towards her as she washed up glasses in a bowl. I told her I knew all about Fred Dickens being in police custody.

Tilly looked at me with resentment on her joyless face and then she said, 'I don't know nothing about what Fred might have done.'

'Ronnie is saying that Fred killed his wife in order to be with you,' I said. 'The police will come and want to speak to you.'

'Well let them come, I ain't got nothing to hide,' Tilly said. 'I ain't done nothing wrong!'

'Yes, but . . .'

'Look,' she said as she screwed her thick features up into a small, resentful ball, 'me, Mr Dickens and Mr Arnold, we liked a drink together. All right? What either of them two might have thought about me is their business. But I just had the odd drop with them and that was that. If Mr Dickens did kill his missus to be with me, then I knew nothing about it.'

What Tilly was saying was probably true. If Fred Dickens had indeed been in love with her, it was possibly something she had never known. No one except Fred probably did know that. But when Ronnie Arnold had burst into the snug earlier, I'd caught him looking at Tilly and I'd definitely seen passion in his eyes.

Nancy, true to her word, went up to Claybury that afternoon to see Nathan Abrahams. While not really having the time to accompany her, I nevertheless asked her if she wanted me to go up there with her. But she said that she didn't. The old man had been very keen to see her again, and only her, and both Nan and myself agreed that Nathan might be more likely to talk about his late daughter and her friends to one of those old comrades of Marie. She promised to be home before dark.

It was getting dusky by the time I left to go up to East Ham at half past five, and Nan still wasn't home. I had a few people to see before I was due to visit Mrs Darling at seven. I wasn't easy in my mind about my sister, but I went anyway. I went first to get some mantles for the gas lamps from Bedwells, and then walked next door to Plaistow police station. Fred Dickens was, according to Sergeant Hill, still in custody, and when I told him about my observation of Ronnie Arnold in the Tidal Basin he wasn't surprised.

'Fred has it that Ronnie's taken with this Tilly and that

Ronnie's telling lies about him so that he can be with her,' Sergeant Hill said. He took his helmet off and wiped some sweat away from his brow. 'I don't know.'

'Are you going to bring Ronnie in?' I asked.

The copper shrugged. 'He's made a statement,' he said. 'It's up to Fred to be forthcoming about this barmaid.'

'You think he is in love with Tilly?'

'Oh, he admits that now,' Sergeant Hill replied. 'What we want to know at the moment is why he lied about it in the first place. I also do wonder, I must be honest, whether he did kill poor old Vi. I mean, her body was up in that attic for weeks. Skinned, seeping blood everywhere . . .'

'Ronnie Arnold was in that house too,' I said.

'Yes, but what motive would Ronnie have had for killing Violet?'

'To put the blame on Fred so he could be free to have his way with Tilly?'

Sergeant Hill shook his head and then just gently laughed. 'These men are drunks, Mr H,' he said. 'They can barely string a sentence together for most of the time. I can't see either of them thinking anything through, as it were.'

'Yes, but if you're saying that Fred killed Violet . . .'

'On the spur of the moment, in a burst of violence . . .'

'You don't skin someone on the spur of the moment!' I said.

Sergeant Hill looked down at the ground and then he said, 'Mr Hancock, all we can do is look at each and every possibility as it arises. East Ham are looking into the death of Marie Abrahams and we're doing what we can with Violet,

Dolly O'Dowd and Nellie Martin. At the moment, with Violet, we have her husband in custody because he had a reason to want her dead.'

I wanted to go on about the other women and the connections that I had made between them, but I knew it was useless to even begin to point such things out. The police work as they work and they operate in very clearly defined and discrete divisions.

It was seven on the dot by the time I got to Margaret Darling's house in East Ham. When I knocked on the door she answered it herself, lumbering slowly down the corridor like a wheezing horse. 'It's just me,' she said as she led me through into her parlour. The table she used for her seances was pushed up against the back wall of the room this time and two comfortable chairs were drawn up in front of a small fire in the grate.

'My husband's fire-watching and everyone else went hours ago,' she said as she offered me one of the chairs and then lowered herself slowly down into the other.

'The note you sent me this morning, Mrs Darling,' I said. 'You wanted to talk to me.'

'Yes.' She offered me a cup of tea, but I declined. I wanted to find out what Mrs Darling wanted and then get home to see whether Nan had turned up back from Claybury or not.

'Mr Hancock, I'm not a woman easily scared,' Mrs Darling said. 'But I am being watched and I don't just have my own feelings to go by with that.'

'Watched?'

'If I'm honest, I had the feeling that someone was observing me well before you came here and we talked about all that White Feather business,' she said. 'I didn't of course know that my being watched might be connected to that then. But when you told me just who had been killed and I realised that I'd known them girls in the Great War . . .'

'Mrs Darling, you're right to be cautious,' I said, 'but what I said about the White Feather girls is only my idea. I could be very wrong. The last thing I wanted to do was really frighten you.'

'Mr Hancock, I am not imagining it,' Mrs Darling continued. 'Linnit told me I was being watched.'

'Linnit?'

'My spirit guide,' she said. Then she added very matter-of-factly, 'She passed over in the last century.'

'Oh.' I failed to keep the disbelief out of my voice, which she picked up on immediately.

'I know how it sounds,' she said. 'But Mr Hancock, Linnit don't get things wrong. Cissy'll tell you, Esme Robinson'll tell you, although I don't suppose you'd be too pleased to see her and her husband again.'

I sighed. She was right, though. I had no desire to see that deluded war-glorying couple ever again. But that didn't mean I wasn't concerned for Esme. I was. I asked if Linnit had mentioned anyone else.

'No, just me,' Mrs Darling said. 'She don't know who's watching or why, beyond saying that whoever it is means me harm.'

'She said that?'

'Yes.'

There was a pause then. I looked into the small fire in the grate struggling to come to life around three tiny coals, and then I said, 'Mrs Darling, you said that you have, besides what Linnit has had to say, felt watched.'

She sighed. 'I don't know how to describe it to you, Mr Hancock,' she said. 'It's just a feeling as if wherever I go and whatever I do, someone is watching me. I've been like it about three months now.'

'And do you ever see anyone?' I asked.

'No.' She shrugged. 'If I had, I would've gone to the police. But I never see anyone. It's just . . .' She leaned towards me, her brow furrowed. 'Everything I do is being noticed,' she said. 'When I'm indoors, when I'm out, when my old man goes to work and . . .'

'Have you told your husband about this, Mrs Darling?'

She pulled a sour face. 'He wouldn't listen!'

'Yes, but . . .'

'Mr Hancock, my Frank goes out to get away from me and all my table-turning, as he calls it,' she said. 'You know, if my Linnit actually manifested in front of him he still wouldn't believe in her.'

'So why are you telling me this?' I asked. 'Might I not be as sceptical as your husband?'

'You know about the White Feather girls,' Mrs Darling said. 'You made those connections before anyone. And besides . . .' she fixed me with a gaze that was rather frighteningly intense, 'you see things.'

I didn't answer her, but I did frown. I felt cold now too. In spite of the little fire I was decidedly chilly.

'Terrible things,' Mrs Darling continued. 'Heads and legs, spirits screaming and tormented from the Great War.'

I turned my head away, but even as I did so I spoke, I had to. 'How do you know what I see?' I said. I'm well known as a bloke not always in possession of his right mind, but very few people know what I see and hear when the terror comes upon me. In fact, only Hannah really knows what I go through, and Hannah, I knew, did not know this woman.

'Linnit tells me what's what,' Mrs Darling said. 'She can see what torments you, Mr Hancock.'

And I knew that according to her own lights, Mrs Darling wasn't lying. Linnit, just as surely as she'd told the medium that she was being watched by someone, had also told Mrs Darling that I heard and saw terrible things from the Great War. But try as I might, I couldn't talk to this woman about that. I just couldn't.

'So, Mrs Darling,' I said, 'what is to be done about your feelings of being watched? The threat you feel from that?'

'Well I can't go to the coppers with just the word of me and Linnit,' the medium said. 'They'd have me put away. No. I know that what I'm feeling is real, and I think you know that it's real too, Mr Hancock. But I don't know who is doing this or really why. What I do know is that I want someone to know that this is happening, in case something should occur.'

'You mean . . .'

'Mr Hancock, I ain't afraid to die . . .'

'But Mrs Darling, if that is how you feel, you must have someone to be with you. Talk to your husband! I'm sure that Cissy would . . .'

'Alone as she is, Cissy has other things to do,' Mrs Darling said. 'She ain't here now because she's grave-tending. Her husband, her parents and her uncle Bob. He had a shop up the Broadway years ago. Cissy loved her uncle. But she's still a home to run, and besides, I need some time on me own. Just me and Linnit and the other spirits. Mediums who surround themselves with the living all the time are no bloody good.'

'Mrs Darling,' I said, 'I would hate it if something happened to you.'

She leaned forward and patted my hand, smiling. But she didn't say anything more apart from reiterating her thanks. Uneasy still, I left shortly afterwards, determined that even if they laughed at me, I'd pass what Mrs Darling had said on to the police when I next got the chance. But then the sirens went and all rational thought left my mind. As I ran back on to East Ham High Street, I heard the screaming of men long since dead follow me into the darkness.

Chapter Thirteen

My sister Nancy did not get home from Claybury Hospital until dawn the following morning. Arriving home just before my sister, I found my mother and cousin Stella almost prostrate with worry.

'She's been strangled by a lunatic!' Stella said as she poured water into the teapot and then stirred the leaves vigorously.

'I am really more worried that she might have been caught up in last night's raid, Stella dear,' the Duchess said.

I said nothing. Worried myself, I didn't know what to say or to think.

'Oh, for Christ's sake!' Aggie said as she wandered in from the parlour, a smoking cigarette in her hand. 'They have shelters at hospitals! Besides, if you look outside you'll see the Jerries were after us again last night, not some hospital out in Essex. Mother, there's a bloody great crater in the road outside! Trust me, Essex did not cop it last night. And as for being strangled by a nutter . . .'

'Who's been strangled by a nutter?' Nan, as large as life

and probably more confident-looking than I'd seen her before, stood in the kitchen doorway, frowning. 'Who . . .'

'You, you stupid girl!' Aggie said as she ran over to Nan and gave her a very brief but very heartfelt hug. 'Mum and Stella thought some nutter up Claybury had done away with you. Where you been?'

'I was just about to leave the hospital when the sirens went,' Nan said. 'We all went down to the cellar.'

Then she looked over at me and quite obviously saw the look of confusion on my face. After all, I had known just how early Nan had left the previous afternoon.

'I spoke to Mr Abrahams again, Frank,' Nan said. 'He told me that his nephew, Edward Abrahams, married Fernanda Mascarenhas. Marie introduced them, apparently. Not on purpose, like, but she was with Edward one day and then along came Fernanda . . .'

'Nan,' I said, 'you can't have been with Mr Abrahams all that time.'

'No, I told you, the raid started and . . .'

'You should've got there by four at the latest . . .'

'Nancy, we were all very worried,' the Duchess said.

Nan took in a very deep breath and then she said to me, 'Frank, this Edward and Fernanda live over south London, miles away. Their families disowned them – including Mr Abrahams, who did, God love him, find it all very difficult to talk about. So Mr Abrahams don't know where they live exactly, but he does know that it is south of the river and he thinks it's Clapham.'

'Nancy!'

Nan turned to the Duchess and for once she looked annoyed with her. 'I got talking to some ladies who work up there at the hospital,' she said. Turning back to me she added, 'They do their bit for the patients.'

'Nurses.'

'No,' Nan said. 'They make tea and clean up. They help out.'

Aggie rolled her eyes. I knew what she was thinking. Middle-class do-gooder ladies no doubt allied to some sort of religious organisation. Sensing this hostility, Nan said, 'I got talking.' Then, to Aggie, 'I'm a working woman, same as you, and you do as you please when you're not at the factory.'

'Nan, we were worried,' I said.

But she was angry now. 'I had a good conversation,' she said to me. 'What's wrong with that? I found out where Fernanda was, didn't I?'

And then she left. The rest of us just looked at each other in silence for a bit. It was Aggie who finally broke it when she came over and said to me, 'You may well live to regret giving her a job, you know, Frank.'

And I had to admit, at least to myself, that Nancy's finding of her feet, as it were, was not an unmixed blessing.

Later on that day, Walter turned up with a garbled story about how Fred Dickens had been charged with the murder of his wife. Most of the day so far had been spent cleaning the two hearses and waxing and polishing the horses' saddles and bridles. But I had a recently bereaved family to visit at midday, and so on my way to where they lived, down by the Boleyn pub, I popped into the police station.

Sergeant Hill wasn't on duty, but another bloke I knew fairly well, a Constable Atkins, was quite happy to talk. He told me that apparently Fred Dickens had confessed. Not to all the murders, just to that of his wife Violet. But it was still a shock.

I said to Atkins, 'But would you think that a bloke like Fred Dickens would mutilate a woman like that? I mean, he might kill his missus, but . . .'

Atkins shrugged. 'He was a boozer, Mr H. Who knows what he'd do?'

And he did have a point. Otherwise quite sane people will do mad things when they're drunk.

I went to see the family down by the Boleyn and then I found myself doing something that even I haven't done before – at least I haven't done it outside of when a raid is on. I walked somewhere automatically. I left the bereaved family's house, and instead of walking back to the shop, I went elsewhere. Only when I got where I was going did I notice where I was. Standing outside Margaret Darling's house in East Ham.

Whether the medium was in or not, I didn't know. But I now realised that I had been drawn to the house on Keppel Road by the anxiety her words the previous evening had raised up inside me. I didn't and still don't know if I believe in spirits, spooks and what have you. But what Mrs Darling had told me about myself had made me think. What had come through to her via her spirit guide had been right on the mark. And if this Linnit character had been right about me, then maybe she or it had been right about Mrs Darling too. Maybe she was being watched as both she and Linnit had claimed. And if she was, then that was reason enough for me to want to be not too far away. Nothing happened beyond a few curtains twitching in neighbouring houses – a tall man with brown skin does not go unnoticed in a place like East Ham. After a while I left. But it wasn't the last time my feet made an attempt to take my only just conscious body out to East Ham. As the days wore on, I found that her words and the beliefs behind them worked more and more upon my brain, increasing my fears for her.

By the time I got back to the shop, the world and its wife was buzzing with the news about Fred Dickens.

'God almighty, Mr H, fancy that Violet Dickens's husband being the Ripper!' Doris said as I looked over her shoulder at the diary for the following day.

'Fred Dickens isn't anybody's "Ripper" Doris,' I replied. 'He's only confessed to killing his wife, and quite honestly I don't think that he did that.'

'Don't you?'

'No.'

'Yes, but people'll be relieved anyway, won't they?' Doris said. 'I mean, now the police've got someone, people'll stop going on about it.'

'Yes, they will,' I said. 'Which will please the government. Mind you, I doubt whether many outside the East End even know it's been happening.'

'You think . . .'

'You try and find anything about these murders in any newspaper, Doris,' I said. 'Bad for morale.'

'Yes, but everybody knows!'

'Everybody knew about the bombing of Hallsville School and the hundreds who died in there,' I said in a now lowered voice. Although it had happened almost six months before, people still spoke about that tragedy in hushed tones. 'But not outside this area. People in Manchester or Plymouth won't know about Hallsville!'

Although used to my occasional rants, poor Doris was obviously quite chastened this time and she looked down at the diary in silence. As I usually do, I quickly realised that I'd gone too far and apologised to her for going off in that fashion. Then I changed the subject.

'We've a lot on tomorrow,' I said.

'Mrs Dobie's funeral at eleven and then those little twins from Grange Road at two.' Doris shook her head sadly. The twins, two girls aged five, had died of dysentery. But then with half the sewers bubbling stinking waste up into the streets, what did people expect, especially people already weakened by hunger and poverty.

'Miss Nancy told me they've got dysentery up at Claybury,' Doris said. 'People in isolation apparently.' Then she looked up at me and frowned. 'You know she's gone up there again, Mr H. Left about half an hour ago.'

'Well, Doris, we cleaned down the vehicles and the tack this morning and so my sister can do as she pleases,' I said. After all, Nancy was only trying out as a member of the firm, and so outside of actual funerals she could come and go, the Duchess permitting, at will. But quite why she'd gone off to Claybury again, unless it was to find out some more from

Nathan Abrahams about the whereabouts of Fernanda Mascarenhas, I couldn't imagine. She had said that she'd met some women she got on well with up there, do-gooders as Aggie would have it. Maybe she'd gone off to see them, or even to do her bit, as she had put it herself. Nancy was quite clearly on a mission to change and possibly mortify her life. I went up to the flat and found the Duchess sitting at the kitchen table looking anxious.

'You know, Francis,' she said as she reached up to kiss me on the cheek, 'I am quite happy for Nancy to make more of her time. But I do fear for her too, you know.'

I sat down beside her and took one of her small, arthritic hands in mine. 'She's gone back to Claybury.'

'Where apparently they have dysentery!' my mother said. 'I told her. I said, "Nancy, you know, back in India, people die in their thousands from dysentery!" But she just said, "Don't worry, Mother," and off she went! She's made friends up there. In a place of mad people!'

I lowered my head. 'Duchess, I'm afraid it was me who took her up there,' I said. 'I . . .'

'Oh, she isn't going to see the elderly Jewish man,' the Duchess said. 'No. Someone called Alice has her attention now. A woman apparently who does good works amongst the deranged.' She leaned in closer to me and said, 'You know, since poor Dolly's death, Nancy has been . . . different.'

'Dolly was her best friend,' I said. 'Her death was bound to hit Nan hard.'

'Yes, but she is never still now!' my mother said. 'And although people are saying that this Ripper character has been arrested, I still fear for my daughter.' She squeezed my hand hard. 'Francis, I know you believe that these killings are connected to that awful White Feather movement your sister was involved in.'

'Mum, I will try...'

'Yes, Francis, I know that you will try to keep your sister safe,' the Duchess said. 'But my son, I feel there is something wilful and dangerous in Nancy at the moment. Not in a bad way; she only ever wants to help and do good. But I fear it is just that part of her that may prove my daughter's undoing.'

Chapter Fourteen

L ike the smell of sewage in the air, the sight of blood on the pavement was nothing unusual to me. There'd been a heavy raid that night, and because Canning Town is so often one of the Luftwaffe's targets I wasn't surprised to see the pavement of Rathbone Street sprinkled with blood. I'd run and run through the night, and the fact that I'd ended up near to Hannah's house was more by instinct than by design. I was nevertheless relieved to see Dot Harris's place still standing, and so when I went to have a butcher's at where all the blood might be coming from, I knew that Hannah wouldn't be involved. I was, as it turned out, wrong.

It came, the thin sprinkle of blood, from a half-ruined house four doors down from Dot's place. Like a lot of places in Canning Town, it was empty, the residents long gone out into the country or to a more outer London manor. What the bombs hadn't destroyed, the looters probably had. And now there was blood on the path up to the street door, and there were people inside the house too. One of them now, I could see, was my Hannah. Pushing the half-destroyed door out of the way, I went in and saw that she was with three elderly men. Holding their caps in their hands, they all looked down at the floor with horrified expressions on their faces. Hannah, weeping almost to hysteria, didn't even see me arrive.

'What's . . .'

And then, like the old men, I glanced down and I saw something that looked almost exactly like the body of Nellie Martin I'd found all that time ago in New City Road. Just a piece of meat, shredded and torn. There was nothing as far as I could see, and I couldn't bring myself to get too close to it, that could have identified this body. No clothes, no face either. But then Nellie Martin hadn't had a face. What Nellie also hadn't had, but which this body did possess, was a man's torso. Though torn and slashed almost beyond recognition, it was most definitely a bloke. I walked over to Hannah and put my arm around her shoulders. Surprised to say the least of it to see me she said, 'H?'

'What's going on here?' I asked.

But Hannah just cried again.

'Mr Patel here found it,' one of the old blokes said as he pointed to what I now saw was an elderly Indian man.

'I saw the blood,' Mr Patel put in. 'It was sprinkled all over the street! Like rain.'

The other old geezer, a short bloke with a boxer's nose, said, 'I live next door. I heard them,' he nodded his head at the other two men, 'so I come out to see what was what.'

'So what are you doing here, Hannah?' I asked my weeping lady friend.

'There was . . . there . . .' She began crying bitterly again and I held her close to my chest. The old men all, in their own ways, gave me funny looks. Obviously local, they had to know what Hannah did for a living.

'Lady heard the commotion and come out to have a butcher's,' the first old man told me. 'We all come in here together.'

'Just after dawn,' Mr Patel said. 'In the first light of the morning.'

'We wanted to help,' the bloke with the boxer's nose said. 'We thought, all of us, that maybe some poor soul was trapped. We thought that p'raps we could help them.'

'But then we found this.'

'The police are coming,' Mr Patel said. 'Mrs Harris, she has gone to get them.'

I looked down at the shredded meat that had once been human and I said, 'Do any of you know . . . Who is this? Who was . . .'

'Gawd knows,' the first old man said sadly. 'Poor bastard! Christ, he must have howled having this done to him!'

Mr Patel shook his thin grey and black head and then said, 'But we would not have heard him in our shelters. All anyone could hear was the bombs.'

'You think that someone did this during last night's raid?' I said.

''Course,' the old boxer replied. 'I live on this street and he weren't here yesterday. Of course someone did it during the raid, when better, eh?'

* * *

Whenever I go to visit Hannah she always makes me a cuppa. This time I was the one who made tea for Hannah. Not that I wasn't shocked by what had been found in the house down the road myself. I was, but Hannah had never seen anything like that before. Also the coppers, when they did finally come, were none too easy on her. They knew Hannah of old, and almost the first thing they asked her was whether what was on the floor in front of all of us could possibly be one of her customers. The last one, a middle-aged 'decent-looking sort', as Hannah had described him, had left just as the raid had begun.

'I don't know who he is but he's been with several of the girls around here,' Hannah said as I put a cup of hot tea into her hands. 'I've seen him before. But H, I don't know whether he was that . . . that thing in that house.'

'You don't know his name? This customer?'

I don't usually ask her anything about the men she goes with – I don't want to know about them – and so Hannah looked at me puzzled. 'No.'

Quite apart from the shock of finding my girl at the scene of a murder, I was thrown completely now with regard to my theory about the White Feather girls. Skinned and mutilated just like the other victims, this one was nevertheless a man. As far as I knew, no men had ever given out white feathers to other men, and besides, my sister's group I knew for certain had consisted solely of young women. I thought about the coppers too. It had been lads from Canning Town who had come to take charge of this latest killing. As well as being disgusted at the sight of the body, they were, I could tell, miffed by it too. With Fred Dickens banged up for the murder of Violet at Plaistow, I imagined they'd hoped the whole business might just miss them and go away. But this new body put that out of the question. Newspapers or no newspapers, word would get out around the manor and all the Ripper madness would get going again.

'Bella was busy with one of her regulars last night,' Hannah continued. 'He left around the same time as my bloke. She might know his name.'

'If she does, she should tell the coppers,' I said. 'They're going to be round again, Hannah, now that this has happened.'

'I know.' She looked cold and broken and miserable.

I wanted to say to her there and then that she could just pack in her whole life if she wanted to and let me marry her, take care of her. But I knew from past experience that that was hopeless. It isn't that Hannah doesn't love me; she does. It isn't even the difference in our religions that stops her taking me as her husband. It is her own lack of worth. Thrown out of her own Orthodox Jewish community for having an affair with a Christian boy, Hannah learned to fend for herself in one of the few ways women could twenty-odd years ago. Now she is, she says, far too 'mucky' for a decent man like me. How wrong she is. But I can't persuade her otherwise.

'You got any further finding that Portuguese woman?' Hannah asked as she sipped her tea and then lit up a fag. 'That one you asked Dot about?'

'I know that she married one of Marie Abrahams's cousins,

Edward Abrahams. But both families disowned them and the last place they were heard of was Clapham,' I said.

'You going over there, are you?' Hannah asked, knowing that in all probability I would be. Except that now I was unsure.

'I don't know,' I said. 'If that body you and the old men found is a man, then where does that leave me and my thoughts about someone killing White Feather girls? Maybe that connection I made between the victims so far was just a coincidence. I mean, I don't want to worry people unnecessarily, do I?'

'No.' But she said it without really thinking. Staring down at the floor with half-closed eyes, she was all done in.

'Why don't you get some sleep, love?' I said. 'We could have another raid tonight. You look really tired.'

Hannah didn't argue. I put her to bed and kissed her before I left at just before eight. Outside the air was foggy and damp, and given the choice, I would have probably turned around, gone back and got into bed with Hannah. But neither the late Mrs Dobie nor the unfortunate little twins who had died of dysentery would or could bury themselves.

Veronica Dobie had been a big woman and so I had to enlist assistance from Doris's Uncle Woofie and his mate George to help Walter and Nancy bear her coffin. Arthur was off for the week to get himself ready for his call-up. But Woofie and, more rarely, George helped out often at the drop of a hat, and so the job got done even if my sister, on this occasion, did look quite pained.

'You all right?' I asked once we'd lowered the coffin into the ground and then moved away to let Father Burton conduct his service.

'She was heavy,' Nan said. Then added very quickly, 'But I'm all right.'

Father Burton crossed himself, and the mourners plus Nancy followed suit.

'So you going off up to Claybury after we've finished this afternoon?' I said into her ear. She hadn't got back from the hospital until just after six the previous evening and I wanted to make sure that she wasn't going to cause our mother to worry again quite so soon.

'No.' She looked at me as if I'd taken leave of my senses. 'I'm not going up there every day, you know!'

'Oh?'

She looked over to make sure that Father Burton wasn't looking at us and then she said, 'Frank, I did what you asked me with regard to Marie Abrahams's dad . . .'

'Who is this Alice woman?' I asked, probably more heatedly than I should have. But I was tired and still upset about the events of the early hours of that morning.

'Alice is a woman on her own, just like me!' Nan whispered angrily back at me. 'She helps out up at the hospital. But she's not there all the time! She's got other things to do, just like I have. And anyway, Frank, why shouldn't I have a friend? I had Dolly, but . . .' I saw her eyes fill with tears and so I put a calming hand on her arm and then silently chastised myself for being so insensitive with her. Nan was right, there was no reason why she shouldn't have a friend. There were thousands of women like her, alone and with very little hope of marriage in the future. Why shouldn't they get together from time to time to talk and go out or whatever? After the Great War, many of the spinsters that had resulted from it were given a hard time, being looked at by society with either pity or hatred. People considered them tragic or queer, but whatever they felt about these women, most couples, and single men for that matter too, shunned them. I hated to think what would have happened to Nan without our family. Some women like her eked out poor livings by typewriting or cleaning and their homes were single damp rooms overseen by fierce and unsympathetic landladies. On the streets, and in fact almost everywhere they went, these women were almost invisible.

'I'm sorry, Nan,' I said after a bit. 'It's just that the Duchess worries and . . .'

'Mum hasn't got anything to worry about with me,' Nan said softly. 'And Frank, I know you had a terrible night last night. I'm sorry I was snappy.'

I looked at her and smiled. I'd told my sisters about what I'd come across in Canning Town. I hadn't gone into detail but I suppose I was preparing them for the fact that I might have been wrong about the White Feather girls all along. Maybe some sort of Ripper striking randomly at all sorts was the truth of what was at large in the East End.

East Ham Broadway was abuzz with people getting in what they could before, possibly, the next raid began. It was just after four when I got there after the kiddies' funeral, damp and shivering as I walked through the fog and the thin, annoying drizzle. As before, and again out of reflex, I was going to make sure that everything was quiet up at Mrs Darling's place. But as I passed by the tobacconist's up by the underground station, a pudgy hand grabbed hold of my arm.

'If I didn't know better, Mr Hancock, I'd think it was you who was watching me!'

I'd already recognised the voice but I looked down to greet a fur-coat-clad Mrs Darling with a smile.

'Old Mrs Fawcett saw you yesterday, hanging about,' she said.

I raised my hat and said, 'I didn't mean to cause you any sort of alarm, Mrs Darling.'

She wound a fat, mink-covered arm around mine and then said, 'Well you can help me take my old man's fags home. Come on.'

On the way back to Keppel Road I asked her whether her feelings of being watched, as well as Linnit's observations, had lessened to any degree. She said that they hadn't. She said that in fact if anything her feelings of dread were increasing.

'And the fact that the coppers found a bloke's body cut to ribbons down Canning Town last night don't make me feel any better,' she said as we began to walk up her small garden path.

I knew that news travelled fast in the East End, but that was quick even by our standards. Amazement on my face I said, 'How . . .'

Mrs Darling tapped the side of her nose with her finger and then said, 'Intuition, Mr Hancock. That and having a cousin who lives on Rathbone Street.' She laughed.

We went through the parlour and into the scullery at the back of the house, where Cissy was boiling a kettle on the range. When she saw me she looked surprised. 'Oh.'

'Cissy, remember Mr Hancock?' the medium said as she puffed and panted her way over to one of the chairs at the table in the corner of the scullery.

'Oh, yes . . .'

'Sit down, Mr Hancock,' Mrs Darling said. She moved a fat hand in the direction of the other chair and I duly sat down.

'I was just making a pot of tea,' Cissy said.

'Oh well, don't let us stand in your way,' Mrs Darling responded with a smile.

For some reason this made Cissy giggle, after which she excused herself and left to go out to the privy in the fog-covered shed at the end of the back yard.

'Wants to be able to speak to her dead husband every day in the end, she says,' Mrs Darling said as she tipped her head in the direction of the privy and Cissy. 'It's why she's here so much of the time. That and she wants to learn.'

'Does her husband come through every day?'

'No.' Mrs Darling shook her head. 'He ain't what you'd call frequent. But anyway, it wouldn't satisfy Cissy even if he did come through easy every day. Not really.'

'Why not?'

'She wants to be able to contact him herself,' Mrs Darling

said. 'It's why she's here. Like I said, she wants to learn. Develop her sensitivity to the spirits.'

'And does she have any?' I said. 'Sensitivity to the spirits?'

Mrs Darling looked at me and laughed. 'Oh, you're a sceptical bleeder, aren't you, Mr Hancock?' Then she said, 'But since you ask, I have to say that I don't know, to be truthful. She can go into a trance and I believe she tries to make some kind of contact, but . . .' She shrugged. 'Between you, me and the gatepost, Mr Hancock, I think that coming here just gives Cissy something to do. She's on her own now, and beyond grave-tending and her own housekeeping, there's little for her to do.'

'She could do war work.'

'What, a thing like her working in a munitions factory or down Tate and Lyle's? Don't make me laugh!' Mrs Darling said. 'She worked in her uncle's shop on the Broadway, but that was donkey's years ago. I remember her back then – just. But then she married, apparently, and that was that. Anyway, outside of my seances and the occasional appearance of my old man, I was very lonely, Mr Hancock. What with me arthritis and what have you . . . When Cissy fetched up at one of me Thursday circles and then said that she wanted to learn some more, I was all for it. She's a funny thing, but . . .'

Cissy returned from the privy then and proceeded, in silence, to make the promised tea.

'So,' I began, 'your cousin in Canning Town . . .'

'Alf's a stevedore,' Mrs Darling said, 'before you start getting ideas I've got a cousin as walks the streets, Mr Hancock.'

I turned my face away just briefly from her then, but I realised as soon as I turned back again that Mrs Darling had taken that in and interpreted it, probably correctly.

'No, Alf don't have nothing to do with no ladies of the night, Mr Hancock,' she said. 'Mind you, according to him, it was one of them same ladies as found the body. Her and some old blokes, one of them a Lascar so it's said. The body was torn to pieces apparently.'

'Yes.'

'How did you know about it, Mr Hancock?'

I told her. I had no reason not to.

'So maybe this killer ain't going after old White Feather girls after all,' Mrs Darling said as Cissy put teacups down in front of both of us.

'Maybe not,' I said.

Mrs Darling shook her head slowly and then said, 'I hear that your sister Nancy is bearing for you now, Mr Hancock. Bit of a turn-up that, isn't it?'

I smiled. 'My young apprentice is off to the forces soon, Mrs Darling,' I said. 'Nancy volunteered.'

'Blimey!' the medium replied. 'A lady undertaker. What next, eh?'

Cissy left the scullery then and went off with her tea towards the parlour.

'And yet I'm still being watched,' Mrs Darling said, changing the subject again. 'I'm still afraid.'

She didn't look afraid, but then Mrs Darling was not the sort of woman who showed emotions like fear with ease. She was too proud for that.

'Are you being watched now, Mrs Darling?' I asked.

'Oh yes, Mr Hancock,' she replied without the slightest hesitation. 'I'm being watched all the time.'

I looked out into the medium's fog-shrouded yard, no longer able to see even the outline of the privy where Cissy had so recently been.

Chapter Fifteen

There was blood all over the bed. Not just the counterpane and the blankets, but the sheets were soaked through too, top and bottom. God, what a mess! I looked down, and although the room was completely blacked out, I could see absolutely everything. My body all thin and long, a pencil-shaped thing inside the bed. The blood, I thought, could only be coming from me. But why was that?

I looked around my bedroom, which, though dark, also seemed to be overlaid with a dusting of fog. Had the shop been hit and some vein or artery in my body exploded by the blast? The blood if anything was pumping out more vigorously. It was dripping down on to the lino on the floor now. I could hear it plop, plopping on to the shiny surface below. Unconfined as I was, I wasn't actually scared. Not until I started to try and get out of my bed, that is.

I couldn't move a muscle. I was completely paralysed. A scream that was a scream inside and stayed that way fought to get out, but couldn't. I began to sweat. Then I began to lose the rhythm of my breathing. I played around with the idea that perhaps I was just dreaming all of this, but I couldn't convince myself of that even when the voices began to crowd into my mind.

The sound of a whistle, followed by a man's voice shouting, 'Charge!' A relic from the trenches, a recurrent terrible thing.

Then, 'Francis Hancock, you are a madman! Get to Claybury, Francis! Get where you belong!'

The urge to scream became very great. It was as if some vast swell of water were building up inside my body, trying and failing to find some sort of exit. I wanted to wake up even though I didn't know whether I was even asleep.

Plop, plop went my blood down on to the lino, and I felt the wetness of my sweat pour down my face in a thick, wide rivulet. *Help me!* I thought. *Someone for God's sake help me!*

'Help you? Why should *I* help you?' It was a girl's voice, young and posh and full of sneering. Terrifying.

Every part of me strained to scream, and then suddenly I felt something that wasn't me, other hands upon my shoulders. My eyes flew open and I looked up into Aggie's pale, frightened face. Her hair was all awry and she wore a terrible tattered old dressing gown. Standing beside Aggie was Nan with a lit candle in her hand. Her hair too was all awry and her face was a dark picture of terror.

'Frank!'

I gasped. Only now finally waking to no blood, no voices, only my sisters in my bedroom in the middle of the night. But then Aggie said something that nearly tipped me back into that nightmare again, because suddenly I knew whose voice had so, so terrified me.

'Who the hell, Frank,' Aggie said, 'is Linnit?'

Of course I didn't tell my sisters who or what Linnit was. That I'd shouted out the name of Mrs Darling's spirit guide in the middle of a nightmare was not something that, after the original shock of it, I put any importance upon. I had been, when I'd gone to bed that night, generally disturbed. We hadn't had a raid, probably due to the thick London fog, and I'd for once slept very heavily. My sisters did stay with me for some time after I woke, however, worried that I might become distressed and scream the place down once again.

'Did I wake the Duchess and Stella?' I said as I sat up in bed to take the cup of water Nan had brought for me.

'Yes, but they're all right now, don't worry,' Aggie said. 'God, Frank, that must've been some nightmare you were having! You bad at the moment, are you?'

When Aggie described me as 'bad', what she meant was disturbed in my mind. Although she'd only been fourteen when I returned home from the Great War in 1918, she'd seen me go through terrible pain both physical and mental. Shocked at my appearance and behaviour, she had neverthe-less taken part in looking after her damaged big brother. And although she is so much younger than I am, she is still as protective of me as she was when she was a child.

'It's all this business with these Ripper murders has upset you,' Aggie said. Then, turning to Nancy, she added, 'And you ain't helped matters either.'

'Me? What have I done?' Nan said. 'I've been helping Frank! I'm taking over from Arthur!'

'Yes, and when you're not here you're off gallivanting up to bloody madhouses with strangers!' Aggie said.

'Well, you go out and . . .'

'I've always gone out and *I* know what I'm doing!' Aggie replied. 'Nan, when you was out with poor old Dolly, none of us was worried.'

Harsh though her words were, they were also true. Nancy's outings with Dolly O'Dowd had consisted of church, church socials, the eel and pie shop on West Ham Lane and, on a warm day, a stroll around East Ham Central Park. The one time, during the Great War, when she had gone out a lot on her own we now knew was a time when she'd done something of which none of us could approve. Now that she was off up to Claybury and possibly around and about with this Alice woman, the family as a whole I could now see was nervous.

'Mum frets,' Aggie continued. 'And so does Frank. Nan, if you're going to go out, always let someone know where you're going. Bloody hell, there's raids all the time! What if you was trapped somewhere and we didn't know?'

'I do tell Mum . . .'

'Yes, but Mother don't always remember,' Aggie said. 'Write it down. Now you're in the firm, you can put it in the works diary. She can put where she's going in the works diary, can't she, Frank?'

'Yes.' I drank my water and then leaned over to the table beside the bed and picked up my fags and matches. I was still shaken by what had been a debilitating nightmare, and really what I wanted was for my two sisters to go. But neither of them would leave until I'd assured them that I really was back to myself once again. Aggie of course had to smoke a fag with me before she would even think about leaving. When they had gone, however, I found that far from settling, my mind began to race once again. I thought about Mrs Darling and Linnit and how and why it was that someone might be watching the medium. I thought about that terrible mutilated male body I'd seen in Canning Town too and wondered who that had once been. In fact all sorts of things churned through my mind – Fred Dickens and his confession to Violet's murder, poor Nellie Martin's butchered body, and of course, Hannah. Had the bloke who had been killed in Canning Town been one of her customers? At that point, as dawn began to break over London, I put a stop to what I was thinking and got up. Thinking about what Hannah does and who she does it with does me no good at all.

Sometimes, even in the midst of war, days pass in something like a dream. It was strange being without Arthur, and although I knew that he was coming back to the firm before he went into the forces, his absence felt like an ending. Nancy, on the other hand, worked hard but was rather quieter than she'd been in recent weeks. She didn't go up to Claybury and apparently only met up with her new friend Alice just the once. From the coppers, no one heard a thing. The Canning Town body was still unidentified, the murderer still clearly at large. But whereas before I'd had maybe rather too clear an idea about why the killings might be taking place, with the murder of a man I was no longer sure. We were busy anyway, and so, like the rest of the firm, I worked. It was only at the end of that week that something happened to make me wish that maybe I'd used some of my time to try and track down Fernanda Mascarenhas.

Just after midday on the Friday, the bell over the front door of the shop clanked violently as a large woman pushed her way sweating into my premises.

'Mr Hancock!' Mrs Darling said breathlessly. 'God help us, thank Christ you're here!'

Doris, who had watched the panting, fur-clad woman fling herself against the door, looked up at me and then immediately went and offered Mrs Darling a chair.

'Mrs Darling . . .'

'Oh, Mr Hancock!' she said as she collapsed into the chair that Doris put behind her. 'I had to come. I had to talk to you.'

I pulled another chair over and sat down beside her. 'Mrs Darling, whatever is wrong?' I said.

She looked over at Doris and then back at me again. I asked Doris if she wouldn't mind stepping out for a moment. Mrs Darling obviously wanted some privacy.

Once Doris had gone, the medium said, 'It's Esme Robinson . . .'

I felt my heart jump inside my chest. 'Oh God, not . . .'

'Oh no, she's all right, if you can call being on your own all right,' Mrs Darling said.

I frowned. Esme Robinson wasn't alone; Esme Robinson had her husband Neville.

'You know that body what you and them others found in Canning Town?' the medium continued.

I had a very cold feeling now. A very cold feeling indeed. 'Yes?'

'That was Neville Robinson,' Mrs Darling said. 'Esme reported him missing the day after the body was found. But only now do they know it certainly was him. What the bloody hell do you think a strait-laced old bore like Neville was doing down on Rathbone Street, Mr Hancock?'

Speechless, I just sat and stared at her. Both myself and Mrs Darling had our own very similar ideas about that.

'God almighty.'

'No one's as strait-laced as Neville was,' Mrs Darling said. 'Not really. They never had kids, him and Esme. Rattling around in that big place of theirs up Forest Gate. Of course they both came to my sittings. She, Esme, liked her garden. Neville obviously liked ladies of the night.'

I looked at the medium's white face but I was thinking about my Hannah.

'But then he was a copper during the Great War,' Mrs Darling said as if this explained Neville's assumed behaviour. 'Weak chest got him out of the forces.'

'Whatever that may mean,' I said.

Mrs Darling frowned.

'If he'd had consumption, the coppers wouldn't have taken him,' I said.

'A touch of bronchitis you think, Mr Hancock?'

'He got out of it somehow, Mrs Darling,' I said. 'But then some of the most patriotic did and do.'

The medium cleared her throat and then she said, 'I'm worried about Esme,' she said. 'She's only ever lived with her family and then with Neville.'

'Won't her family look after her?' I asked.

'Her parents died in Canada and Rosemary's still over there.'

'Well isn't . . .'

'Neither the Martins or the Harpers will speak to her on account of her belief in the spirit world, and her mother's people come from up north somewhere.' She looked up at me with troubled eyes and was about to speak again when suddenly a figure pushed through the curtains at the back of the shop. It was Nan.

'Oh.' My sister hadn't seen Margaret Darling, or Margaret Cousins as she had known her, probably since the end of the Great War. The girls, it seemed to me, had disbanded very quickly once the conflict was over.

'Nancy.' Margaret Darling smiled. It wasn't an easy gesture for her but she did it in what seemed to me a sincere fashion.

'Margaret.' Nancy had known that I was seeing her old friends although I had never spoken to her about actually getting in contact with them herself. Now she turned immediately away from Margaret Darling and said to me, 'Frank, I'm going out. We've no work on today and so I'm off.'

'Where to?' I was embarrassed by what seemed to me my sister's rudeness. But then, looking up at her, it was obvious from the redness of her face that she was embarrassed too.

Nancy's eyes shifted from me to Mrs Darling and then nervously back to me once again. 'I put it in the diary, like you told me,' she said.

'Yes, but . . .'

'I'm going up the hospital!' Nancy said angrily.

'Oh, right, er . . .'

'Do my little bit,' she said. Very stiffly she nodded her head at Mrs Darling, said, 'Margaret,' and then pushed her way back through the black shop curtains and was gone.

The medium looked at me, I looked helplessly at the medium, and then she thankfully resumed our earlier conversation.

'Because of the way that I feel, that I'm being watched or followed or . . . you know what I told you the other day, Mr Hancock . . .'

'You still . . .'

'Oh, I still feel, well, hunted I suppose you'd call it,' she said. 'As if someone is looking at me through the sights of a gun.' She shook her head as if to try and dislodge something unpleasant in her mind. 'Something or someone is blocking me spiritually. I mean, I can still speak to spirit, Linnit is still with me, but it's hard, like talking through water. But that to one side, even with that on me mind I'm thinking of taking Esme in, Mr Hancock. She ain't got no one, she's dedicated to spirit and I am afraid for her.'

I didn't even begin to broach the subject of my apparently having spoken to Linnit myself in a dream. That would have to wait.

'Afraid? Why?'

Mrs Darling took a deep breath in and then crossed her arms over her chest. 'Esme was always highly strung,' she said. 'As a girl she had problems eating, and then . . .' She looked around the office to make sure no one was either about or outside the shop waiting to come in. 'Years ago, Rosemary told me that Esme tried to . . . well, she . . . she cut her wrists, you know.'

'Ah.'

'I'm afraid that with Neville gone and in the circumstances that he went, Esme might, well, she might do something silly,' Mrs Darling said.

'Well, Mrs Darling,' I said, 'I can't tell you what to do with regard to Esme. If you and your husband want to take her in . . .'

'Oh, he don't mind what happens as long as he can get his pint and his fags!' the medium said. Mention of her husband obviously made her tetchy. Then she added, 'Mr Hancock, what does it mean? Killing Neville. If this Ripper wants us White Feather girls, why murder Neville? I know he was boring and said silly things, but he never gave out white feathers to my knowledge. Why kill him?'

She was right. Looked at from the point of view that Neville was the only male victim in a series of ladies, his death could be seen as completely separate from the others. But then given the manner of his death, that was unlikely. And the fact that he was or had been the husband of a White Feather girl had to be significant. Something else occurred to me too, something so calculated that it made my blood almost freeze solid in my veins. 'Mrs Darling,' I said, 'if anything happened to Esme, how do you think Rosemary would take it?'

The medium narrowed her eyes. 'Happen?'

'Like if her wrists got cut or . . .' I sometimes wish that we could talk openly about suicide in this country. I know it's a crime, but it happens. It happens, in my experience, quite a lot.

'Well, Rosemary couldn't come over, could she?' Mrs Darling said. 'Not from Canada, not now.'

The days when civilians could still travel across the Atlantic are well past. I knew that.

'But she would be devastated,' the medium continued. 'They're twins, Rosemary and Esme, so there's a psychic bond between them. If one died the other would know, you mark my words! If one died it would be as if the other had lost part of herself. It would be torture.'

The psychic bond aside, that was what I had thought. If Esme died, then Rosemary would be punished too. Two for the price of one provided Esme took her own life, which seemed, from what Mrs Darling had said, a probability at least. And all achieved via the death of one rather hypocritical and boring man. If indeed I was correct. I hoped sincerely that I wasn't.

Chapter Sixteen

When Mrs Darling finally left me, it was to get a bus up to Forest Gate and the home of Esme Robinson. She made some play of trying to reward me for listening to her by saying that she'd try to secure Neville Robinson's funeral for our firm. I told her she didn't have to do that, but she didn't appear to want to hear. To tell the truth, I didn't particularly want the Robinson business. Where Neville had been found and the fact that Hannah had been one of those who had discovered him didn't sit well. She had by her own admission worked the night Robinson had died. I didn't want to know any more about it than that, and that included burying his body.

That afternoon I spent doing bookwork with Doris. It's not my favourite occupation as it often involves geeing up bereaved relatives for payment. I freely admit that without Doris, Hancock's would be bankrupt. I don't like asking for money, which means that I'm not very good at it. But it has to be done, and so after a good telling-off from Doris, I did trawl around to a couple of poor addresses and share tea and sometimes a drop of ginger wine too with people still in heavy mourning. I got a bit of money, here and there. When I returned, Doris had gone home but Nancy had returned, with visitors. Sitting up very straight in our parlour was a tall, average-looking Jewish bloke and a lady of breathtaking beauty. The woman, whose long blonde hair hung down her back in a thick, straight sheet, did not smile when she saw me come into the room. Black eyes in a face as pale as the moon regarded me steadily but without any sort of emotion. Nan and my mother, who were, it seemed, sharing tea with these people, both put their cups down when I entered the room.

'This is my brother Frank,' Nan said to the amazing blonde woman. 'Frank, this is my old friend Fernanda.'

Very often beautiful women know that they're beautiful to the extent that it interferes with the way they are with ordinary mortals. Fernanda Abrahams was one such lady. She was pleasant enough and very far from rude, but there was a superiority about her that seemed to preclude any sort of facial movement. Every time she spoke, she looked down her perfect nose at the world and most people, I imagined, that were in it. Her husband Edward, on the other hand, was, or seemed to be, a very easy-going and natural person.

'I've a cousin, Dave, who keeps me abreast of family matters,' Edward Abrahams said. 'Told me about poor Marie and Uncle Nathan.'

'David never had a problem with our marriage, unlike everyone else,' Fernanda said from a face as cold and unmoving as that of an idol. Faces like that I'd seen in my parents' photographs of Calcutta's many Hindu temples. But then India was or had been Fernanda's country too.

'As it happened, poor old Nathan found us suddenly fetching up out of the blue a bit too much,' Edward Abrahams said as he offered me a fag and then took one for himself.

'Old Mr Abrahams screamed the place down,' Nan put in.

'Screamed?'

'He's lost his wits,' Fernanda said. 'But then a parent don't expect to lose its child, do it?'

She was also trying, I now noticed, to be posh. An affected accent together with ropy grammar is always a dead give-away. But then for Fernanda Mascarenhas, as was, even Clapham North, where she and Edward lived in a flat 'over-looking the Common', was a step up from Canning Town. Even without asking, I knew she was not going to go back there. Plaistow was one thing, she'd tolerate our slightly better part of West Ham, but Canning Town was, I felt, a step too far.

'Nancy was helping out on the ward, and when we come in the two girls recognised each other,' Edward Abrahams said good-naturedly. 'She'd just turned up and so had we, and so when Uncle Nathan was brought in we were all together. Nancy tried to introduce us, but . . .'

'He just screamed, Frank,' my sister said. Then, shaking her head at the memory of it, she added, 'It was horrible.'

'It must've been,' I said as I puffed on the Passing Cloud that Edward had just given me.

'Never screamed before,' Nan said.

'Oh, I expect it was the shock of seeing us,' Fernanda said. 'Me and Edward, we have that effect on members of his family.' Turning to my mother, she added, 'You must know that effect, Mrs Hancock, don't you? When one marries out . . .'

The Duchess smiled. 'My dear, I pay no heed to the silly opinions of others, whoever they may be.'

Fernanda Abrahams sniffed. She knew that what my mother had just said was by way of a put-down. But then the Duchess, for all her natural fine manners, has never had any time for those who appear to put such things on for the benefit of others. Quite where Nan stood, I didn't know, but I had the feeling that both the Duchess and myself were well and truly put off by this woman.

Smiling, Edward said, 'So when Nancy here offered us tea, Frank, we took her up on it straight away.' He frowned. 'Poor Uncle Nathan. Shook me right up, the state of him, I can tell you. But then for our Marie to die like that . . . Nancy says you've been trying to find us.'

I told them what I knew – about Marie and Mrs Darling, about the White Feather girls. As I spoke, Nan put her head down in what I could see was shame. But Fernanda Abrahams was unmoved. Not in the silly, giggly way that Esme Robinson had been unmoved – it was much more measured and profound than that. Fernanda Abrahams I felt just didn't care. She had experienced far too much suffering herself, or so she felt, to be bothered with the pain of others. When I reached the end of the story as I knew it, Edward Abrahams said, 'Well, Frank, that's quite a tale you tell and I am obliged to you for telling it. Of course I knew that Fernanda was a

White Feather girl when she was young; it was how she met Marie.' He held a finger up to silence any protestation I might make about this. 'I never approved, of course,' he added. 'I was on the Somme and, well . . .' He looked at me with the eyes everyone who was in that carnage has.

'I don't know that whoever is killing these people is doing it because of the White Feather connection,' I said.

'Police don't say much these days,' Abrahams said as he slowly and sadly nodded his head.

'The coppers are treating each death as a separate incident unless they happen in the same division,' I said. 'There's a bloke here in Plaistow who's owned up to one of the killings. But only one, and whether he's telling the truth, no one seems to know.'

'They keep quiet about such things now because of the war,' the Duchess said.

I looked at Edward Abrahams and said, 'All I wanted to do was to warn you. Keep your wife safe.'

'Oh, you can be sure I'll do that, mate!' Abrahams winked at his wife as he said it. She turned aside in what looked like disgust. He was still besotted with her, but she was more in love with the clothes and make-up that he obviously had to work hard to get for her. Edward Abrahams, he told me just before they left, was a tailor. He'd learned his trade in the sweatshops of Spitalfields; now he had his own shop on the Clapham High Street. He also did his turn as a fire-watcher down in Clapham.

'I have to go out at night,' he said to me when we found ourselves alone at the shop door for the few moments just before they left. 'There's our daughter, Phillipa, but she works, driving ambulances.'

'Mr Abrahams,' I said, 'I don't know if your wife is really in danger.'

They left. I was glad that I'd managed to get to speak to them, even if Fernanda Abrahams was an unpleasant character. When we were back up in the parlour again, Nan said, 'You know, Frank I nearly jumped out of my skin when I saw Fernanda at the hospital. She hadn't changed a bit!'

'What, the look of her or how she behaved?' I said.

Nancy rolled her eyes. 'Oh, she was always a madam,' she said. She looked down at the floor and went on, "Course she never wanted to be seen with *me*. Not standing next to me or nothing. She made a beeline for girls like Marie and the Harper twins because they was fair. You know, Frank, when I told Fernanda that Dolly had died, she never said a thing, not one thing. Blimey, I was so glad when I saw her and her husband up at Claybury! I was so relieved.' She sighed. 'Although why old Mr Abrahams screamed when he saw them I don't know. He'd been quite calm when he talked to me about them. But then she was so cold, Fernanda, so very, very cold!'

That night the fog put paid to any designs Hitler might have had on us. But the fire-watchers went up as usual, on the roof of the bank next door. Mr Deeks the bank manager and his boys scanned the skies as they always do, while my mother, Nan and cousin Stella sat in the parlour knitting and mending. Once I'd stabled the horses for the night I stood down in the yard with Aggie, smoking. Aggie more than any of us gets out and about: to work, shopping and socially in pubs. I wanted to know if she'd heard anything.

'About the murders? Yeah, plenty,' she said as she rolled herself a fag from my tin of tobacco. 'They can censor what they like, people will always talk. Especially round here. Not that you'll want to hear any of it, Frank.'

'Why not?'

'Because all they ever talk about is the Ripper,' Aggie said. 'All the Jews up Brick Lane are quaking in their boots thinking he's come back again. Bleedin' ghosts!'

'But Jack the Ripper never attacked any Jewish women,' I said.

'I know that! But a lot of people blamed the Jews, thought he was one of them at the time.'

'Yes, but that was nonsense.'

'Was it?' Aggie pulled her chin back and gave me a very wry look indeed. 'Who told you that, your lady friend? Frank, no one knows who the Ripper was or is. He could be Jewish, he could be Irish, Welsh or sky blue pink. He could even be a she.'

'Aggie, Jack the Ripper cut women open and then pulled their innards out,' I said.

'Women can do that,' Aggie replied.

My younger sister has become a very different person from the girl who married and had children years ago. It's partly the war and the opportunities it has certainly given women to work that has changed her. But the humiliation she suffered at the hands of her faithless old man played its part too. He just left her and her children for another woman, just disappeared off the face of the earth.

'I'd never let a bloke get close enough to cut me up,' Aggie said as she ground her fag butt into the mud beneath her feet.

'But Aggie,' I said, 'don't you want to feel . . .'

'Frank, I go to the pub, I have a laugh and a sing-song, but that's the finish of it as far as blokes are concerned,' Aggie said. She crossed her arms over her chest and then muttered, 'They can bloody sing for anything else.'

'But Ag, everyone wants to be loved,' I said.

'Well you do because you're as soft as butter!' my sister said. 'But you know, Frank, that when this war is over, things are going to be a lot different.'

'Well, if Hitler . . .'

'No, when, *when* we win, Frank, after that the world will change. Won't be no more women doing as they're told all the time. We've had some freedom and we like it! And you know what, too?'

'What?'

'There won't be no more silly talk about ghosts and spirits when the war is over,' Aggie said. 'Because you know what? There's no such things. No ghosts, no God, no Blessed Virgins and no resurrected Jack the Rippers!'

'Well don't let Nan hear you say that!' I said.

Aggie's face suddenly fell into something very serious. 'You know that since Dolly's death Nan's been a different person too, Frank. Oh, she's still devoted to God, the Virgin and all that, but she's working for you and she's putting her back into it. Time was when she'd barely leave the house. She's changing, Frank. Even she's changing.'

And I knew that Aggie was right. Nancy, albeit by degrees, was moving out into the world. Even a month before, I couldn't have seen her grafting for me or doing good works up at a hospital, much less a hospital outside of West Ham. Maybe at last she was getting on top of the way she'd always felt about her colour and her looks. To be truthful, and as I had always known, deep down she was a strangely beautiful woman, especially when wearing the dark suit of our profession. Handsomer than Aggie in her way, Nancy was also, I thought, now somewhat more appealing than Fernanda Abrahams. Such chilliness in that woman! And yet she had a nice husband, a daughter who worked driving ambulances, a home – the Abrahams quite clearly had money.

But something rankled. A beautiful woman with beautiful white skin, she nevertheless knew where she came from, if no one else did. Both she and Edward had chosen to leave their pasts behind when they got together, and that included their families. But Edward, unlike Fernanda, had come from a white world. In spite of the fact that his family had disowned him, he was still a Jew, still who he had been before. But Fernanda . . . I didn't know this for certain, but by the look of her I imagined that she lived her life as a white lady, as something she really was not. That had been her choice, but I wondered what she felt about it deep down inside. According to Nancy, Fernanda had always been a 'madam' and had avoided my sister because of the colour of her skin. But Fernanda's parents and siblings had been brown, and however ambitious she might have been in the past, as the years went by she must have thought about them. Maybe it was a sense of being alone in the world, which she must have felt from time to time, that made her seem so hard and cold and without feeling? If indeed Fernanda Abrahams was really like that.

Chapter Seventeen

'They say the police have a man in custody for these Ripper murders. Down in your manor, Mr Hancock,' Esme Robinson said to me as Cissy handed me a cup of tea and a very old water biscuit.

Mrs Darling, across the table from me, sitting next to the widow Robinson, said, 'Cissy love, will you get the sugar bowl, please?'

Cissy smiled and went off to the kitchen. I'd come back, a little reluctantly it must be said, to the medium's house because, true to her word, Mrs Darling had persuaded Esme Robinson to use our firm to perform Neville's funeral. Because I had actively disliked Neville, this didn't sit easily with me. But as my dad always said, 'a job is a job'. Neville's funeral was to take place at Manor Park Cemetery on the following Tuesday.

'Well, Mrs Robinson,' I said, 'the man in question has admitted to the murder of his wife.'

'Violet Dickens,' Mrs Darling put in.

'Oh, poor Vi!' Esme Robinson's eyes filled with tears.

She looked, understandably, bad. She was pale and had clearly lost weight. Also, her face, although covered by a layer of tan-coloured powder, was covered with lots of angry red scratches. I wondered if in her grief she had done those herself.

'But Fred Dickens can't have killed your husband, Mrs Robinson,' I said. 'He was in police custody when Mr Robinson was killed. Personally, I don't think that Fred killed anyone.'

'Neither do I,' Mrs Darling said. But she didn't elaborate upon why. I assumed it had something to do with the feeling of being watched she had told me about. That or something the spirits were telling her.

'Why do you think Vi's husband might be innocent?' Esme said. 'Why would he own up to something he didn't do?'

'Well, Mr Dickens is a drinker . . .'

'Coppers want an easy life, especially now,' Mrs Darling said. 'They have ways to force out confessions.'

Cissy came back into the room just as the medium was finishing what she was saying. She put the sugar bowl on the table and sat down. I left the sugar on this occasion myself and let the women have it. Conscious of the fact that I needed to get back to the shop for a funeral in the afternoon, I said, 'Mrs Robinson, I will need to know where Neville is now.'

I knew his height and could gauge the size of coffin that I needed for him. But I needed to know where to take it before I either brought Neville back to the shop or left him wherever he was until the day of the funeral. I imagined, given the circumstances, he was in Whipps Cross Hospital.

'Oh, he's up at Claybury,' she said. 'They ran out of space at Whipps Cross.'

'So . . .'

'Oh, they said they'd keep him there until the funeral,' Esme said. 'But Mr Hancock, on the day, if it's all right, I would like to go and pick him up with you and . . . I've got money. I can pay for a car as well as the hearse.'

Esme Robinson was now sole owner of a big house on the edge of Epping Forest.

'You'll come with me, won't you, Margaret?' she said to Mrs Darling. 'And you, Cissy?'

As I wrote all this down in my notebook, I heard the medium say, 'Yes, Esme love.'

'So the cortège will start at Claybury Hospital?' I said.

'Yes.'

As soon as I'd finished my tea and we'd chatted over a few more details, I got up to go. Unusually it wasn't Cissy who saw me out but Esme Robinson. She thanked me profusely for my help all the way to the front door. Then suddenly her face went very blank and she said, 'I will do right by my Neville, Mr Hancock. A good send-off for a good man. What happens afterwards . . .'

She shut the door behind me, and in spite of the relative warmth of that day, I shuddered.

'You so much as touch my sister again and I'll knock your teeth out, you mare!'

Aggie in full flight was not a sight I'd imagined seeing when I got back to the shop. What I'd hoped to see was the hearse and the horses, along with the coffin containing the deceased, and my bearers, including Nancy, ready to go. And that was what I got. But I also got Aggie screaming at a very well-dressed and not terribly frightened-looking Fernanda Abrahams in the back yard. Nancy, I now noticed, had been crying.

'Aggie?'

'Oh, Mr Hancock,' Fernanda Abrahams said calmly, 'I didn't know your younger sister was so pretty.'

Like Fernanda, fair as a lily, Aggie nevertheless had a temper that was far from pale.

'This one,' Aggie said pointing to Fernanda, 'come here and started mouthing off! Threatening!'

'It's all right,' I heard Nan say gently.

Aggie turned to look at her and said, 'All right? No it ain't, Nan. No one comes here and threatens us! Not on our own property. No one!'

She looked back at Fernanda again and narrowed her eyes for the next onslaught. I took a hand. Walking between Aggie and Fernanda I said, 'Now, ladies, let's have a bit of respect, shall we? This is hardly dignified as a start to the last journey for the late Mr Compton here, is it? Come on, let's go inside and discuss this.'

Herbert Compton was due at the East London Cemetery in half an hour, and so I knew I was cutting it fine to delay our departure. But I had to get this thing with Fernanda Abrahams and my sisters sorted out.

Once we were all, including Nan, in the small room that leads out to the yard, I said, 'Now what's all this about?'

Aggie pointed to Fernanda and said, 'Madam here threatening Nan!'

'Threatening?'

'No, it wasn't threatening, Aggie,' Nancy said as she looked down very pointedly at the floor.

'Yes, it . . .'

'No, Fernanda came to see me because she was upset,' Nan said.

'You were bawling your eyes out by the time I turned up,' Aggie said. And then she turned to me and added, 'All dressed up lovely for Mr Compton's funeral, then tears all down her face, sobbing fit to break her heart!'

'Aggie,' I began, 'will you . . .'

'Mr Hancock!' The imperious voice of Fernanda Abrahams broke through our family squabble and demanded attention – which it got. 'Mr Hancock,' she said, 'I came to visit Nancy firstly because I was upset that she had just come up to my husband and me while we were visiting his uncle in Claybury and broke up what Edward hoped might be a nice reconciliation with the old bloke. As it was, Nancy turning up frightened the wits out of the old man, and then we had the screaming and such like.'

'Mrs Abrahams,' I said, 'you told us only yesterday that Mr Nathan Abrahams reacted badly to you and your husband, not my sister. When I was with my sister and Mr Abrahams up at Claybury the other day, he took very well to Nancy.'

'Yes, well,' Fernanda said sulkily, 'I couldn't say nothing in front of your mother, could I? And anyway, raking up all that

White Feather business, that upset my old man. Had a right hard time with him about it when we got home.'

'I said I was sorry,' I heard Nancy say.

Aggie looked daggers at her sister, probably because she felt that Nan was being weak. 'Yeah,' she said to Fernanda, 'didn't have to make her cry, though, did you? Didn't have to say you never wanted to see her again.'

'But I don't want to see her again,' Fernanda Abrahams said, yet again very calmly. 'You've warned Ed and me that someone out there might want to harm me, so we can take care of ourselves now. Nancy and I were never friends. We don't need each other.'

This did make me angry. 'Now look here,' I said, 'my sister didn't have to invite you and your husband back here yesterday. Although I think your husband was rather grateful after what happened up at Claybury. Mrs Abrahams, Nancy got you back here specifically so that I could warn you about the danger you may be in. She didn't want any harm to come to you.'

'Yes, well . . .' She was still infuriatingly unconcerned.

I wanted to ask her straight out whether her dislike of Nancy was connected to the colour of my sister's skin. I knew that it probably was, but I just couldn't get myself together to say it. In the end, I didn't have to.

'You know, Fernanda,' Nancy said gently, 'just because when you look at me you see everything that you hate about yourself, that doesn't mean I'm a bad person. As my brother said, I did what I did because I don't want anything bad to happen to you.'

There was a long silence. Even Aggie shut up then. Aggie like me had tears in her eyes. Neither of us had ever seen Nan stand up for herself with anyone outside the family before. Again it was Nan who changed the atmosphere in that little room when she finally looked at me and said, 'Frank, we must get on now. Mr Compton needs burying.'

Later, when Herbert Compton had finally been laid to rest, Nan said to me, 'You know, of all of us it was Fernanda who was the least bothered about giving out white feathers. Not that I think she thought it was wrong at the time. Margaret I think did – not Fernanda, though. But the rest of us, though far from posh, came from much better-off families than she did. Just knowing she came from Canning Town told you that. I think she got in with us because she wanted to better herself. Which of course she did with Marie's cousin Edward. Calculating is what Fernanda is. I never told anyone, but she always gave me a shudder.'

Mrs Darling had told me something not dissimilar to this when we'd first spoken about Fernanda. There was something about her that got people's backs up.

Bella, one of the other old girls who lived with Hannah in Dot Harris's house, had spent more time than she liked at Canning Town police station.

'Some copper called Hartley,' she said in her deep, smoke-dried voice. 'Constable Hartley. He took me in. I said, "Get your sergeant here. I won't talk to no one apart from him." Mama! What a fuss! I said, "If you want me to talk about some man I may have entertained, then I need to talk to the organ-grinder, not the monkey!'"

Not a day under fifty, Bella is Italian on her father's side and is therefore as expressive and expansive as those people do tend to be. I only know this, however, because Hannah has told me. Italian people don't tend to draw attention to themselves these days.

I'd gone over to Hannah's just to see her and had found my girl having tea with Bella in front of her range. The two women were talking about Neville Robinson and the fact that he had been one of Bella's regulars. Neville had apparently been identified by his clothes, something Bella knew quite a bit about.

'Tartan socks he always wore, I told Sergeant Raymond,' she said. 'Tartan socks, horrible dark green suspenders, and he always had a packet of du Maurier fags in his jacket – his old lady wouldn't let him smoke in the house, can you imagine? There was always some saucy postcard he'd want me to look at too. Don't know where he got those.'

Bella had known me for years, and so my presence and my questions were not any sort of problem for her.

"Course, it weren't just his clothes what helped to identify him,' Bella said as she picked a tiny piece of tobacco off her wrinkled red lips. 'I always had to call him Nevvie. Weren't hard to know what his real name was. Then when I told Sergeant Raymond that Nevvie liked to play at being a copper, well that clinched it!'

Neville Robinson had been a policeman in Islington in

the First Lot. That, apparently, had left a lasting impression upon him, or rather on his intimate life.

'Bella,' I said as I took the cup of tea that Hannah gave me, 'I know that Sergeant Raymond probably asked you this already, but did you see anyone about when Neville left the night that he died?'

'What, on the street? No. Only girls out for business,' Bella said.

'Girls that you recognised?'

She shrugged. 'I dunno, Frank. Girls!' She shrugged again. 'I was tired. Nevvie was hard work.' She looked briefly over at Hannah, who said, 'Bella, just tell him. It's Frank! He knows what's what.'

'Nevvie hadn't had anything intimate with his wife since just after they got married,' Bella said. 'She didn't like it, apparently. But he did, 'cept he only liked it if he pretended he was arresting me. Like being in a fucking play, it was!'

'Yes, but . . .'

'As I said, Frank, it took it out of me!' Bella said. 'I'm not as young as I was.'

'Who is?' Hannah put in gloomily.

'Once we'd finished, I took Nevvie down to the front door and waved him off as he walked in the direction of the Barking Road,' Bella said. 'There were some girls about but I didn't look at any of them because I was tired and wanted to get some kip. Anyway, the youngsters out on the street don't talk to us old-timers.'

'Were they all young girls out on the street then, Bella?' I asked.

'Well I can't swear to it because I never looked at them, Frank. But they usually are just bits of kids, ain't they?'

Hannah nodded in agreement.

'No men?'

'Not that I could see, although men would have been about at some time because of the girls,' Bella said. She lit up a fag and leaned towards me. 'Frank, Nevvie always come to me once a week, same time, same day. Told his wife he went to some retired coppers affair.'

'So he was very predictable,' I said.

'Nevvie,' Bella said, 'was always the same. Hard work, punctual to the second and probably the most boring bleeder in the world.'

I looked through the open hatch at the small fire inside Hannah's range and thought about all the other victims and how no one in any of those cases had ever seen anything. I included the case of Violet Dickens in this because although her husband was, according to my mate Sergeant Hill, to be sent to trial for her murder, I didn't believe that Fred was or could be guilty. Somehow whoever was killing these people was blending in with whatever was around the victim. People saw this person, but because of where he was or what was happening, no one really *saw* him. He had to be safe, not threatening in any way, to achieve what I was beginning to feel was a kind of invisibility. In my head I made a list – coppers, nuns, *women* . . . A copper in Rathbone Street would have stuck out like a sore thumb. But a woman? Aggie had seen nothing wrong with the idea of a woman killing and mutilating bodies. But I still drew back from it. After all, why would a woman want to kill a group of old White Feather girls? All that had happened a long time ago and no women, to my knowledge, had been harmed by it. In fact most women at the time, as I recalled now, had rather approved of what the White Feather movement had done.

Chapter Eighteen

Ever since Dolly O'Dowd's funeral, none of the so-called Ripper victims had had flowers with horrible messages placed upon their graves. However, as I looked through the small bunches of blooms that had been delivered for Neville Robinson, I was prepared. But there was nothing, and so we all, including Arthur once again now, set off with the hearse and Walter (God help me!) at the wheel of the car. When we arrived at Claybury, we found the coffin already in the corridor outside the mortuary, waiting to be taken away. Apparently, due to the outbreak of dysentery on some of the wards, Claybury had too many bodies of its own to store now. We could have taken off then, but strangely neither Esme, Mrs Darling or Cissy were anywhere to be seen.

'Well it is a bit odd having the cortège run from a hospital,' Nan said as she looked around anxiously. 'You sure this was what Esme wanted, Frank?'

'Yes.'

Walter, in the car, said, 'Well it's a good job it ain't summer.

Stuck out here in the middle of nowhere, the corpse stinking like . . .'

'Yes, thank you for that, Walter,' I said. Walter doesn't do well outside of West Ham. He believes, I think, that anywhere beyond the borough is hostile land. In reply he muttered something about being sorry for saying what he had in front of a lady. But neither Nan, Arthur or myself responded. Personally I was just grateful that he was sober.

'I should have arranged to pick the ladies up from Mrs Darling's house,' I said as I scanned the area just beyond the front gates of the hospital. 'I don't even know how they were going to get here. I hope nothing's wrong.'

But as the minutes began to mount up I became more and more alarmed. This wasn't helped by the fact that people – staff and even, I think, a few patients too – began to stare at us. Walter tried to deal with this in his usual manner by taking out his hip flask. But I told him to put it away on pain of death. Sober, he's not the best driver in the world; drunk, he's bloody awful.

I had, I admit, just started to imagine what the coppers were going to find at Mrs Darling's house when the lady herself and Esme Robinson came puffing up the long gravel path. Their faces, red from the effort of walking fast or running, were in stark contrast to their deep black mourning.

'Oh, Mr Hancock, we are so sorry!' Mrs Darling said as she came over and put a gloved hand on my arm. 'We were waiting for Cissy! Waited and waited but the silly girl never turned up! Can't think why!'

I was so relieved just to see them, I smiled. After all, Cissy, wherever she was, hadn't been a White Feather girl and so was probably quite safe. I ushered the ladies into the car and then climbed up on to the box behind the horses with Nancy and Arthur.

Once we were moving, my sister said to me, 'Esme Harper didn't even acknowledge me then, you know, Frank.'

'I expect,' I said, 'Mrs Robinson has other things on her mind.'

Neville Robinson's wake took place at the house he'd shared with his wife on Hampton Road, Forest Gate. Although backing on to the railway line from Liverpool Street to Southend-on-Sea, the house was big and detached and had a considerable coach house to one side. Apparently it had belonged to Esme's parents who, like their relatives the Martins, had made their money in the greengrocery trade. As I looked around what was a very fine building, I wondered about how much more money the family had taken with them when they went to Canada.

Mrs Darling, reading my thoughts, said, 'Esme's mother had means. Her people was in jewellery. Jews, some say, although not now of course.'

I thought about Neville as I sipped from the little glass of sherry Esme had given me. I thought about his strange sexual life and felt that I now knew why he had put up with his wife's rejection of him. When Neville had met Esme, he had clearly landed on his feet.

There weren't many at the wake, just really friends from Mrs Darling's seances. No one, I noticed, came from

Islington or any other police force. As usual all of my workers were invited, including Nancy, who was nevertheless very uncomfortable.

'I remember coming here years ago,' she said to me as we moved from the drawing room into what appeared to be a small library. 'Esme and Rosemary were well off. I felt so bad here then.'

'About not being well off?' I said.

'That and . . .' She didn't finish her sentence; she didn't have to. I knew. 'Frank, I don't think I can stay,' she continued. 'I'd like to go home. I'll catch a bus or . . .'

'Someone needs to take the horses back soon,' I said. 'I'll get Arthur to drive you home.'

'Will you come back in the car?'

'I should stay for a little bit longer,' I said. 'Just to make sure the ladies are all right. I'll stick Walter in the car later and drive him home.'

'You know, Esme still hasn't spoken to me,' Nan said sadly as I led her out of the library and towards the front door.

Not believing for a moment what I was saying, I said, 'She probably doesn't recognise you, love. Not now you're a gorgeous working lady.'

Nan and Arthur left, and then about ten minutes later, another guest arrived. Esme Robinson answered the door. It was Cissy.

'Oh, Esme,' she said as she nervously twittered outside the front door. 'I am so, so sorry. I was taken bad in the night and . . . Something I ate, I think. I am so very sorry.'

She did look pale, even for her. Esme Robinson took her friend into her arms, and stroking Cissy's hair, she finally broke down and wept.

'Oh well,' Mrs Darling said as she looked at the scene unfolding on the doorstep, 'at least the silly ha'p'orth didn't go to the wrong place.' Then she turned to me and said, 'Here, Mr Hancock, did you have any joy with finding Fernanda Mascarenhas?'

I hadn't had a chance to tell her. Now I did. Mrs Darling frowned. 'That sounds like her,' she said. 'Does as she pleases, always has done. Nothing ever gets in the way of Fernanda's life, so if your Nancy popped up to remind her husband about what she once was . . .'

'Mr Abrahams was clearly not as forgiving of his wife as Neville Robinson,' I said.

'Well, if he's had to live with Fernanda all these years, there's few as can fault him for that,' the medium said. 'I'm glad you've found her and she's safe, but Fernanda Mascarenhas always was and probably still is a right mare!'

Fernanda Mascarenhas clearly still evoked very strong opinions in all those that knew her. Not long after my conversation with Mrs Darling, we all left. Esme Robinson was going to stay in her own house from now on, and it soon became apparent that she needed some time by herself. Three times Mrs Darling asked her whether she was sure about this, and three times the bereaved woman said that she was. Just because it worked out that way, I was actually the last person to leave. As I bade her farewell in the elegant hall of her elegant house, Esme Robinson took one of my hands in hers and said, 'Goodbye, Mr Hancock. You have been very, very kind.'

The drive back to the shop was long and bleak and depressing. Although Forest Gate itself had sustained little bomb damage, as we went further south, the scars of war began to multiply fast. First one, then two and then countless sites that had once been houses and shops reduced to piles of bricks and burnt mortar. Odd remnants of lives either gone or relocated: curtains, teapots, washing bowls scattered across the debris like lost thoughts. The closer we got towards home the more it all reminded me of Flanders, and as a consequence, the more I began to wonder how I was enduring it. Back in 1918, just before I left the continent, I remember looking around at the churned-up land, the flattened towns and villages, and knowing that the world would never, ever be the one I had known before the Great War. And I was quite right. Driving down from Forest Gate to Plaistow, I had that feeling all over again. What is being done now will never be undone. Buildings may be patched up or made over again, but what the sight of those devastated homes and churches will do to the people who loved them, I don't know. I wonder sometimes whether everyone will not just end up like me. Mad and sad and really, at the core of my soul, quite alone.

Walter, asleep and snoring in the back of the car, didn't see a thing. But then alcohol can be a very merciful substance. Driving on, my thoughts shifted to the notion of what whoever might be killing the White Feather girls might be like. I had in mind a fellow not entirely unlike myself.

Someone whose insides had been scarred beyond all recognition by the sights and sounds of the First World War. A chap who volunteered – unlike me, who was a silly kid at the time – for the sake of form and against his better judgement. A man, in short, bullied into destroying his own life. The more I thought about this theoretical man, the more I, in a sense, sympathised with him. And yet what I couldn't shift out of my mind, the question I'd been puzzling over since the beginning of these killings, was why now? Why leave it twenty-three years? If the rage he felt against these women was so great as to make him literally rip their bodies apart, then surely it was no fiercer now than it had been just after the Great War ended?

Something clearly had to have happened. If the killer had suppressed his anger for all those years, then an event must have taken place that made or allowed that fury to come out. But what? I thought that maybe the killer had recently been released from either a prison or an asylum. Not that either of those things could cover all the possibilities that had to exist under the title of 'Things Happening' to people. Births, deaths, marriages, divorces, sickness of all and any sort . . . The possibilities were endless and there was no chance that I could even start to think about them all. But I would, I decided, tell Sergeant Hill what my thoughts on the matter were about someone coming out of prison or an asylum. Even if he didn't do anything, Sergeant Hill always listened.

For the moment, I took my mind quite away from the victims.

Chapter Nineteen

*E*verything was ready. She'd pulled the blackout curtains
and put a freshly washed counterpane on the bed, and
now she lit a candle on her bedside table. She could have
had more than one really, she could easily afford it, but Esme didn't
need a lot of light to do what she was about to do. She'd already
poured the filthy green liquid from the can in the shed into an
empty Ribena bottle. There was still a faint smell around the
bottle but she'd just have to put up with that.

Esme lay down on her bed and thought about Neville. In all
the ways that were important to her, he'd been a good husband.
He'd always supported her, had done generally whatever she asked
and had maintained a respectable façade with their neighbours,
family and friends. He couldn't really help it if he liked that dirty
stuff. Men generally did. And although it was distasteful that he
should do that with cheap, common street women, that was far
better than if he'd had an actual mistress. Neville had never
brought any of that into their marriage. Esme need never have
even known. But no one could possibly attend so many retired
police officers' meetings, and one night she'd paid to have him

followed. He'd gone to a known bawdy house in Canning Town to visit, apparently, a prostitute who was no longer young. Eventually, around that rough and distasteful company, Neville had met his death. Esme sighed. If only her husband could have been content with kisses! If only he could have settled himself to his real retired police officers' meetings, and the circles at Margaret Darling's place in East Ham of course. Poor Margaret! She'd tried so hard to look after Esme in the wake of Neville's death. Esme was really going to disappoint her. But she couldn't go on without Neville, she didn't want to. She didn't want to be one of those burdensome single women that people always pitied! And besides, every time she thought about carrying on without Neville she got a pain in her chest so harsh and severe it completely took her breath away. Esme propped herself up on her pillows and took the lid off the Ribena bottle. The smell of the disinfectant made her gag. But there was no point in delaying things. She'd made up her mind. It was now or never.

Esme poured the rank green liquid into her mouth and began to cough immediately. Coughing and gagging again now, she fought to swallow what she could feel was burning a hole in her throat. Somehow she got some down, even though she spat what looked like most of it out over her nice clean counterpane. Eyes watering and bulging with the strain and the pain, Esme's mind raced as she thought about what to do next. The pain and just the sheer difficulty, not to mention the messiness of the act, was making her panic. For some reason she wanted to speak, to hear her own voice one last time, but all that came out of her was a hot, agonising rattle. God, she hadn't wanted to die like this! Retching and vomiting and turning her lovely bedroom into some sort of ghastly, filthy abattoir! She leaned forward so she could cough more easily and saw that most of what she was bringing up now was blood. Esme began to cry, and in spite of the fact that she still really, really wanted to go beyond the veil and be with her Neville once again, she began to whisper, 'Help! Help me!'

The pain in her wrecked throat moved to her chest and increased in intensity so that Esme began to howl, a long, fierce, tattered scream.

For the next two nights the raids were long and hellish. My night-time runs were lit up by massive fires all over the docks and especially in the manors closest to them: North Woolwich and Silvertown. As usual I can't be absolutely certain about what I did when I was out fleeing from the bombs. But I know that at one point I was in Central Park, East Ham. I remember plants of some sort wrapping themselves around my feet and tripping me up. At the time this was just simply annoying. But later I realised that what I'd probably tramped through with my great big boots was some poor sod's allotment. A lot of the parks are turned over to the growing of veg for the war effort – have been ever since the start.

By that Friday morning, I was dead on my feet. Aside from the raids, we'd done three funerals the day after Neville Robinson's, and then on the Thursday I'd spent a good eight hours talking to bereaved families and making arrangements with them. Nan, apparently, had managed to fit in a visit to Claybury.

'Old Mr Abrahams don't talk even to me no more,' she said sadly.

I was cleaning my boots at the time and looked up at her with what I knew were horribly bloodshot eyes.

'I don't care what Fernanda Mascarenhas might say,' my sister continued, 'it wasn't me who gave the poor old thing such a start last week. It was when he saw them two.'

'I know,' I said, 'My understanding is that Mr Abrahams began to scream when Fernanda and her husband and you were all together. Although why he should do so after, according to you, talking about Edward quite comfortably, I don't know.'

'Yes, well . . .'

'Nan, was there anyone else with you?' I asked. 'Any of the other ladies who help out up there, or maybe a nurse? A patient?'

On the Wednesday, one of our funerals had been for an ex-Plaistow copper. Sergeant Hill had attended on behalf of the division and so I'd spoken to him about the possibility of the so-called Ripper being an ex-prisoner or asylum inmate. He'd said that if he found the time he'd look into that. Here I was doing my own little bit towards that.

'No. Mrs Ravens and Nurse Belmont were up the other end of the ward and Alice was helping Bernie to drink some soup. Nothing was happening.'

Beyond knowing the name Alice, I didn't have a clue about who any of these people were.

'Oh, I'm going over to Alice's tomorrow,' Nancy continued. 'She's invited me to tea with her and her mother.'

'That's nice,' I said. My brain was really still thinking about Nathan Abrahams. If he had indeed screamed when Fernanda,

Edward and Nancy went to talk to him, did that have any significance? Nathan had never said whether or not he'd seen anyone who could possibly have killed his daughter the night that Marie died. All he'd managed to blurt out was that a woman friend had visited his girl earlier in the evening. Of course there were problems between Nathan's family and Edward, and the actual sight of his errant nephew might very well have upset the old man enough to make him scream. But what if the couple from Clapham had brought to mind something else? Something about his daughter's killer?

Nan, looking into my seemingly blank face, said, 'I'll put Alice's address in the diary.' Then she left.

'All right, love,' I said to the thin air she left in her wake. I decided that I'd go out on Saturday too. In the morning I'd have one last shot at speaking to Nathan Abrahams.

It wasn't even starting to get dark by the time Doris began to close up the shop for the night. I wanted her and Walter to be able to get home before the sirens went. She was just getting the key to lock up the front door when a bloke of about fifty-five walked in. I was sitting at Doris's desk and was the first to see him. A bit of a grimy, rough-looking geezer. I frowned at him and said, 'Yes?'

'You 'Ancock, are you?' he said in what some would have taken for an aggressive way. But I'm an East Ender, I know that this is the way with some of us, particularly the men.

'Yes,' I said. 'How can I help you?'

'You can't,' he said. 'I brought a message from my missus.'

'Your missus?'

Doris, who had been hovering beside the desk with the door key in her hand, said, 'Mr Hancock, do you want me to lock up or . . .'

I took the key from her and said, 'That's all right, Doris, I'll do it. You get off now.'

With a quick, uncertain glance at our visitor, Doris got her coat and left. As soon as the door closed behind her I said, 'Your missus?'

'Mrs Darling,' he replied. So this was the famous 'old man' who shared a Christian name with me. 'I'm her messenger boy, postman, whatever she wants me to be.' He didn't look that happy about it. 'But anyway, my old lady thought you should know that Esme Robinson is dead.'

I was shocked, even if I wasn't that surprised. As well as what Mrs Darling had told me about Esme's past, there was also the very final way, after Neville's funeral, in which Esme had bade me goodbye. And the medium herself had been unsure, I knew. She had almost begged Esme to come back and continue her stay with her in East Ham. But Esme had insisted upon being alone. Had she indeed done something to herself, or had someone else done it for her? I took in a deep breath in order to try and calm myself.

Then Mr Darling provided the stark truth. 'Topped herself,' he said in a whisper. 'Disinfectant.'

'God help us!' I said. 'Jesus Christ!' Drinking disinfectant isn't a clean or a quick way to go. I've dealt with a few disinfectant deaths in my time, I'm sorry to say. It is an agonising and desperate way to die. Poor Esme, she must have truly felt utterly unable to go on without her husband. I gestured for Mr Darling to sit down, which, after first taking the flat cap off his head, he did. 'When? How did Mrs Darling find out?'

'Coppers,' Mr Darling said.

'Coppers contacted you?'

'Come to speak to Maggie,' he said. 'Right after her husband's funeral, Esme Robinson done it.'

'How did the coppers know?' I said. 'I mean, this did take place in her house, didn't it?'

'Yus.' Mr Darling looked around to make sure no one else could possibly be listening, then said, 'Neighbours called the coppers in the evening because of the screaming. She must have drank it and then when the pain started . . .'

'God almighty!' Unfortunately I could only too easily imagine what she must have gone through. Tears came into my eyes, and although they remained unshed, I cried inside for this woman I had known only slightly and not even liked particularly well. Some things just transcend any bad feelings people might have towards each other. An untimely and painful suicide is one of them.

'They tried to save her,' Mr Darling said. 'Took her over Whipps Cross by all accounts. But she was dead by the morning. Left a note for her sister in Canada and one for my old woman. The one to Maggie said that she, Esme, wants you to do her funeral.'

'Oh God, what a thing to do. I . . .' I was still shocked. She must have been, as Mrs Darling had predicted, unable to face existence without her husband. Without intimacy or even faithfulness on his part – if indeed Esme had known about what Neville did with prostitutes – she had nevertheless loved him and could not imagine a life without him.

'Good money in it for you,' Mr Darling continued. 'Esme and her old man was not short of a bob or two.'

He was unmoved, some would say callous. But the Darlings weren't rich and he, poor bloke, had his own cross to bear. He wasn't interested in 'spirit'. I didn't think he even probably had much notion of what spiritualism was about. And yet he had a houseful of spiritualists most evenings as far as I could tell. Cissy was in and out during the day too.

'Maggie says if you could come over tomorrow morning to discuss arrangements, she'd be obliged,' he said.

'Yes, well . . .' I didn't need to look at the diary to see what I was doing the following morning. I had planned to go and see Mr Abrahams at Claybury. Now that would have to wait. 'Of course,' I said. 'If you could let Mrs Darling know that I'll be with her by nine. We, er, we must all do right by Mrs Robinson now. Like every living creature she deserves a decent burial.'

'All right.'

'And of course offer your wife and everyone concerned my sincerest condolences,' I said.

Mr Darling shrugged. 'Bit of a funny one, Esme, if you ask me,' he said. 'Until her husband started coming along with her, I thought she was another old maid. Maggie picks up old maids. They're usually interested in what lies beyond the veil.'

He said it with a straight, miserable face. It made me wonder, for a moment, whether Mr Darling did in fact believe in his wife's circle and seances. But he soon put me right on that.

'Well, my dear old lady excepted, but who but silly spinsters or soppy irons like that Mr Watkins fella would believe in something as daft as spirits and angels playing their harps sat on clouds and all that nonsense?' he said. Then he leaned forward and added conspiratorially, 'If you ask me, all these single women want to be paired up and soon. Hysterical.'

'Mr Darling,' I said, 'our young men are fighting.' Now that the initial shock of Esme Robinson's death had passed, I was starting to feel angry, as I often do in the wake of a suicide. I've no religious objections to it; I just feel sad and frustrated at the waste.

'Oh, not the young girls!' he said scornfully. 'I mean it's the old maids want to be paired up. Women our age. A bleeding nuisance, all of 'em!'

To my way of thinking Mr Darling was being silly and prejudiced and I wasn't having it. I let my anger, if in a rather limited form, have its way. 'And who would you pair these women up with, Mr Darling?' I said. 'I assume, sir, you were in the forces in the First . . .'

'Royal Navy,' Mr Darling cut in sharply.

'Then you know that women our age outnumber men to a vast degree,' I said. 'There's no one for them to marry. I have a spinster sister myself. My younger sister has married and has children, but my older sister has always been single. It isn't ideal, but there's very little she or anyone else can do about it.'

For a moment he sat in silence, not exactly ashamed of

what he had said, but cowed nonetheless. Eventually he said, 'Yus, well . . . Well, they should do normal things as hobbies like sewing and knitting, not flapping about hysterically all over the place!'

I didn't make the obvious comment about the fact that Mrs Darling's sitters, spinsters included, paid for the privilege of attending her seances. He had to know that, and so as he left I said no more about it to him beyond reiterating that I'd see his wife in the morning. But he'd really annoyed me. Spinsters like Nancy, cousin Stella and strictly my Hannah too, together with widows like Doris, make up a big and very industrious part of the population. Doris I would say is probably the backbone of our firm; without her I would quickly get into a tizz with my appointments and everything. But people still shun single ladies over the age of thirty in a way they don't do to blokes of the same vintage. People look at me a bit funny from time to time, but that isn't because I'm single. I behave strangely and I look a bit different to most people and so I have come to expect and accept that. But spinsters are treated as unnatural and looked upon either as tarts or mad or queer. I thought again about Esme Robinson and wondered whether not just her grief but the way people see single women had informed what she had done so very painfully to herself.

I looked at the diary for the following day to see if I had anything on in the afternoon. I didn't, so I resolved to go up to Claybury after I'd visited Mrs Darling in the morning. Nan had, I noticed, put her appointment with her friend in the book just as Aggie had told her. It said, *2 o'clock, Alice,*

Abbey Lane. I smiled. Well, there was one spinster not either sewing or talking to the spirits, I thought. There was also one spinster with a job too. I had already decided that provided Nan was happy to work for the firm, I was happy to have her. She had certainly at least started to emerge from her shell in recent weeks.

But then suddenly that thought turned sour. Nan had started to get out because her best friend, Dolly O'Dowd, had been stabbed, beaten and hacked to death. And now yet another of their friends had died very horribly too.

That night the skies were clear again and so we had another visit from the Luftwaffe. Unusually for me, I was so tired I couldn't even think about running away. Very occasionally this happens, and when it does, I usually take myself off up on to the roof over Aggie's bedroom window. Seems barmy, I know, but my reasoning is that if a bomb should drop with my name on it, if I'm out in the open at least I will go quickly. On top of a roof I stand far less chance of being buried alive than I'd have in an Anderson or a public shelter. Mr Deeks the bank manager and his little group of fire-watchers on the roof of the bank next door are used to my doing this from time to time.

'Good evening, Mr Hancock!' I heard Mr Deeks call out just after the first bomb hit somewhere down North Woolwich way.

'G-g-good evening, Mr Deeks.'

He scratched his head underneath his tin hat and said, 'Good lord, these wretched Nazis, eh?'

'Y-yes,' I said.

By the light of the now mounting explosions as well as the beams of the searchlights overhead, I saw him smile. His duty as a neighbour done, he then went off to be with his lads at the southern end of the rooftop. Normally I would have lain down and closed my eyes, but on this occasion I sat up and looked down into the street below. Without being able to see any details, I knew that no one would be walking the Barking Road now that a raid was in full swing. Not even dogs and cats, kept indoors since the beginning of the war, wandered at night now. One creature I did know that was out and about, however, was the rat. As our sewers collapse and we die, so they grow in numbers. Just as they did in the trenches, thriving on the filth that gets into every corner of our lives. On this night, however, it wasn't just the rats that were down on the Barking Road. Amazingly there was a person down there too, and, although at first I couldn't make out what the noise was, eventually I realised that this character was knocking on my shop door. As soon as there was a slight lessening of the noise from guns and aeroplanes and explosions I shouted down, 'Who is it? What do you want?'

Knowing my luck it was a warden or a copper who had spotted a slight chink of light at one of our windows. Aggie in particular can be a bit careless about turning off the gas when she goes down to the shelter. But no answer was forthcoming. I shuffled a little closer to the edge of the roof and yelled, 'Oi!'

As I did so, the person looked up just as a great explosion of red, orange and yellow illuminated the sky, the street and probably the whole manor. Somewhere, I reckoned just south of the East London Cemetery, blew apart in a hail of brick, wood, slate and flesh.

'Bloody hell!'

But it wasn't the explosion that shocked me. It was my visitor. Her face pale as the moon, her long blonde hair flowing down over her shoulders, rendered gold by the death and destruction of who knew how many others, there, large as life, was Fernanda Abrahams. Even though I had a terrible feeling afterwards that maybe I imagined the whole thing, my eyes most certainly met hers and I would have sworn at that moment she was real. But just in case I was dreaming the whole bloody thing, I closed my eyes for a moment, by which time Fernanda, or whatever I had seen down there, had gone.

'Fucking hell!' I heard one of the fire-watchers say shortly afterwards. 'That looks like that was Manor Road!'

I'd been right. Not far from the East London Cemetery. I wondered who amongst the dear departed the Luftwaffe had blown from their graves this time. That one is not even at peace in death is so very common now. As for the living? I couldn't see any of them, apart from the fire-watchers, and that included Fernanda Abrahams.

Chapter Twenty

'Partly I blame myself,' Mrs Darling said as she offered me a piece of cake that was heavy and grey and probably made from parsnips. Pleading a late breakfast, I refused.

Mrs Darling shrugged, sipped her tea and then said, 'Esme should never have been left on her own. I knew it at the time, but . . .'

'Mrs Robinson was adamant,' I said. 'I was there too, Mrs Darling. There wasn't anything anyone could have done.' We both went silent for a moment until I asked, 'Did they, er, in hospital . . . did she have, um, a hard time? Were they . . .'

'Coppers told her she was on her way to prison. Some doctor told her she was on her way to hell. What did you expect, Mr Hancock?'

What I'd expected had been just about what she had told me. War or no war, nothing much changes for those who choose to take their own lives. Maybe now, given that so many are dying not out of choice or by their own hands, attitudes to suicide are even worse. An embarrassment for a family, a sin for the religious, it is also a crime and probably always will be.

'Esme had money and a will, apparently, and I expect that most of what she had will be left to her sister Rosemary,' Mrs Darling said. 'But that said, Mr Hancock, she did leave a note for me which gives instructions related to her funeral.'

'She wanted me to perform it.'

'Yes,' the medium said. She sighed. 'Wants to be buried next to Neville, God help her.'

'You don't think . . .'

'Why would a bloke like Neville Robinson go down Rathbone Street in the middle of the night unless he was after some hanky-panky?' Mrs Darling said.

I hadn't been about to defend Neville in any way. I knew without any shadow of a doubt that he had indeed gone down to Rathbone Street for sex. What I wondered was whether Esme had known, and if she had, whether she had been the sort of woman who would forgive her husband such a thing. But Mrs Darling didn't give me a chance to ask and just rattled on about the funeral.

'There's plenty of money of course,' she said. 'So we'll all be expecting a good do. I think Neville's monument's being done now, isn't it?'

'Yes,' I said. I'd organised that myself, with the monumental masons on Grange Road. 'I'll go and see Mr Piper and get him to add Mrs Robinson in. Date of birth was 1890, wasn't it?'

'Yes.'

The same year as my sister Nancy.

'Did Mrs Robinson ever say either to you or in her letter anything about wanting any other words or phrases on her monument?'

'No,' she said. ''Course, her family over in Canada may well want some other sort of dedication or what have you, but Gawd knows when they'll get to know the poor woman's even dead! I mean, the coppers say they're informing Rosemary, and I've written to her myself, but whether my letter will ever get there . . .' She shrugged. 'Them U-boats are like sharks, aren't they, Mr Hancock? Always waiting for our ships, always knowing where they are.'

Whether sharks do indeed lie in wait for their prey, I don't know, but I understood what she meant. My old bearer Walter had been talking about the same thing earlier. He has a brother in America, his only living relative I believe, who he likes to write to and receive letters from. Walter moans about most things, but the interruption to his correspondence with his brother by deadly U-boats is one that I can sympathise with. Poor and lonely, Walter Bridges boozes for a reason, just like he comes into work often when I don't need him for a reason.

Mrs Darling and myself discussed funeral arrangements while her husband brought in more tea and then, apparently, headed off up to his allotment.

'Green fingers, he's got,' she said once Frank Darling had finally made his lugubrious exit. 'Gawd knows where he gets them from. His father was hopeless, couldn't grow weeds he couldn't. Sometimes I wonder whether some of my sitters just turn up to get the odd carrot or parsnip from my old man's allotment. Especially Cissy.'

'Cissy likes vegetables?' I said.

'I don't know,' the medium said with yet another shrug. 'Who can fathom someone like her, eh? Who can fathom most of my sitters. But Cissy's always first in line if my Frank's got something from the allotment. That said, it can't be easy for a woman all alone in the world, can it?'

'No.'

It wasn't easy for Nan, but at least she had Aggie, the Duchess, Stella and myself.

'And how is Cissy getting on with contacting her husband?' I said. More than anything else I was making conversation, even if my motives for doing so did eventually change.

'Oh, I don't think he wants to come through,' Mrs Darling said as she shook her head sadly. 'I mean, Cissy, God love her, she don't have no gift as far as I can tell. But when I try to get through to him myself there's something blocking'. Then, possibly realising that what she'd just said didn't sound entirely professional, she added, ''Course, I make contact, but . . . but he's like I say . . . distant.'

It was then that I asked her whether Esme Robinson had been in touch in a spiritual sense. Mrs Darling eyed me narrowly. 'Why would you want to know that, Mr Hancock?' she said. 'You don't hold with what I do, do you?'

I didn't answer her. We both knew that what she'd just said was true. Mrs Darling cleared her throat. 'When a soul dies violently by their own hand, often they have no memory of it,' she said. 'So why Esme done herself in or what she might have known of Neville and his doings – which I know interests you, Mr Hancock – I don't know.'

250

'But she has contacted you?'

'Esme has safely passed over,' Mrs Darling said, not answering my question at all. But then had I really thought she might have something useful to tell me about Esme's death? Did I really think that the Great Beyond might provide me with any answers to anything? Of course I didn't, but I'd been compelled to ask because by this time I truly didn't know what to do next. Five women, including Esme Robinson, plus her husband Neville had died seemingly because of their connection to the White Feather movement. The police, either because they didn't feel that the White Feathers really were a connection or simply because they couldn't cope with the notion of one person killing so many, hadn't done much beyond arrest poor old Fred Dickens. He may well of course have killed his wife, Violet, so that he could court the barmaid Tilly, but I was doubtful even about that. What, after all, are drunken confessions really worth?

There was another mystery, though not of a supernatural nature, that Mrs Darling I felt might give me some assistance on. Having said that, I still didn't discount the notion that it could all have been in my head. 'Mrs Darling, I think that Fernanda Abrahams might have come to my shop last night.'

'Might?'

I took a deep breath in and then I said, 'Well, the raid was on and you know that sometimes I . . . well, I see things and . . .'

'If you're having visions, Mr Hancock, I would hope they'd

be about something a bit more worthwhile than that old cow!' Mrs Darling said heatedly.

'Yes, but . . .'

'Probably come not to see you but your Nancy,' Mrs Darling said. Then, recalling the conversation I'd had with her at Neville Robinson's funeral, she continued, 'If your Nancy had reminded her old fella of things she didn't want him reminded of, she probably came to tell her off.'

'She's already done that,' I said. Nan, Aggie and Fernanda rowing out in the yard wasn't something I was likely to forget.

'Well then, I don't know,' the medium said. 'All I can say is that whatever it was, it probably involved grief for someone. Such a nasty woman she always was! I liked her at first. Very keen to get in with me. But then when I found out how cold and unpleasant she was . . . Never knew why Marie took to her so. Too tender-hearted she was! You know, Mr Hancock, it is my opinion that if you was on fire in the street, Fernanda Mascarenhas is the sort of person who'd leave you to burn!'

As I walked up East Ham High Street to see if I could get a bus from Manor Park up to Claybury, I thought about something Aggie had said about the possibility of a woman being able to commit violent murder. She had been convinced it was possible. And in theory I agreed. In the case of these White Feather murders, however, I did wonder how a woman would be able to do quite so much damage to the bodies of the female victims, much less to Neville Robinson. Also, I had assumed that a man had to be the culprit because only men had been affected by the White Feather movement. Women were not and still aren't required to fight. But what if the murderer's motive was something else? What if the motive had more to do with obliterating a past that was unwanted than in wreaking revenge? Not that Fernanda Abrahams's husband was unaware of what she'd been. But what if she was trying to hide her past from someone other than her husband? It was a very unusual, some would say bonkers, idea, but it was one that was sticking in my head. Everyone I'd spoken to about Fernanda Mascarenhas agreed that she was unpleasant, self-centred and ruthless. But did that make her a murderess capable of killing and then mutilating her victims?

I got up to Claybury just after the patients finished having their lunch. I asked if I could see Nathan Abrahams but was told that since his fit of agitation when his nephew had come to visit, his doctor had thought it better if he didn't have any visitors for a while. To say I was disappointed was an understatement. I had wanted to talk to old Nathan so that I could, if possible, find out just who or what had made him react so badly. I wanted to know whether suddenly seeing Fernanda again had recalled his daughter Marie's death to him. After all, the person who was murdering these women was getting into their homes very easily and without comment from others. Just like a female friend might do. But the nurse on duty was adamant. I couldn't see Mr Abrahams and that was that.

'Well, can I see the nurse who was on duty when Mr Abrahams became agitated?' I asked.

She thought for a moment and then said, 'That was Nurse Belmont. No. She's not on today.'

I tried to think of the other woman Nan had mentioned

when she'd told me about the incident. Alice had of course been there too, but I knew that she was out with my sister. Try as I might, I couldn't remember the woman's name until . . .

'Mrs Ravens, one of our helpers, is on today,' the nurse said. 'She was there when Mr Abrahams became agitated. Would you like to speak to her?'

Mrs Ravens! Yes, that was it! I said that I would very much like to speak to her. I waited in the corridor outside the ward for about five minutes. Though far from silent, there was no screaming coming from inside on this occasion. I imagined that the food probably had much to do with that. Although my own sojourn in hospital after the Great War had been mercifully short, I still remembered that food had been important. When there is nothing else to look forward to, even a plate of watery soup can make your day.

'Mr Hancock?'

I looked up and found myself staring into the face of a rather pleasant-looking woman of about sixty. Slim, with thin iron-grey hair, she had a very lined, very genuine smile. 'I'm Mrs Ravens,' she said. 'Nurse Wallis said you wanted to talk to me about Mr Abrahams. You're Miss Hancock's brother.'

'Yes,' I said. 'It's about when Mr Abrahams became agitated when his nephew came to visit.'

'Oh yes.' Mrs Ravens frowned. 'Yes, that was distressing for all concerned. His nephew didn't know what to do and your sister, Miss Hancock, well, it all came out of the blue at her. She was trying to be pleasant and friendly to Mr Abrahams's nephew and his wife.'

'Mr Abrahams started to scream.'

'Yes.'

'Do you know why?'

Mrs Ravens frowned. 'At the time I thought I did,' she said. 'It seemed he was upset by his nephew and his wife turning up. But then nothing really happened until a few seconds after his nephew arrived. In fact Mr Abrahams seemed to be really very content until your sister left Mr Bannerman, who she was helping to feed, and came over to speak to the couple.'

This was not what I had expected to hear. I said, 'So it was my sister who caused Mr Abrahams to become agitated.'

'At first I thought that yes, it was Miss Hancock who upset him, but . . .'

Mr Abrahams had seen Nancy before. He'd spoken to her! For him to suddenly take so violently against her had never made any sense to me.

'It's my belief it was Miss Hoskin he was looking at as he screamed,' Mrs Ravens said. 'Like he'd seen the devil it was! Of course I didn't say anything myself. Patients can take against people for no reason at all and Miss Hoskin hadn't been on this ward for a long time, since before Mr Abrahams arrived I think. But I have noticed that she hasn't been back on the ward since. Maybe Matron won't let her. I don't know. I don't know if anyone, apart from me, even noticed.'

Nancy had said that her friend Alice had been on the ward feeding a patient called Bernie. I also had a recollection of hearing the name Hoskin in the not very distant past.

'Mrs Ravens,' I said, 'is the gentleman my sister and Miss Hoskin were feeding called Bernie, or Bernard?'

'Yes,' she said. 'Bernie rather than Bernard, although . . .'

'And Miss Hoskin, is her name Alice?'

'Yes,' she said with a smile. 'Yes, it is. I think it was in fact Miss Hoskin who encouraged your sister to join the rest of us ladies in helping the patients.'

'Yes.' Something at the back of my mind felt bad. 'Mrs Ravens,' I said, 'do you know Alice Hoskin very well?'

'No,' she said. 'Why?'

'Well it's just that my sister has . . .' It sounded so ridiculous to say that my fifty-one-year-old sister was out with her and that now, suddenly, I wasn't comfortable with that. But that was the truth, even though I couldn't really say, beyond the fact that none of my family had met Alice, and Mr Abrahams's reported reaction to her, exactly why. Mrs Ravens must have appreciated how much I was struggling and so she put a hand on my arm and said, 'I'll go and get Nurse Milburn. She's known Alice for years.'

Mrs Ravens went away and was replaced a few minutes later by Nurse Milburn. A stout woman in her mid-fifties, Nurse Milburn sat down next to me and said, 'You want to know about Alice?'

'Yes,' I said. 'My sister has . . . well, she is friends with Alice . . .'

'Miss Hancock.' Nurse Milburn smiled. 'We always need more helpers, given the war and, of course, our situation as an asylum. Not very popular places, asylums. But,' she shrugged, 'thank God for people like Mrs Ravens, your sister and of course our Alice.'

'Our Alice' implied a kind of ownership or great familiarity. I said as much to Nurse Milburn.

'Well, Alice has been associated with the hospital since nineteen nineteen,' the nurse replied. 'When her sweetheart came to us.'

'Her sweetheart?'

Her face assumed a sombre expression. 'He'd been in the Great War, on the artillery guns,' she said. 'Unfortunately the poor man was deafened and . . . well, as you can tell from the fact that he was sent to us, his mind did not survive the experience either. Alice, to whom he'd been engaged before the war, came to see him every day until the day he died. Not that he ever said anything except her name, but . . .'

'He died? When?'

Nurse Milburn paused for thought for a moment and then said, 'Oh, it has to be almost a year ago now. For some time afterwards Alice didn't come here at all, which I can understand. But then she came back to visit, spoke to a couple of our volunteers that she already knew, and then decided to come and help out herself. It was a very brave decision.'

'Yes.' It was a tragic story. It wasn't one the like of which I hadn't heard before. Stories like Alice's are all too common. Not every story of this kind, however, chills me as this one seemed to be doing.

'But then so many ladies of . . . well, of my age and Alice's are obliged as it were to try to make something of lives that were really curtailed by the Great War.' She smiled again. 'So many men went away, so few came back. Poor Cissy, she . . .'

'Cissy?' It was as if an electric current went through me.

'Cissy is what her sweetheart called her, and old members

of staff like me who've known her for years. Alice Hoskin, Cissy.'

Cissy Hoskin, Mrs Darling's mousy protégée. Cissy trying in vain to make contact with her dead sweetheart. Cissy who had caused Mr Abrahams, father of poor dead Marie, to scream. Why had such an inoffensive person made Mr Abrahams scream? Had he seen her before, perhaps? Had he seen her the night his daughter Marie died?

I felt sick. Cissy Hoskin, out and about somewhere with my sister . . .

Chapter Twenty-One

N ancy had written in the firm's diary that she was due to meet her friend Alice on Abbey Lane, which is up around the back of the River Lee, and beside the Abbey pumping station. The nearest station is West Ham underground. But before I could even think about jumping on to the District Line, provided it were running, I had to get out of the middle of nowhere.

I thought at first I'd ask to use the hospital telephone and call the police. Nurse Milburn, who gave me a bit of a funny look as she did so – I'd gone rather pale by this time – went and asked if this were possible. But as so often happens these days, the lines were down, and so I just ran out of there and kept on going until I finally found a bus. As I ran, I thought. Not that that helped my sense of panic very much. Cissy had had direct access to some of the dead women, indirect access to others. Being around Mrs Darling and her seances had put her immediately in touch with Esme Robinson and her husband and Violet Dickens. Through Esme she could have heard of the whereabouts of her estranged cousin, Nellie

Martin. Marie Abrahams had, according to Esme Robinson during my first meeting with her, been getting interested in spiritualism just before her death, which implied contact on some sort of level. But then there was Dolly O'Dowd. How, if I were right about any of this, had Cissy got to her? And why, if indeed she had killed all of these women, had Cissy done it at all? As I emerged out of the countryside and into the back end of Gants Hill, I stopped for a moment to give my poor tired lungs a rest. Some little bloke in a long black overcoat, a Homburg perched on his unnaturally large head, stopped and looked at me, frowning. Because I'd gone to see Mrs Darling on business, I was wearing my work suit with my black tie plus my top hat complete with mourning veil. It isn't the kind of outfit you often see people wearing when they run. But I ignored him. I braced my hands against my knees and rested for a couple of minutes before heading further south, looking all the time for a bus to take me faster towards my home.

As soon as Nurse Milburn had first said the name Cissy, my mind had immediately flown to the idea of getting the police. I'd been frustrated that the telephone lines were down yet again. But thinking about it as I ran had changed my mind. For all that Cissy's position in Mrs Darling's circle seemed to fit with that of a person able to murder the White Feather girls, I couldn't imagine how, physically, she could perform such acts or why she should do them at this point in time. I could see *why* she might kill, however. It was only a thought, but I felt I knew that if Cissy had killed these women it had been because of her sweetheart. Had this group, my sister's group of White Feather girls, goaded that young man into fighting, maybe against his better judgement or in the face of ill health? It was of course very possible. But if that were the case, why didn't any of the girls recognise Cissy? Mrs Darling knew her from way back when Cissy, as a girl, used to work in her uncle's shop on East Ham Broadway. But not once had she mentioned her in connection with White Feather business. And had she had any fears about anyone, I knew that Mrs Darling would have said something. She was as worried as I was. No, if Cissy were indeed guilty of these crimes, I was either missing something or I simply did not know enough to connect her completely with what had happened.

I finally managed to flag down a bus on the Cranbrook Road. It was packed, as buses always are these days. The little lady conductor came towards me and said, 'Tickets, please!'

I asked to go to Barking, where I knew I could get a bus direct to Plaistow. Like the man in the Homburg back in Gants Hill, as well as, really, most of the other passengers, the conductor gave me a funny look. But she took my money and gave me a ticket, and slowly but surely we made our way into Barking. As soon as the bus stopped, I pushed my way towards the door. It's not like me to be so rude and it didn't go unnoticed. A woman in a fox-fur coat said to a woman in a threadbare jacket, 'God, look at that! You wouldn't expect behaviour like that from an undertaker!'

But I didn't care. I had to get home, get in my car and go and find my sister.

* * *

When Walter washes down the Lancia, he doesn't strain himself to finish the job quickly. He likes the car and enjoys making a good job of getting all the dirt and dust off the paintwork as well as buffing the chromium trim until it sparkles. It doesn't stay clean for very long, but that isn't the point. A clean car pleases Walter, and it is the only part of his job, I would say, he really takes pride in. He was just sloshing a clean chamois over the windscreen when I came hurtling in, breathless, through the back gate.

'Cor blimey, Mr H!' Walter said as he looked up at me. 'Who's on your tail?'

'No one,' I gasped. 'Walter, has Miss Nancy gone out yet?'

'To see her friend? Yes, about an hour and a half ago,' he said.

'Oh God!' I barrelled past him and threw myself into the back of the shop. I grabbed the car keys which hung to the side of the back door and then called up the stairs to the flat. Aggie I knew was not at work and so I said, 'Ag, I'm just going out for a bit. Taking the car.'

In the second it took me to turn to go, Aggie flew down the stairs and said, 'The car? Frank, you're only supposed to use it for work. The petrol . . .'

'Bugger the petrol!' I said. Then, thinking how stupid it was to say that because it might alarm her, I added to the problem by saying, 'Oh shit!'

'Frank!'

But by this time I was out in the yard and on my way over to the Lancia. As I moved past him I told Walter to get in the car, and then I slipped myself into the driver's seat.

'Get . . .'

'Just get in, Walter,' I said. 'It's an emergency.'

'An emergency?'

'An emergency? What's an emergency?' I heard Aggie say as a very troubled Walter got into the car beside me.

'What's up, Mr H?' he asked.

'I'll explain on the way,' I said as I fired up the engine and took off out of the yard before Aggie could even begin to stop me. The last I saw of her was her screaming face through the back window, shouting my name.

Abbey Lane is just to the north of West Ham station. It's in an area of almost countrified ground that exists around the many creeks and tributaries of the River Lee at this point. If it wasn't for the stink from the sewage or the almost constant fog that hangs over the area, it could be somewhere out in the wilds of Essex. But this is London, and so signs of industry are never far away. In this case, such a sign is in the very ornate form of the Abbey Mills Sewage Pumping Station. Decorated in that really intricate way only Victorian buildings can be, Abbey Mills is a great big place set in grounds enclosed by high walls and fences. Even though England was such a rich country in the last century, the idea that such an amazing thing – looks like a mansion to my way of thinking – could be built for industrial purposes is incredible. Years ago my dad knew an old bloke who'd worked at the Mills who told him that inside, everything was engineered to perfection. Everywhere he went inside that building, so he said, gleamed with the lustre of polished brass. Outside there used to be two very fancy towers that carried the smoke away when the station was powered by steam. Now it's all electric and the towers were demolished anyway on account of the fact that they gave the Luftwaffe a rather too easy target.

And it wasn't just the pumping station itself that was good to look at. The houses for the workers, which fronted directly on to the road, were big and, although nowhere near as ornate as the pumping station itself, had that slightly churchy or mansion style of architecture to them. There are no other houses on Abbey Lane, and so I assumed that Cissy had to live in one of those. Although how she was managing to do that if she didn't work at the pumping station, I couldn't imagine.

Walter, who I had now told much of what he needed to know to help me search, if necessary, for the women, said, 'Miss Nancy's friend must have a brother or a father working in the station, Mr H. You generally have to to have one of these houses.'

'I've heard she lives alone,' I said. Cissy's parents were dead according to Mrs Darling.

'I'll go and ask that geezer just going into that house there,' Walter said as I pulled the car up to the pavement outside the row of houses. 'What did you say the lady's name was?'

'Alice Hoskin. Cissy.'

Walter went off and spoke to a middle-aged bloke with ginger hair. He looked over, warily I thought, at the car a couple of times, but he spoke to Walter nonetheless. When he came back Walter said, 'Geezer says that the Hoskins live at number three. A mum and a daughter. The daughter's called Alice. But he ain't seen her today.'

Alice/Cissy had lied about living alone if nothing else. Although like Walter I did wonder how the women managed to live in a house that was connected to the pumping station. But as we walked up the path towards number three, Walter told me that the chap he'd just spoken to had provided him with something of an answer.

'Apparently the old woman's a cripple. Don't go out much,' he said. 'The old man worked in the station for years, and when he died the family was allowed to stay on.'

'Well, if they pay the rent . . .' I knocked on the dark wooden front door with my fist and called out, 'Mrs Hoskin!'

With luck I'd soon find Cissy, her mother and my sister all safely inside together, with rational explanations from Cissy for everything. But my knock had sounded ominously hollow and was followed by absolutely no sound from inside at all. Walter, who had taken it upon himself to look in through the front window, said, 'Can't see nothing. They've got the blackout up.'

Most people take their blackout curtains or blinds down in the daytime. Most people want to see some light whenever they can. But not everyone. I shrugged, knocked again and then, when that didn't summon anyone, said to Walter, 'Come on, let's go round the back.'

We went down the side way between the Hoskins' house and the place next door. We found a large garden which most people would have given over to the growing of vegetables. But not this one. Though large, it was just a disorganised pile of mud with a chicken coop at the far end next to what I recognised as the entrance to an Anderson shelter.

Mrs Darling had said that Cissy was always first in line for any spare vegetables from her husband's allotment. But I couldn't, at that point, see why she didn't grow her own.

'Blimey, they live well out here, don't they, Mr H?' Walter said as he looked through the window in the back door. 'Been eating tea and cake by the look of it.'

I joined him at the back door and saw a wooden table in the middle of a large kitchen that was indeed set for quite a dainty-looking tea. I knocked and called out, 'Mrs Hoskin!' once again. But to no avail. It was then that I tried the door-knob, which moved easily and without hindrance in my hand. Still calling out lest I frighten the women inside, I walked into the kitchen followed by Walter. It smelt of tea and baking but also of damp too. Around the sink there was a scum of mould which belied the dainty cakes that sat very invitingly on the china stand in the middle of the table. I wondered, if Nan had been here, what she would have made of it. Both of my sisters are practical but fastidious. After a swift butcher's around, Walter said to me, 'Shall we go and have a look at the rest of the place, Mr H?'

I said, 'Yes.'

All the rooms except the kitchen were blacked out. They were all dusty, damp and in the case of the bedroom at the front of the house, full up with cardboard boxes and wooden crates filled with God knew what. They're big places, the workers' houses on Abbey Lane, and so all three bedrooms were large. Only two, however, had beds in and only one, the one over the kitchen at the back, looked as if it could be in use.

'Bit of a two an' eight, ain't it, Mr H?' Walter said as he looked around the top floor with me. 'And where's the old girl anyway? That bloke I spoke to said that Mrs Hoskin was some sort of cripple.'

'I don't know,' I said. 'Maybe her daughter and Nancy took the old woman out in a wheelchair.'

But then I remembered that I'd seen one of those in the chaotic parlour downstairs. Everything felt bad and wrong and I found that now my heart was really pounding. We went back downstairs again, for want really of anything else to do. Back in the kitchen, it was Walter who put his hand on the side of the teapot and said, ''Ere, this is still warm!'

'So whoever made the tea can't be very far away,' I said.

'Don't seem like it.'

We went to the four houses nearest to the Hoskins' place to ask if anyone had seen Alice, but only one person, a bloke of about sixty, was in. He said he'd seen no one all day except the bloke we'd already spoken to.

'Well they can't have gone far, given that the teapot was still warm,' I said to Walter as we walked down the path of the last house we visited.

'There's a lot of ground around here, Mr H,' Walter replied gloomily. 'Down by the Lee and around the back of the pumping station. People get lost over here. Gangsters, some say, get rid of the bodies of their rivals here.'

'And some say, no doubt, that the last Tsar of Russia and his family are buried down by West Ham underground station,' I responded crossly. 'Walter, we are looking for my sister! I'm very concerned about her. If you can't say anything helpful, then don't say anything at all!'

A bit shamefaced now, Walter said, 'I'm sorry, Mr H.'

I looked up and down Abbey Lane twice before I decided that we'd go left towards the pumping station. Just before the station there is a bridge over the road that carries the great pipes full of sewage from the city to the plant. On top of the bridge there is a little lane that I can remember playing about on with my mates as a kid. It always stank up there and was known very aptly as 'the Sewer Bank'. This path stretches in fact as far as my home in Plaistow. It is of course at Abbey Mills that it is at its most pungent. I knew there was a staircase just before the bridge, which Walter and I headed for now. As we got there, a thin young woman in blue work trousers, her head covered with a green scarf wound into a turban, came down the steps towards us. Her face was made up, bright and red, like an American film star, and she smoked a fag with all the aplomb of the lovely Greta Garbo. She gave me a bit of an old-fashioned stare as she looked down on Walter and myself, which of course was because of what I was wearing.

'Miss,' I said, 'have you seen a lady or maybe two ladies walking about up there or maybe down by the water?'

She frowned. 'Why?'

'One of them is my sister,' I said. 'And I need to speak to her urgently. She's gone, I think, for a walk with a lady called Miss Hoskin.'

'What, Cissy?'

'Yes!'

'Why?'

'What?'

'Cissy's my neighbour, and she might be a funny old thing but I can't just go giving out her whereabouts to two blokes I don't know,' the woman said. 'I mean, you could be anyone, couldn't you? You could be Nazis.'

I looked at Walter and said, 'God almighty!' I know that careless talk can cost lives, but government instructions together with natural East End suspicion were holding me up.

'Now listen, love,' Walter said, 'we need to find these ladies as a matter of importance. Life and death.'

'Yeah, well . . .'

'Do I look like a fucking Nazi!' I finally exploded. 'Miss, I am an undertaker with skin the colour of tea. Nazis, you'll find, won't usually go around in hearses and will probably be blond. Now . . .'

'Blimey, keep you bleedin' hair on!' she said. 'As it happens I've just seen Cissy. Up on the bank picking dandelion leaves for tea, she said.'

Neither Walter nor myself said another word. We just ran past that woman and up those stairs as fast as our legs would carry us.

Chapter Twenty-Two

From the Sewer Bank it's possible to see the top of the pumping station. Even in the thick, smoggy afternoon light I could see that its decoration in blue, red and gold was still in large part intact. What I couldn't see, for just a moment, was anyone about. It was actually Walter who first noticed the small figure crouching down apparently picking dandelion leaves from the side of the pathway.

'Mr H, look!'

It was definitely Cissy. Wearing a limp floral dress several sizes too big for her, her thin hair hanging over her face as she pulled the plants up from the ground with long, skinny fingers. I went up to her and said, 'Cissy?'

She put a hand on the bag she was apparently collecting dandelion into before she looked up at me and then smiled. 'Mr Hancock!'

'Cissy, where is my sister?' I said. There was no point beating about the bush. 'Where is Nancy?'

'Your sister? I don't know what you mean,' she replied. 'I'm here on my own.'

'Where's your mum, love?' Walter put in as I stared at this woman I knew absolutely had to be lying.

'My mum? She's at home,' Cissy said. 'Tucked up in bed where I left her. Mother is an invalid.'

'Yes, we know.'

'We also know that your mum ain't at your house,' Walter said. 'No one's at your house, love.'

Although I would have said it was impossible before it happened, Cissy paled.

'Well . . .'

'Just take me to where Nancy is,' I said. It wasn't easy to control the anger that I could feel rising inside of me now.

Cissy stood up and pulled her bag close in towards her chest.

'I don't know what you're talking about,' she said. 'I don't know anyone by the name of Nancy.'

'Yes, you do, you . . .' I stepped towards her, but Walter, seeing that I was probably too full of anger to be reasonable, got in between us.

'Now look, love,' he said, 'we ain't asking here. Mr H knows that his sister come to see you. Now where is she? Don't muck us about, love!'

Cissy put a trembling hand into her bag and said, 'Don't threaten me! How dare you threaten a woman on her own!'

'We're not . . .'

All I saw was a bright flash pass in front of my eyes. Walter flung an arm up as if to ward something off, and then with a rapidity not normally associated with Walter Bridges, he hit the ground like a sack, clinging on to his arm with his one free hand and screaming.

'Bloody hell, she's got a knife!'

Cissy, a large, bloody knife in her hand, began to run. I looked down at Walter, who was clutching his forearm while trying simultaneously to wrap it up in his neck muffler. 'Get after her!' he said. 'Fucking mare stabbed me!'

I flung myself forwards. Cissy, the knife in her hand trailing a thin drool of blood behind her, was going hell for leather in front of me. It had been decades since I'd actually played on this stretch of the bank, and I didn't have a clue as to where she might be going.

'Walter!' I called behind me, gasping as I did so. 'Get down to the houses! Get help!'

I didn't know whether he'd heard me, or even if it were possible for the poor old sod to move at all. I just kept on ploughing forwards, gaining just a little on the woman in front of me as my lungs began to burn and feel as if they were about to burst. It came as a huge shock to me when Cissy suddenly took a dive to the left, off the path and down the side of the bank towards one of the tributaries of the River Lee. When I did finally pull level with where she'd disappeared, I glanced down and found myself looking only at brackish, sewage-filled water.

There were bushes, brambles and lots of long grass on the way down to that sad little elbow of the River Lee. We hadn't had that much rain, but all the fog and smog and drizzle we had suffered had taken its toll, and my way down was wet and muddy. By the time I hit the slush at the river's edge, my work suit was filthy. Inwardly I cursed. I would have done so out loud if I hadn't been worried about hopefully coming upon Cissy by surprise. But as it happened she was waiting for me, propped up against an old woody bush. There was a long, thin, black-clad figure draped across her lap. It had thick black hair, and when I got closer, I could see the very familiar face easily. Nan, it appeared, was sleeping, or so I hoped.

'Laudanum,' Cissy said as she held the knife still stained with Walter's blood up to Nancy's neck. It was a large and serious piece of equipment. I remember that at the time I thought it might be something used by a butcher or a slaughterman. 'My mum had bottles and bottles of it for her arthritis.'

The Duchess had been prescribed laudanum for her pain years ago too. But she'd put a stop to it. She didn't like being asleep so much.

'Where is your mother, Cissy?' I asked as I looked down at my sister to make sure that she was indeed still breathing. To my relief she was. But she was still in the hands of this murderous woman and I knew that if I was to have any chance of getting the knife away from Cissy I'd have to try and keep her talking. I also didn't know whether Walter had managed to stand up to go and get help. 'Where is your mother?' I repeated.

Cissy's face creased up and she said, 'She's dead.'

'Your neighbours don't think she's dead,' I said as I struggled to keep my balance on the steep slope underneath my feet.

'The week after Albert,' Cissy said.

'Albert?'

She looked up at me with eyes just on the edge of tears and said, 'My young man. He died.'

'In Claybury Hospital.'

'You know,' she replied as a statement of fact.

If her mother had died a week after her sweetheart, then she must have been dead for about a year. It had to have been a terrible blow for Cissy to lose her mother and her sweetheart all in one go. But if that were so, and notwithstanding the fact that Mrs Darling believed both of Cissy's parents to be dead, why did her neighbours not seem to know?

'Is that what all this is about?' I said to Cissy. 'Your young man who died?'

She turned her head to one side. Nan, her throat just lightly creased by Cissy's knife, coughed a little before settling down into silence once again.

'It's about all of it,' Cissy said. She looked at me, and not understanding what she meant, I frowned.

'Everyone around me goes away or dies,' she said. 'I lose everything!' It was said with such passion. 'Nobody loses everything like I do!' she continued. 'Not Nellie Martin, not Marie Abrahams, not Violet Dickens not even that stupid, stupid Dolly O'Dowd!'

I inched slightly forwards, but then stopped when I saw the terrible look that Cissy was giving me. If she had killed as frequently and as viciously as I thought she had, I knew she'd have no compunction about murdering me or my sister.

'Because you know what, Mr Hancock? You know what your sister and her friends did in the Great War? You know the damage that they caused to men all over the East End of London?'

'Nancy and her friends were White Feather girls,' I said. 'I didn't know until just recently. I was away at the time, fighting in the trenches. Cissy, I don't approve. Had I known, I would have put a stop to it, but . . .'

'I've got no quarrel with you,' Cissy said. 'But those women have to pay for what they did to Albert.' She looked up at me with eyes full of pain. 'He wasn't strong, he didn't have to fight. And yet those girls, they went on and on and on at him every time they saw him! "Why aren't you in uniform, young man?" "Don't you want to fight for King and country?" "What kind of man is it who doesn't want to defend his country's honour?" He said they used to follow him. I told him not to take any notice.'

'But he joined up anyway.'

'He lost his mind out there in those trenches. He couldn't do it! He couldn't do what they wanted him to do, he wasn't strong enough.' Her eyes filled with tears. 'When first he came back, he didn't know me! Then when he did, all he could do was say my name! We never spoke again after he went away. Not like you and me are speaking now – never!'

'Cissy, I do understand . . .'

'I visited him in Claybury every day,' she said. 'While I was doing that, although I was still angry, I could manage. But then one day Albert died. He got that dysentery so many of the patients get in that type of hospital, and he died.

276

He should never have been there! If he hadn't been in the asylum he would still be alive!'

'And then your mum?'

Cissy was crying now. 'They just died! Both of them! I didn't know what to do!'

I moved slightly closer to her.

'I lost the people I loved the most! I knew I'd lose the house too! We could only stay there as long as Mum was alive! I had to pretend. Day in and day out, I had to pretend – to everyone!' Her face darkened again and she said, 'They had to pay, those women! They had to know what it felt like to lose!'

'Cissy . . .'

'I will get them all eventually, you know,' she said. 'Even Rosemary out in Canada. I'll get her too. I will.'

'Cissy.' I leaned down towards her, and in spite of myself I smiled. 'Cissy, you can't carry on like this, love,' I said. 'It doesn't help. My sister Nancy was a silly girl when she was younger, but she knows now that she was in the wrong. It was nothing personal against you or Albert. I don't think they knew either of you, did they? The soppy things just did what they did because they thought they were being patriotic.'

I saw Nancy's eyelids flicker for a moment. But I tried to ignore her and concentrate on Cissy.

'They used to go down Custom House,' Cissy said. 'Albert lived there, on Garvary Road. I used to see Margaret Cousins, as she was then, and Marie Abrahams when they came into my Uncle Bob's shop on East Ham Broadway. Waving their white feathers!'

'Why didn't you say anything?' I said.

She looked at me now with hatred. 'I'd only just lost my dad! I had to work at Uncle Bob's to help make ends meet. I couldn't go upsetting his customers. He wasn't keen to have me working there anyway. He wanted a lad. He'd have thrown me out on my ear'ole!'

'Frank?' It was a little, very tired voice and it came from my sister, into whose bleary eyes I was now looking.

Cissy in response to this tightened her grip and shoved the knife even harder against Nancy's throat.

'Frank!'

I looked down at my sister and said, 'Just keep still, Nan!'

'I am going to kill her,' Cissy said in a voice that was so cold it almost made me pull my jacket tighter about my shoulders.

'And I am going to stop you,' I said.

She frowned, and I saw the knuckles of her fingers holding the knife turn white.

I made a dive for her wrist but she was a lot stronger than I had imagined and so I grabbed what I could of the knife itself. God, it was sharp! The blade cut into my fingers with such ease it was almost as if they were made of butter not flesh.

'Nan!' I shouted as I tried to pull Cissy's arm away from my sister's neck. 'Get out of it!'

But she was far too drugged to move. With the blood from my fingers dripping down on to Nancy's face, I moved my one good hand away from Cissy's wrist and then pulled my sister down towards the riverbank. I grabbed her skirt and just heaved. Luckily, what with her being so light and the ground so wet, Nancy just slithered down until her legs and body dangled into the filthy water of the creek. I was just aware of her coughing as I flung myself forwards on to Cissy.

'Give me the knife!' I said as I tried in vain to get a hold of the damn thing. But my hand was so badly cut that I couldn't get any purchase, while my other, undamaged hand had to try and pin this now screaming woman to the ground. God almighty, if Walter wasn't dead or dying, where the hell was he?

There was blood everywhere now and all of it was mine. Cissy's face screwed up with effort as she tried with some success to push me away. But I used the weight of my body to pin her to the ground even as she turned the knife in my injured fingers and fought to get the end of the blade close to my face. I thought that she might even succeed too as I felt my head go light and dizzy with the effort. Not that failure was an option for me under these circumstances. But then it wasn't an option for Cissy either.

'You are not going to stop me!' she shrieked.

I didn't answer, I couldn't. I managed to heave my head out of the way of the slashing blade beneath me but I knew that by this time I was fading. I couldn't even spare any energy to abuse her and she knew it. I knew she knew it because she smiled. I thought at that point that I was as good as dead. But that shriek of hers, so I later learned, changed the direction of Walter and the little group of men who were looking for us up above on the bank. That shriek gave away where we were.

Seconds later someone pulled me off and away and two blokes I didn't know from Adam wrestled the knife out of Cissy's hand. I just heard Walter's voice say, 'Fucking hell, Mr H!' before I passed out cold.

Chapter Twenty-Three

The men from the pumping station took Walter, Nancy and me to the nearest hospital, St Andrew's at Bromley-by-Bow. Cissy they took to Plaistow police station, which wasn't the closest. It was Walter who insisted they do that. The sooner Cissy got into the hands of Sergeant Hill and his boys, the sooner everyone could find out whether poor old Fred Dickens still needed to be in one of Plaistow's cells or not.

The nurse who attended to both me and Walter was a sweet girl who looked to me to be just barely into her twenties. We did see a doctor briefly, but all he told us was that we'd both lost a lot of blood and that we'd have to rest. Neither of us could drive, but thankfully the ginger-haired neighbour of Cissy Hoskin we'd first met when we went to Abbey Lane, and who Walter had run to when the woman had attacked him, had taken us to the hospital. Now he volunteered to drive the Lancia and us home to Plaistow. Nancy was to be kept in St Andrew's for the time being. Not because she was injured in any way but simply because it appeared she'd been given a very large amount of laudanum. She wasn't used to it and the medical people wanted to keep an eye on her, for which I was grateful. Before we left St Andrew's, however, I did just have to go and see her.

She was deathly pale. Lying in a narrow metal bed in a ward full of equally pale but also bloodied and injured women, she looked tiny, worn out and old. Not that the way she looked bothered me. And besides, as soon as I got close to her, she opened her eyes and smiled and she was my beautiful sister all over again.

'Frank.'

I kissed one of her hands and then sat down on the chair beside her bed.

'Frank, what . . .' Her eyes suddenly widened and she said, 'I was drinking tea! Drinking tea and then I felt odd and . . .'

'Ssh, ssh, ssh!' I put a finger from my one good hand up to her lips and said, 'Don't you worry yourself with anything. You're all right now. They'll look after you here tonight and then you can come home tomorrow.'

Nan frowned. 'Tomorrow?'

'Sunday,' I said. 'They just need to keep you in to . . .'

'But I have to go to Mass!' Panicked, she tried to sit up, but thankfully, for it wasn't good for her to do so, she found that she couldn't rise easily and so just slumped back helplessly on to her pillow once again.

'You've had a shock,' I said gently. 'God'll understand.'

'Yes, but . . .' And then her eyes narrowed and she said, 'I was having tea with Alice. That's right. She'd made some very nice cakes, although her house was ever so dirty. Ever so dirty.'

'Nan, we can talk about this later,' I said as I saw Walter and Mr Holland, the chap with the red hair, beckon me towards them. It was, so it seemed, time for me to go home.

I bent forward to kiss my sister on the cheek. But she didn't notice, as she was already asleep again. As I stood up, I wiped a tear away from my eye and tried not to think about what would have happened had I not visited Mr Abrahams up at Claybury. Because Cissy Hoskin would have killed my sister, she would have mutilated her body and my mother would never have been able to kiss her oldest child goodbye.

Walter, who lives alone in a rooming house down by the Boleyn pub, stayed with us in the flat that night. The Duchess wouldn't even entertain the idea of his going back to his digs.

'Good gracious, no!' she said when Walter tried to make an exit. 'After you saved the lives of my son and my daughter? I should think not, Mr Bridges! You will stay and we will take care of you.'

Aggie was working and so still didn't know. But Walter and me regaled my mother and cousin Stella with the story of our recent adventures. Stella, who is a great believer in the power of blood tonics and the like, went over to the Abbey Arms and brought us both back bottles of stout. 'It'll build you up,' she said as she handed us pint glasses. 'Good for making blood.'

Walter, who is more than partial to a drop, smiled. Later, and just before Aggie finally made it home from Tate and

Lyle's, Sergeant Hill came over and asked to speak to me. Walter was asleep in my bedroom by this time and so it was just the Duchess and me and the silence when Stella went down to answer the door.

'Oh, I don't know about seeing Frank yet, Sergeant Hill,' I heard her say. 'He's been through a shocking time. Attacked he was! By a lady!'

'Oh.'

I looked over at my mother, who had also heard the exchange, and I said, 'Could you please go and sort Stella out, Duchess? And ask Sergeant Hill to come up, will you?'

'Are you sure, Francis?'

'Yes.'

After some protest from Stella, who felt that she was better placed to make decisions for me than anyone else, Sergeant Hill was shown up into the parlour. He asked, if at all possible, if he could talk to me on my own. The Duchess was tired anyway and so she went off to bed. Stella, after making both Sergeant Hill and myself cups of tea, went to the kitchen to be with Aggie, who had just that second got home. Once the parlour door was shut, Sergeant Hill said, 'Well, Mr H, what a day, eh? You and Mr Bridges attacked by a madwoman who now it seems is almost struck dumb.'

I frowned.

'Alice Hoskin says she'll only talk to you,' he continued. 'We can hold on to her because she was found by the gents from the pumping station laying into you with a knife. I imagine you and Mr Bridges will want to press charges.'

'Yes.'

'But about the attack on your sister and the other ladies I understand you say she admitted to killing, she won't say anything.'

When the pumping station workers had taken Cissy up to Plaistow, Walter and myself had told them what to say.

'All she will say is that she'll only talk if you are present. Says she owes it to you to provide an explanation,' Sergeant Hill said. 'Oh, and she wants to see a lady she's given as her next of kin, a Mrs Darling . . .'

'You mustn't let her see Mrs Darling!' I said. 'She's one of the women Cissy wants to kill!'

'Oh, we haven't let anyone see Miss Hoskin yet,' Sergeant Hill replied. 'Mrs Darling has been told where Miss Hoskin is but she's not as yet been told why. Now, Mr Hancock . . .'

'I'll come,' I said as I slowly and painfully began to rise to my feet. Sergeant Hill put a hand on my shoulder and pushed me gently back into my seat once again.

'Tomorrow morning will do, Mr Hancock,' he said. 'You need to get some rest, you've been through quite an ordeal.' He lowered his head, looking down into the depths of his copper's helmet. 'If you're right about this Hoskin woman, then . . .'

'She's been killing the White Feather girls,' I said. 'They made her fiancé go to war and then he lost his mind and . . . I don't know too many details, Sergeant Hill, but I do know that she named Violet Dickens.'

'Did she actually admit to killing her?'

'Well no, not exactly, but . . . Sergeant, I've never thought that Fred . . .'

'We can't let Fred Dickens go until this woman confesses to Violet's murder,' Sergeant Hill said.

'So I'll come . . .'

'In the morning is good enough,' Sergeant Hill said with a smile. 'But if you can come early, Mr H . . .'

'Of course,' I said. Stella had already said that she'd go and pick up Nancy from the hospital, and Walter's job for the following morning was to go and talk to Albert Cox up in Canning Town. Neither Walter nor myself could drive or lift on account of our injuries, ditto Nancy, so Walter needed to get another undertaking firm, Cox's I hoped, to take over our work for a week or so.

'Well, I'll leave you to rest now,' Sergeant Hill said as he stood up and put his helmet back on to his head.

I was exhausted and so I was grateful that I didn't have to go into the police station right away, even if I did feel a little bit guilty about poor old Fred Dickens. There was something, however, that had puzzled me and continued to do so.

'It's the viciousness of it all that I can't fathom,' I said. 'I mean, how one small woman could do such terrible things to her victims. Mutilation and . . .'

Sergeant Hill smiled. 'I spoke to that Mrs Darling that Miss Hoskin named as her next of kin. She told me straight away that she wasn't Alice's real family, of course. Told me Alice's family were all dead, and that included her Uncle Bob, who used to own a butcher's shop on East Ham Broadway. Alice apparently used to work in Uncle Bob's shop some years ago.'

Now that I knew what kind of shop Uncle Bob had had, some things about Cissy and what she'd done did make sense.

Although quite how, angry and grieving or not, she could have done what she did was still absolutely beyond me. As Sergeant Hill left, so Aggie arrived.

For a few moments she didn't say anything, she just looked at me. Then, as she languidly pushed herself away from the door frame, she said, 'Oh Frank, what are we going to do with you?'

Before I could even begin to answer, she ran towards me and flung her arms around my shoulders. I felt rather than heard the tears of relief that she shed.

Chapter Twenty-Four

S he looked very composed. She had, I imagined, spent a not entirely comfortable night down in one of Plaistow police station's no doubt freezing cold cells. But Cissy Hoskin, I had to admit, looked none the worse for it. In fact she looked to me rather better than she had done ever since I'd first known her. There is a saying about the truth setting you free, and maybe that was why. Maybe by getting all of her crimes off her chest, Cissy was, as it were, coming back to life once again.

'When Mum died, I didn't know what to do,' she said once Sergeant Hill and myself had sat down at the table opposite her. 'I'd only just buried Albert and . . .' She looked up into my face. 'I couldn't do that again. You understand, Mr Hancock, I'm sure. If there are too many funerals, well . . . The departed are too far away in cemeteries. They lie cold and alone in unfamiliar places.'

I wondered where she'd put the old woman. Sergeant Hill wrote down what Cissy said without either looking up or commenting. Cissy had said she'd only speak to me.

'I buried Mum in the garden,' she said. Her eyes filled with tears. 'I had to do it at night, in a raid as it happened. I had to dig up all the cauliflowers to do it. No one saw. But then . . .' She paused in order to scratch her face, then she said, 'In the morning, because of the vibrations from the bombing, part of her had come up again and so I had to rebury her. I pretended to be digging up more caulis. But nothing else has grown there since Mum died, and nothing will.' She looked up into my face. 'That happened for several weeks – burying her, reburying her. Crying all the time and apologising to her for not getting it right! Couldn't sleep, couldn't eat! No one came! No one!'

'It must have been a terrible time,' I said. And I really did feel sympathy with her in spite of what she'd done.

'But I wasn't angry then. That didn't happen until after . . . Mum . . . After I finally got her into the ground.' She cleared her throat. 'I was in Canning Town, shopping. I saw a face from the past.'

'Who?'

'Marie Abrahams. Used to come into my uncle's shop with her friend, Margaret Darling. She was talking to another woman, some little dried-up cripple she was, outside Murkoffs.'

'Did you speak to Marie?'

'No. But I heard some of their conversation. Marie called the woman Violet. There'd been a Violet in that group of White Feather girls Marie and Margaret had been in. I hadn't known her, but I remembered the name. They used to talk about Violet, Nellie and Nancy, the Harper girls and Fernanda when they came into the shop. Used to ignore me. My blood boiled then. If it hadn't been for those girls, I'd've had my Albert to comfort me through my poor mother's death! I would've been able to let Mum go in the normal way and get on with my life. Maybe I would even have had children!' Cissy swallowed hard, her skinny throat shaking and pulsing with emotion. 'It was like a dream when I followed that Violet home to her place on Freemasons Road. Walking through the smoking ruins of other people's lives . . .' She looked up again. 'She lived with two men, Violet. Two!' she said. 'And when I got there, she took a bottle of something out of her shopping bag and the three of them got drunk. I watched them falling around outside the street door, drinking and laughing and enjoying themselves!'

There was a pause during which I looked hard into Cissy Hoskin's impassive face.

'Why didn't you follow Marie?' I said. 'You remembered her.'

Cissy shrugged. 'Yes, but I knew where Marie lived,' she said. 'And Margaret. That Violet I didn't know, not until that day.'

'Seeing her with her husband and their lodger made you angry?'

'Yes.' Her face reddened with fury. 'I thought, "My life's in ruins because of people like you!" I hated her, with her husband and her drink and the way she laughed all the time! I began to watch her, see what she did. One time she went to where I remembered Margaret Cousins used to live. She was still there. Holding seances. I thought about that a lot then.'

'About the seances?'

'I decided that I'd go too,' Cissy said. 'That way I could see that Violet and Margaret Cousins as well. I could decide what I wanted to do with them.'

'Do with them?'

'To punish them,' she said. 'I had to find a way of punishing them for what they'd done to Albert and me.'

Cissy stared ahead for a few seconds, and when she began to talk again it was in a whisper. 'Margaret remembered me from Uncle Bob's shop. I said that my husband had passed and so she offered to contact him for me. As if she could contact anyone on the other side! She's a fraud! But her circles allowed me to meet the Robinsons. Esme. I didn't remember her as such, but that Neville talked very freely about where his wife had first met Margaret. Boasting he was. Said she was a Harper. And so then I knew.'

'And did you get friendly with Violet Dickens?'

'No, just on acquaintance terms,' she said. 'But I watched her for weeks. I got to know when her husband and the lodger went out. Violet didn't always go with them, especially if she'd already had a skinful.'

'You killed her . . .'

'Shut up,' she snapped at Sergeant Hill. 'I'll talk to Mr Hancock and only to him!' She folded her arms across her thin chest as a furious expression crossed her face.

Sergeant Hill looked over at me, then at Cissy, and then he said, 'I apologise, Miss Hoskin.'

Cissy leaned forward in her seat, her eyes fixed upon Sergeant Hill and said, 'If you interrupt again, I'm not saying another word, understand?'

Sergeant Hill is a copper, a person accustomed to ordering others about, and so it wasn't easy, I knew, for him to say what he did, which was, 'Of course, Miss Hoskin. I won't do it again.'

'Good.' Then she turned back to me and said, 'I went to see Violet. I went with one of Uncle Bob's old knives, prepared if you like. She was drunk. Of course she recognised me from Margaret's circles. I told her I'd been a White Feather girl too. I said I remembered her.'

'And did she believe you?'

'Like I say, she was drunk, she'd've believed it if I'd told her I was Winnie himself! We talked, she gave me a drink. Then she said she thought she had some old photographs from her White Feather days up in the attic. I said I'd go up with her, to help, like – her being crippled.' Cissy gulped.

'And?'

She looked deeply into my eyes. 'We sat on the floor up there. Violet had a torch. She pointed out girls whose names I didn't know or ones maybe I'd forgotten. Nellie Martin – she apparently worked in her family's shop on Prince Regent Lane. A widow, but she was coping so Violet said. Then there was Dolly O'Dowd. A spinster. I thought I might feel some sympathy for her. I thought I might find some sort of connection between her and me. But then Violet said that she had the church and good works and the friendship of another old White Feather girl. Your sister.' She licked her dry lips with her dry tongue and said, 'Violet asked where I was in those photographs. I said I wasn't in them. I think Violet was afraid then, but I was very quick after that and she couldn't move too sharpish even when she was sober. I cut her throat and she died very quickly. Too quickly.'

She looked down at the floor and I let her be for a few moments before I asked, 'Is that why you cut her body up, Cissy? Were you angry that she died so quickly?'

'Partly,' she said. 'A bit. But mainly because I just wanted her gone. Alive or dead, I just wanted her to be unrecognisable.'

'But there must have been blood . . .'

'Oh, there was a lot at first,' Cissy said. 'I had to move out of the way quick. But you know that once a creature is dead you can cut it up without much more mess. Uncle Bob taught me that. "If you kill a chicken then leave it for a few minutes so the blood stops pumping, you can have its legs off and its gizzard out without hardly dirtying your hands," he used to say.'

'So you waited until her blood had stopped pumping.'

'Yes.' She sat back in her chair and cleared her throat. 'She wasn't human. What she done to me . . . Just a piece of meat. I took her photographs, left her up in the attic, closed the door behind me and went. No one notices a woman with a bit of blood on her clothes these days, do they?'

She was right about that. Sergeant Hill tapped me on the elbow and then pointed down to a word on the paper he was writing on. It said, *Confession?*

I looked up at Cissy and said, 'So, Cissy, are you confessing to the murder of Violet Dickens, then?'

'Oh yes,' she said. She looked at Sergeant Hill and added, 'You can let her husband go. I killed Violet, not him. I don't know why he confessed to something he didn't do. Unless of course you lot knocked him about. Oh, and I put flowers on her grave too, horrible flowers with a horrible message. Violet died too quickly, you see, far too quickly. I felt she wasn't finished somehow, her and Dolly.'

Sergeant Hill, true to his earlier promise, said nothing. But Cissy looked straight at him as she said, 'I confess to the other killings too. Nellie Martin. I followed her home from her family's shop in the blackout. It was so cold! We got talking and I offered her a nip of brandy from my hip flask. She was guilty because of how religious she was, but she took it anyway. It was the first time I used Mum's laudanum. It worked ever so well. I don't think Nellie really knew very much about what happened to her after I pushed her into that bombed-out house on New City Road. Dolly O'Dowd I engaged in conversation about her church and how I was alone and unhappy and wanted to join. She invited me into her house for tea. While she could talk, she spoke about your sister, Mr Hancock. Did you know that Dolly was jealous of Nancy? Thought her hair was lovely, envied your family. Jealous cat.' *Jealous cat* had been written on the card attached to those violets Cissy had obviously sent to poor Dolly's funeral. She stared glassily at the table in front of her before continuing. 'Marie Abrahams knew me a little bit, when I reminded her of who I was. I said we should meet up some-time and so we did. We had tea as well. But her dad saw me, which was a shame. I suppose I should've sorted him out too at the time. But old Nathan is a bit simple and so I just told him that Marie had gone to bed. He never knew no different until the morning. Neville Robinson? Esme never went out on her own, never opened the door if she was alone. But her Neville was very easy to find. He'd just had his way with a prostitute, but he was still up for some more when I found him. Even though he knew me, because of where we were he still propositioned me in the street. How wrong can you be about someone! Neville I didn't drug, though. I smashed him over the head with a hammer when he turned away to lead me into that empty house. Such an animal! My Albert would never have done such a thing! Never!'

She looked mad, whatever mad looks like. Obsessed and triumphant. I left it a moment before I spoke again.

'Did you know that Esme Robinson would kill herself if her husband died?' I asked.

'No. I just wanted her to suffer, as I had,' Cissy said as she looked back at me once again. 'I knew she'd take it hard even though Neville was a faithless, useless article.'

'So you didn't want Esme Robinson to die?' I asked.

'Oh yes, eventually,' Cissy said. 'And I would have done her in. But Mr Hancock, while Neville was alive it was almost impossible. I didn't want to get caught, did I? Not before I'd done for the lot of them! I was always careful not to be noticed.' She looked up at me and frowned. 'Not that I had to work too hard at it.'

'What do you mean?' I asked. Although by that time I felt I knew anyway. I wasn't wrong.

'A single middle-aged woman doesn't attract a lot of comment,' Cissy said bitterly. 'Especially if we're out visiting other women. No one looks, no one cares. There were millions of us at the end of the Great War. Women who had lost their men in battle, women who'd never had anyone and now never would, women like me who cared for men who'd lost their youth, their health and their minds out in Flanders.'

Of course this was familiar. Nan had never met anyone before the Great War, and by the time it was over, she had missed the boat. Whether her friend Dolly would ever have found anyone whatever the circumstances of her life I had always doubted. But probably the Great War and what had happened after it hadn't helped her.

'People pity us or call us queer,' Cissy continued. 'We're a nuisance and an embarrassment. I've got cousins and aunts over Bow way who I know would've taken me in if I'd asked after Mum died. But what would I have been to them, eh? A poor, sad spinster who would've done all the housework to show how grateful she was. That or I'd've had to get a job somewhere and live in lodgings with other single women, paying extra on my rent every week for the privilege of one cold bath and a kettle of boiling water to wash out my smalls. I didn't bury Mum in the garden just because I wanted her close; I didn't want to lose my house either. I didn't want to become some mousy little thing in the corner of someone else's parlour that everyone pities! I didn't want to become invisible!'

I thought about Nan again, but mostly I thought about cousin Stella. I hoped she didn't see her life like that. Annoying though she often is, I hoped she knew that she was also loved.

'You weren't invisible to everyone, though, were you, Cissy?'

There was a moment during which I thought she might leap across the table and go for me, so hate-filled did her eyes become. Even if I hadn't seen her in action, as it were, down behind the pumping station, I would have known without any doubt in that moment that she was a killer. But somehow Cissy took hold of herself and said, 'Mr Abrahams was my only mistake.'

'It was you who made him afraid up at Claybury,' I said. 'He recognised you, made the connection between his daughter's death and your face.'

'I should never have stayed on there after Albert died! But when Mum passed away, what was I to do?' As she spoke, she shook with emotion. 'Marie's dad was known all over for being silly! He didn't know who I was! Didn't know my name! But then his nephew came and that . . . that woman . . .'

'Fernanda Mascarenhas.'

'Swanning about with Margaret and Marie and the others as if she was one of them! People said she was white but she wasn't. I could tell! Albert knew the family, he knew she was a darkie! Like your sister she was,' she said as she looked up at me. 'Neither one thing nor the other. I remembered them two faces immediately when Violet showed me her pictures.'

Cissy crossed her arms over her chest in what looked to me a gesture of satisfaction – at her own powers of deduction, at her lack of sympathy for 'the other'. I suddenly felt wild with fury and I was sure that my cheeks, if only momentarily, flushed.

'I should've given up visiting the hospital,' Cissy continued. 'I was going less often once I started going to Margaret's.

But I didn't like being with that faker! I went to the hospital to do my bit!'

'You think that Mrs Darling is a fake?' I asked.

I knew what I believed but I was interested to know what Cissy really thought and why. Not that this I felt went down too well with Sergeant Hill, who cleared his throat in a very obvious way. Cissy, interpreting what the copper did in exactly the same way as myself, said, 'Well of course she is! The dead don't talk to *her*! You have to have loved them who've passed over for them to talk to you. She tried to talk to my mother once but Mum wouldn't speak to her! Mum talks to me.'

I saw the frown pass over Sergeant Hill's face as soon as she'd finished speaking and I said, 'Cissy, how often does your mother speak to you?'

She looked at me as if I was mad and said, 'Well, all the time!'

'What, even when you kill . . .'

'All the time! *All* the time.' And then she smiled and looked over at Sergeant Hill. 'Got enough yet to hang me, have you?'

Chapter Twenty-Five

Although Mrs Darling was both surprised and horrified by what Cissy had done, she did admit that some things about Cissy only now made sense.

'Her mother was completely mute when I tried to contact her,' she said, referring to her efforts to raise Cissy's dead relative.

'Cissy said that that was because her mother was too busy talking to her,' I said.

Once Sergeant Hill had called a halt to my meeting with Cissy, I'd gone outside, where I'd found Mrs Darling waiting to see me. The coppers now had the confession they wanted, and so my part in all that was over. Not that I didn't still have some questions of my own.

'Well I don't know about that,' Mrs Darling said, 'but in that muteness, that silence around her mother, there was a terrible malevolence, Mr Hancock. Terrible.'

She shuddered. Whether she was just putting that on for my benefit or not I didn't know. I don't know what I feel about those who claim to be able to contact the dead. I was and remain certain, however, that Cissy did hear her mother's voice. Although whether it was indeed malevolent and whether in some way perhaps it made her do what she did, I don't suppose anyone will ever discover.

''Course, if she was seeing your sister up Claybury it explains why she was late for Neville's funeral,' Mrs Darling said.

'Yes?'

'Yes. Well your Nancy was working that one, weren't she.' She drew her fur coat closer round her shoulders as we walked past the Abbey Arms. 'When you come round to mine to organise the funeral with Esme, Cissy was there all the time. She must've realised then that she couldn't be seen by both me and Esme and your Nancy at the funeral; would have given some of her lies away. I reckon Cissy had to have been waiting somewhere outside Esme's until either the lot of you or your Nancy left. Only then could she come in. She couldn't let people make connections to other parts of her life. Things tucked away in there she wouldn't want anyone to know about.'

'Like Mr Abrahams.'

'Yes.' She frowned. 'As it was, she must've been under all sorts of strain.'

'In what way?'

We were outside the shop now. Mrs Darling looked with some disapproval at our dusty, blacked-out windows.

'Well I remembered her from her Uncle Bob's shop, as you know,' she said. 'I don't remember her young man or her being with him when, as she has it, we tried to shame him into fighting. But just because I didn't remember didn't mean that no one else would.'

'Her young man came from Custom House.'

She shrugged. 'We went down there, but I don't remember who we talked to or what we done. There was a lot of men about, you know, Mr Hancock,' she said. 'And to our shame, us girls went and harassed many of them. I can say that we was young and young people will have their passions and what not. But I know it don't go any way towards excusing it. We ruined lives.'

'You had a hand in ruining Cissy's, and of course her young man's too.'

'If we only done that then that's enough, isn't it?'

'I'm not excusing what you did, Mrs Darling,' I said.

'Good.'

'But I'm not condoning what Cissy did either.'

We'd been standing outside the shop for a little while now. It became obvious that those inside had seen us when I saw one of the first-floor parlour windows open and Stella poke her head out.

'Are you coming up, Frank?' she said. 'Nancy's home. Isn't that lovely?'

I smiled. 'Up in a minute,' I said. 'One extra for tea please, Stella.'

'All right, Frank. Whatever you say.' She closed the window as my face fell into a frown. Another disregarded spinster who wanted to be useful. Stella made me sad.

'You know, Mrs Darling,' I said, 'if all of these murders teach us anything, it's that we overlook people at our peril. And I don't just mean all the mad and wounded and just plain sad old soldiers who made it back from the First Lot.

I mean the women who'll never recover from that terrible carnage too. You know what Cissy said she feared the most when her mother died? Becoming a lonely spinster, a woman just tolerated by her family, a woman deemed sad or worthless or queer by our society. Outside of loving families these women are treated like dirt, Mrs Darling.'

'Not by me, love,' Mrs Darling said as she pushed on the shop door and began to go inside. 'Believe what you like about what I do, but my circles give spinsters something, Mr Hancock. The dead don't judge, remember. But then neither do I.' She smiled. 'I'll go and visit Cissy in the condemned cell if they'll let me.'

'I think she may still want to kill you,' I said.

She smiled again. 'I expect she does, God love her,' she said. 'But the guards won't let her, and anyway, I ain't afraid no more. I ain't being watched any more now, am I?'

'You and Linnit are free?' I said with a smile.

'Oh yes,' she said, 'although Linnit says you're still very troubled in your mind, Mr Hancock, and she knows you know!'

I thought about telling Mrs Darling about the dream I'd had where I'd heard her spirit guide's voice, but then I decided against it. After all, I didn't want to actually get involved with spiritualism myself, did I?

Cissy Hoskin made one attempt on her life before she even left Plaistow police station. Once in Holloway prison, according to Mrs Darling, she tried it twice in the first week. What she'll be like at her trial I dare not imagine. Again according to Mrs Darling, Cissy's mother talks to her all the time now, not always in the nicest of terms either.

Life for Hancock's goes on much as before although now Arthur has gone and Nancy has, to some extent, taken his place. She can't really bear as well as a man. She admits that now she's not so keen to mortify her flesh any more. We've another lad, Sidney, to do the bearing now. But Nancy does help out with the horses and the cleaning, and she is quite a desirable feature for some people at their loved ones' funerals. Even in these tough times there are people who are affected by the sight of a sad-looking woman by a graveside. I suppose it goes back to the old days when mutes were popular at funerals. And my sister, it has to be said, is still sad. Her best friend is dead, a fact due directly to a dark secret Nan, Dolly and all the other White Feather girls once shared. I never tell her what Cissy told me about Dolly being jealous of her, though. I never would. What I do tell her and tell her, even though I know she doesn't believe me, is that I've forgiven her. But then maybe at the very back of my mind I haven't.

One real mystery did however remain, and that concerned whether or nor I had really seen Fernanda Abrahams knocking on the door of the shop the night before Walter and I were attacked by Cissy. For several weeks after Cissy's arrest I'd been expecting to maybe hear from Fernanda. After all, my name, as well as Cissy's, had been in all the papers. Once criminals are caught, the censor goes out the window! But she didn't come, and this seemed to confirm to me that she either didn't care, which was very possible, or she'd put the whole thing out of her mind. Whatever the cause, I assumed that Fernanda hadn't come to the shop that night except inside my head. But one bright morning towards the middle of March she proved me wrong.

'Mr Hancock?'

I'd just walked through the curtains and into the shop to speak to Doris when she came in. I recognised her immediately, even though her hair, or so it seemed, was slightly darker than it had been before.

'Mrs Abrahams,' I said. 'What can I do for you?'

She looked over at Doris and then back at me and said, 'Mr Hancock, I need to talk to you. In private.'

I took her upstairs to the parlour. The girls were out shopping and the Duchess was taking a nap, so we were likely to be left alone. Once she'd sat herself down and put her handbag on her lap, Fernanda Abrahams said, 'I expect you've been wondering why I came here that night when you called down to me from the roof. There was a lot of bombing . . .'

'I thought I dreamed you!' I said. 'Blimey, Mrs Abrahams, you've no idea how good it feels to know it wasn't just all in my head!'

'Oh.' She leaned towards me. 'Mr Hancock . . .'

'Good heavens, I haven't offered you a cup of tea!' I started to get up. 'God, what . . .'

'Mr Hancock, I came that night to see Nancy!' Fernanda Abrahams cut in. There was a desperation in her tone that made me stop and sit back down again. 'I'd rowed with Ed and I flew out of the house, and by the time I got here it was dark!'

'Why did you come to see Nancy?' She'd been contemptuous, even hostile towards my sister last time she'd seen her.

'Last time I saw Nancy, when we had that row with your other sister and . . . Nancy said something about my not wanting to know her because she is everything I hate about myself. She meant her colour . . . what she . . . what she so obviously is and what I am so obviously not.'

'Mrs Abrahams,' I said, 'like me and my sisters you are . . . well, you're . . .'

'I am more Indian than you, Mr Hancock,' she said. 'Both my parents are from India! Where this skin and this hair that I have come from I don't know. My sisters were always jealous of me for it. My parents spoiled me because of it when I was tiny! From God knows how young, I lived my life as far as I could as a white person. I wanted that!'

I'd wanted that once, but that had been many years before. You get used to being 'the wog' to some people. You put a smile on your face and you say nothing.

'My old man wanted me to be white too. If he hadn't, I would never have married him,' she said. 'That we're white is important to Ed an' all. Our daughter's white. She's a lovely girl.'

This time there was no arrogance in her. Just sadness.

'But you know, Mr Hancock, it was only when I come here and saw Nancy and all the rest of you again that it struck me that my daughter, Phillipa, only knows half her family. My parents disowned me when I went with Ed. His family didn't want to know either, but some of his relatives do still speak to us. Phillipa has been brought up in their faith.'

I knew. 'Mrs Abrahams,' I said, 'Nancy isn't here at the moment . . .'

'It doesn't matter. I just have to talk to someone, to . . .' She gulped. 'Look, my daughter don't know my family, they don't know her. My daughter, Mr Hancock, don't even know what my family are. She's a nice Jewish girl, she is! A nice Jewish girl from Clapham!' Her eyes bulged with tears as the words caught painfully in her throat. 'I always kept away from your sister when we was in the White Feather girls. Some of the others would whisper about her behind her back, about her being brown . . . I didn't want them to do that to me! Although I expect some of them did. They all knew – I think they did. But only Marie really got through to me, you know. Margaret never! She was a nice person, Marie, kind. I trusted her.'

'Marie was good to you?'

'She helped me! She introduced me to Ed and so she helped me, indirectly like, to be a white lady in Clapham! And, and . . .' She began to cry. I let her weep for quite some time before I spoke again.

'So what happened to change that when you came here?' I said. As I recalled them, both her appearances in my home had been fraught and far from pleasant.

She looked at me over the top of her handkerchief and said, 'I saw that you didn't care. You, all of you, just get on . . .'

'We don't really have much of a choice . . .'

'Yes, but what you are don't matter! You all love each other, you help each other. Your sister Aggie is as white as I am, although,' she smiled through her tears now, 'her hair's probably a damn sight lighter than mine at the moment!

Can't get hold of the peroxide.' She put her head down a little. 'Maybe not sure that I want to . . .'

'Mrs Abrahams . . .'

'I came that night to apologise to all of you,' she said. 'Also I wanted to tell Nancy that she was so kind to do what she did to warn me. She never liked me, Mr Hancock. I know that. And to be fair, I wasn't likeable. I wasn't nice to your sister when we were young, and yet in spite of that she still put herself out to help me when Ed and me saw her up Claybury.'

'But Mrs Abrahams,' I said, 'when you came here after you'd met up with Nancy at Claybury you were furious at us for bringing up the White Feather subject in front of your husband because it made him angry.'

'It did! But what he was also angry about was being here with you!' she said. 'I know he hid it well; he's a polite man, my husband. But being so close to Canning Town with people your colour . . . Ed's never got over the way most of his family disowned him. He blames the colour my skin should be, do you understand? He blames my skin for taking him away from his family, for making our Phillipa something she isn't, just like me!'

This time her tears stopped her from saying any more. I didn't feel able to comfort her, either with my voice or with a friendly arm around her shoulders. I let her weep until she was spent. I said very little when she finally did rise to go. But she did.

'Mr Hancock,' she said, 'that night I come here in the raid, I was running away. As I said, I had a row with Ed and . . . Suddenly I didn't want the white life any more! I wanted to be who *I* am . . . But then I saw you up there on the roof, your brown face and your strange black clothes, and I, I couldn't.' She sniffed. 'I saw you as different. I couldn't belong to people like you – God forgive me!'

I wasn't upset by what she said. I knew what she meant. 'Mrs Abrahams,' I said, 'you've lived most of your life as a white lady. You can't just stop doing that now.'

'Yes, but my daughter . . .'

'Your daughter is a white girl,' I said. 'You made that choice, Mrs Abrahams. A very long time ago.'

Suddenly she looked crushed. If she'd come wanting me to take her in to some kind of Anglo-Indian community, help her find her parents maybe and talk to her daughter, she was now very disappointed. But then maybe she hadn't just come to see if I or my sister would do that. Maybe she'd come to have us confirm some things to her too. I said, 'You know, your husband must love you very much. He gave up most of his family for you.'

She looked at me, her eyes glazed with tears.

'I will tell Nancy that you came and that you thanked her for what she did,' I said.

And then she left. But just before that, she pulled my head down towards her face and she kissed me on the cheek. It was, she said, just for a moment like kissing her father's face once again.

That night there was a raid and so I went out running. My feet pounding down on the pavements that threatened to melt underneath me, I thought about Cissy Hoskin and how her life had been taken away from her by a few silly girls. We all do what we think is best at the time, and yet so often we make mistakes! Nancy and, I imagined, the other remaining White Feather girls were trapped to some extent in their guilt; Fernanda Abrahams was trapped inside a skin she felt she was no longer comfortable with. And Cissy? Cissy Hoskin's trial will begin next month, it appears. After it she will be sent to the condemned cell and then there will be silence. In a way, I do believe it is probably what she wants.

After the Mourning

Barbara Nadel

It's the London Blitz of 1940, and undertaker Francis Hancock has seen the worst that humanity can do to itself. Why then does the murder of a young gypsy girl in Epping Forest move him so much?

Travellers, gypsies, the homeless, deserters and German spies inhabit this stretch of open ground that was once her home. Francis knows it's not wise to delve into this human melting pot, but he is drawn to the exotic customs of the gypsies, their music and magic.

But as he further investigates the slaughter of the girl, the death toll rises and Francis begins to uncover a much bigger conspiracy, at the heart of which lies something even the German *Führer* is prepared to kill for . . .

Praise for *Last Rights*, the first in the Francis Hancock series:

'A great depiction of the period and a touchingly involuntary new sleuth' *Guardian*

'A gripping and unusual detective story, vivid and poignant' *Literary Review*

'She confidently and convincingly paints a grim picture of a bombed-out east London . . . curious and memorable' *Time Out*

978 0 7553 2138 4

headline

Last Rights

Barbara Nadel

October 1940: The London borough of West Ham is suffering another night of horrific bombing and undertaker Francis Hancock is caught in the chaos. A man lurches towards him through the rubble screaming about being stabbed but there's no visible wound and Francis dismisses him as a madman . . . until the man's body turns up at his funeral parlour, two days later.

Suspecting foul play, Francis feels compelled to discover what really happened that night – but as he finds himself pitted against violent thugs, an impenetrable network of lies and his own fragile sanity, he realises that there are people who want the truth to stay dead and buried . . .

Praise for Barbara Nadel's novels:

'Unusual and very well-written' *Sunday Telegraph*

'Impeccable mystery plotting, exotic and atmospheric' *Guardian*

'Gripping and highly recommended' *Time Out*

'Intelligent and captivating' *The Sunday Times*

978 0 7553 2136 0

headline

Now you can buy any of these other
Barbara Nadel titles from your bookshop
or *direct from her publisher*.

FREE P&P AND UK DELIVERY
(Overseas and Ireland £3.50 per book)

TO ORDER SIMPLY CALL THIS NUMBER

01235 400 414
or visit our website: www.headline.co.uk

Prices and availability subject to change without notice.